Comfort of the Hills

Barbara Gold

Gledsnest Books

Publisher: Gledsnest Books

ISBN: 978-1-0686738-0-1

A CIP catalogue record for this title is available from the British Library.

Any errors in the book are entirely my own.

In memory of Raymond who loved the Borders countryside.

There is a glossary of farming terms and Scottish words at the end of the novel.

Prologue

Monday 22nd January 2018: Australia

Kirsty Ainsworth stood in the crowded departure lounge of Sydney airport. She gripped her phone and took a deep, steadying breath then hit call.

'Mum, I—'

'Good grief, girlie,' her mother yelled. 'What the hell are you playing at? Why have you had your mobile phone switched off? I've been frantic. You've not returned any of my dozen calls. You know your great-uncle is really poorly. What if he'd died?'

'I don't care if the old alchie has finally drunk himself to death.'

'What?! You can't speak about him like that. He's been like a father to you.'

'Well, it's your fault I've never had a father of my own.'

'Not that again. Kirsty, you're obsessed. When I couldn't contact you, I thought you were in trouble with the police. I was expecting to have to come and bail you out again.'

'Trust you to think the worst of me.'

'Where are you anyway?'

'I'm at the airport. I'm going to Scotland to find my father. I've been feeling guilty about going away and leaving you, but now I'm glad I've made my decision. I'll be on the plane in half an hour.'

'What?! Did you say you are going to Scotland?'

'Yes. That's exactly what I said.' Kirsty held her phone away from her ear waiting for the verbal onslaught.

'What the hell are you playing at? What about your physiotherapy course? Aren't you due to start at the beginning of next month? You'll ruin your career.'

'I've put my place on hold. I'm taking a gap year.'

'How did you find the money for your fare?

'Actually you did. I've used some of the money in the savings account you set up for me. Thank you very much. I'm going whether you like it or not.'

'But Kirsty why now? What's brought all this on?'

'You have. Maybe if you'd told me anything about my father, anything at all, I wouldn't be forced to travel to the other side of the world to find him for myself.'

'Oh darling. Don't say that. I never meant to hurt you. It was complicated. Please say you'll stay and we can talk about it.'

'No, it's too late. I don't believe you. You can't stop me. I'm going walkabout,' she shouted down the phone.

She ended the call blocking her mother's number before she could change her mind. She slumped into the nearest seat, breathing fast and shallow. She'd only ever spoken to her mother once like that before and had instantly regretted it. Now she felt sick with guilt, yet lighter at the same time, because she had voiced all the things she should have said years ago. She was finally taking charge of her own life.

Chapter 1

The Young Family

The brown burns of the Border,
They hasten down the vale
In shallows through the sunlight,
In spates before the gale.
Grey dawn and rosy sunset
Lie mirrored in their breast,
Who call us forth to labour,
And lead us home to rest.

The Brown Burns by Will H Ogilvie

Tuesday 23rd January 2018: Newcastle Airport, England

As soon as the plane landed Kirsty felt chilled; she fastened her jacket, picked up the bright red and orange scarf her cousin, Emma, had bought her and wound it round her neck. Pulling on the matching beanie hat, she popped a vegan candy into her mouth and sucked on it hard, hoping it would settle her queasy stomach. A mixture of emotions spun around her insides like a roller coaster; excitement about the possibility of finally meeting her father but at the same time apprehension. Grabbing her hand luggage, she set off on her Scottish walkabout.

She'd arranged to meet the farmer's son at the airport and he'd sent her a photo of himself wearing a tartan hat, so that she wouldn't miss him at the arrivals gate. In reply she'd sent a photo of herself wearing a cork-brimmed bush hat; her hair was longer then and the dyed-pink ends could clearly be seen popping out from under the brim. The airport was crowded, but she couldn't miss her host waiting for her; she smiled when she saw him wearing the red and green hat as promised. He spotted her in the crowd and came hesitantly towards her.

'Hi. Kirsty Ainsworth? I'm Euan Young. Delighted to meet you. I didn't recognise you at first; I was half expecting you to be wearing the bush hat like in your photo.' He gave a little bow, took off his hat, ruffled up his thick blond hair, then held out his hand.

Kirsty laughed and shook his outstretched hand. Her insides flipped over; he was good looking in a rugged, rugby player kind of way, but a romantic liaison during her stay in Scotland would distract from her plans. She'd already compromised her principles to take the job on the farm; involvement with a farmer was out of the question, no matter how good looking.

'G'day,' she replied giving him her best smile. 'I'm pleased to meet you at long last. There was no room in my luggage for a bush hat.' Patting the Bennie hat, she added, 'I expect this hat will be far more useful in Scotland.'

Euan loaded her bags into the back of the mud-splattered Land Rover; she watched bemused as he flung his tartan hat into the back, as if he were skimming stones across a pond.

'How was your journey?'

'The flight was better than I'd expected. It was a relief

to have the stopover in Dubai, but to be honest I slept a lot of the way.' When she was settled in her seat she asked, 'What's the story with the tartan hat then?'

'It's called a "Tammie", after a character called Tam o'Shanter, in a famous poem by Robert Burns. I don't suppose you were taught it at school.'

'Eh, no, I'm not keen on poetry, but I have heard of Burns Night. But I don't know much about it.'

'I can't say I'm an expert either. It's more my dad's scene. There's a Burns night in the village hall on Thursday night if you want to try some haggis. It'll be a *gie braw* do.'

'Eh... a what kind of do?'

'Sorry, I mean it will be a really good evening.'

'Eh, thanks, but I think I'll give it a miss. I'll still be jet lagged.'

'No worries. I'm not that keen myself, but I can always ask my Ma if she'll make a *wee* Burns Supper at home.'

'That's kind of you, but eh, no thanks, I'm sure your mother has enough to do.' She shook her head wishing she'd never asked about the ridiculous hat.

'I hope you're warm enough. The heater is on the blink. I'll need to get it fixed.'

'I'm fine just now, thanks. The temperature's a relief after the heat of Sydney. I got a bit too much sun when I met up with my mates from school. They made a farewell picnic for me at Bondi Beach.' She rubbed her shoulder where it was still tender from where she'd caught the sun despite wearing a wide-brimmed hat and slathering herself with sun cream.

'Wow. I'm jealous. Mind you, I'm not one for lazing on the beach, but a day off now and then would be good. Anyway, less about me, you must be exhausted after your long flight. Don't worry, lambing won't start till early March, so you'll have plenty of chance to get familiar with everything. But there are a lot of tasks to do beforehand. Eh, there's just one thing... you might want to do something about your nails.'

'My nails?' Puzzled, she looked down at her long green fingernails.

'*Aye*, they are *gie braw*, but they'll soon get chipped once you start doing jobs round the farm.'

Kirsty grimaced and tried to smother her annoyance. 'My cousin treated me to a manicure for Christmas. As you said, "they're *gie braw*." I'd planned to "do something about them," as you said, once I got here.'

Euan turned to her and smiled. She blushed, then taking a deep breath confessed, 'Hmm, Euan, there's something I need to tell you... I'm veggie.'

'You're what?' Euan asked, keeping his eye firmly on the road.

'Sorry I didn't tell you when you offered me the job, but I'm vegetarian. I know it's a farm so you will eat lots of meat. I've no problem with that. Is there a supermarket or decent village shop I can get veggie sausages and pizzas? Then I can make my own meals.'

'Mum will be disappointed. She likes cooking for folk, but I suppose it might take some pressure off her. It gets pretty hectic during lambing. But I should warn you my *faither* might want to know what's wrong with a good lamb dinner.'

As Euan drove out of the city towards Scotland, they chatted about their respective lives. Kirsty was selective about what she shared and wondered if Euan was doing the same. He was easy to talk to and after the initial tension about her nails and eating habits, she relaxed in his company. Curious about her hosts she asked, 'What made you want to take on someone to help on the farm?'

'My father is suffering from arthritis in his knees and is finding it increasingly difficult to manage, which is why we've been looking for some extra help. Your contact via the Young Farmers came just at the right time. It must have been serendipity.'

After a while they fell silent. Kirsty had a chance to concentrate on the view unfolding in front of her. Enthralled, she stared at the lush scenery; patches of ice lingered along the sides of the hillside facing away from the sunlight, streams ran in brown torrents hurtling along tree-clad ravines towards the valleys. It was such a contrast from the hot, bustling city she'd left behind and from the parched and isolated landscape of her great-uncle's sheep station where she had spent so much of her childhood.

They travelled along miles of narrow country roads, through a patchwork of scattered farmhouses, quaint cottages and tiny hamlets. She felt she was being driven through one of the poems she'd been reading on the plane. She sighed contentedly.

Eventually they passed a dark blue and red sign saying, 'Welcome to the Scottish Borders.'

'It won't be too far now,' Euan assured her, giving her a running commentary of the various villages that they passed through, until at last they reached a sign that said STANTON HOLM, 1 mile. The road became narrower and more winding as it followed the curve of a river, with wooded hills on one side and fields of sheep on the other. They travelled over a humpbacked bridge and passed a single-story stone building with a sign on the grass verge in front of it advertising:

BURNS SUPPER
Thursday 25th January.
7.00 for 7.30.
£10 per person

'That's the village hall. The roof has been leaking and the guttering needs replacing, so the village hall committee have been raising money to fix it. The farm isn't far now, we'll be there in a wee bit.'

Euan followed the road till they came to a small finger sign on the right saying, 'Stanton Holm Farm.' He turned sharply and followed the road as it passed between several fields of sheep until a large house, surrounded by a cluster of sheds and outbuildings, appeared ahead of them.

Kirsty wondered where Stanton Hall was in relation to the farm but didn't risk asking. As they approached Holm Farm, she felt the tension spread throughout her body and willed herself not to panic. She took a deep steadying breath. She was nervous about meeting Euan's family and the tasks she had in front of her. The reality was she'd not much of a clue of how to handle a sheep in spite of the time she'd spent on her great-uncle's sheep station during her school holidays and wondered if she'd have enough time to carry out her plan to connect with her father and grandmother before her hosts saw through her ruse.

They travelled up a short, tree-lined drive. The garden surrounding the old farmhouse was dormant, except for some pretty white flowers growing either side of the front door which were in full bloom. She gasped in delight.

‘Oh, what are those lovely flowers? They look so delicate.’

Euan replied proudly, ‘They’re my mother’s favourite; they are called Hellebores, Christmas Roses. They’re hardy and she says that they bring the garden to life even in the dead of winter when nothing else is in bloom.’

Jim and Lizzie Young were at the front door to welcome her. His mother was dressed in a baby blue cashmere sweater, worn loosely over a pair of ill-fitting denim jeans. The outfit was completed by a pair of pink candlewick slippers. His father was wearing a blue denim shirt under a yellow sweater, embossed with a black Pringle of Scotland logo. His long legs were encased in a pair of brown cord trousers flapping over worn leather slippers. Kirsty thought the farm must be doing well for them to be able to afford luxury sweaters.

‘Mum, Dad, this is Kirsty. She was sunbathing on Bondi Beach a few days ago.’

‘Pleased to meet you both.’ Kirsty gave them a broad smile. ‘Euan’s right, the temperature here is a lot different from back home.’

His mother stepped forward, arms outstretched to hug her, enveloping her in the warm scent of home baking.

‘Hi, I’m Lizzie. Welcome to our home. You’re shivering, lass. Come in and get yourself warm by the fire.’

With her arm still round her, Lizzie led Kirsty into the kitchen. His father hung back, before following them into the house, humming a catchy tune. As they made their way down the dark, narrow hallway, the smell of damp hit her nostrils. Kirsty struggled to contain a sneeze, and took several deep breaths.

‘You’re honoured today coming through the front door,’

Euan told her. 'We usually come through the farmyard at the back of the house straight into the boot room. That's where we leave our muddy Wellingtons and dirty outdoor clothes. And from there go directly into the kitchen.'

There was a large table in the centre of the kitchen set for afternoon tea, with a plate piled high with an assortment of sandwiches and another loaded with sausage rolls. In the centre of the table was a plate of cakes arranged on a white paper doily.

'Wow,' Kirsty gasped in total surprise. 'I see you have made Lamingtons.'

Lizzie beamed. 'I'm thrilled you recognised them. They were a bit fiddly to make, I nearly covered myself in chocolate.' She laughed nervously and picked up the plate with the squares of sponge cake which she'd carefully covered with chocolate then rolled in desiccated coconut.

'Help yourself. I made them especially to make you feel at home. I know it's Australia Day on Friday, but it's not the weather for a barbie or fireworks.'

Kirsty nodded her agreement and forced a smile.

'Thanks for the cakes, but I'll have one later.' She'd long held mixed feelings about Australia Day. When she'd attended an Invasion Day Rally on the 26th January last year with her friends from school, Tahnee and Ash, both First Nations Australians, she'd never expected to be eating Lamingtons in Scotland a year later.

They sat in the warm kitchen and chatted. The family couldn't have been kinder. Euan's mother was outgoing, but his father was quiet. He had a kindly face and she looked forward to getting to know him. She felt a twinge of guilt about using them to further her plan.

After they had eaten, Lizzie got up from the table. 'You

take it easy, lass, for a day or two till you get over any jet lag. Now, I'll show you to your room and you can get yourself settled in.'

Kirsty followed Lizzie to the top floor of the house. The bare wooden stairs narrowed as they ascended to what would have been the attic. The old house felt dark and musty; totally different from the bright fourth floor flat she and her mother lived in.

Lizzie continued her tour of the top floor. 'There are two bedrooms that we set aside for visiting farm workers. This is the larger room,' she said, opening the door to a room with twin beds and a set of bunk beds. 'We use this if we have shearers staying over. But I've put you in the single room. Our Euan decorated it last year. We call it the "blue room" for obvious reasons.'

Lizzie laughed as she opened the door. Kirsty glanced round the tiny room. 'Wow it's perfect,' she gasped. The room was painted pale blue. There was a single white wooden bed with a white quilt folded over the end and a small blue rug on the wooden floor next to it. Lizzie pressed down on the blue and white check duvet covering the bed. 'The bed is nice and supportive... what you need after a long hard day on the hills. I've given you a spare quilt for extra warmth... you will probably find it cold at night after the hot temperatures you are used to. About an hour before bed I'll give you a hot water bottle to take the chill off. There's a shower room next door for your sole use. I've laid out some towels and there's a change of bedding in the wardrobe and plenty of extra towels. Now you get yourself settled in, lass, then come down when you are ready.'

'Thanks. You have been most kind. Oh, I forgot to ask,

what's the Wi-Fi signal like?'

'We have broadband, but you won't get it up here, but you may get a mobile signal if you put your phone by the window.'

'Thanks. I'll put my phone to charge and try it later.'

Kirsty switched on the bedside lamp then unpacked her belongings. She hung her jeans and tops in a small wardrobe that was fitted into a recess in the wall. She carefully placed the precious book, *The Border Poems of Will H Ogilvie,* that had brought her halfway around the world on the white bedside cabinet next to a clock radio.

The bedroom ceiling dipped low by the sash window, which was fitted with a pale blue Roman blind. She didn't want to risk trying to open the window to see if she could get a better signal, in case the window fell out. It was getting dark, but she could just make out the lights of a large house in the distance; it was surrounded by trees and was at the end of a long drive. She wondered if it was Stanton Hall. When she'd agreed to take the job, she'd never expected it to be so close by, but perhaps it would make her plans easier. Before going downstairs to spend the evening with the Young family, she sent a quick text to her cousin, Emma.

Hi Em, I've arrived. Farmhouse is cold and damp. Family very nice. Son good looking, but not my type. Let Mum know I've arrived safely but remember your promise and don't tell her where about I am. Looking forward to getting on with my plans as soon as I'm settled. See ya. Kx.

Chapter 2

The Poetry Book

Even though she was tired after her long journey, Kirsty fell into an uneasy sleep and woke with a start; the bedside clock read 1.00am. The hot water bottle Lizzie had given her had gone cold and she shivered. She got out of bed and immediately pulled back her foot as soon as it touched the cold wooden floor. Sitting on the edge of the bed she rubbed her icy feet and pulled on a pair of socks. She padded to the wardrobe and put on a couple of T-shirts and the one jumper she'd brought with her, over her thin cotton pyjamas. She wrapped herself in the white quilt and looked out of the window towards Stanton Hall. She saw a light through the trees and was curious if the father she'd travelled half way round the world to find couldn't sleep either. She wondered how she'd ended up in Scotland rather than getting ready to start university.

Friday 12th January 2018: Sydney

After the family Christmas at her great-uncle's sheep station in the Outback, her mother stayed on to help look after him during his illness. Kirsty returned to their flat in the suburbs of Sydney, to check her finances before finalising arrangements for her physiotherapy course at Melbourne University, due to start in February.

'Now where is it?' She lifted piles of paper and yanked open the drawers in her mother's desk in the hunt for the details of the savings account her mother had set up towards her education. As she pulled open the final drawer it snagged on something jammed underneath. With a bit of juggling, she managed to free it up. A slim red book fell out. It looked old and well read but fortunately wasn't damaged by her attempts to release it. She suspected it had been deliberately hidden there rather than having simply slipped out from the back of the half empty drawer above. Curious, she read the title in black lettering.

The Border Poems of Will H Ogilvie

She looked inside the cover and saw that the book was published in 1959. She held her breath as she read the inscription.

To my dearest Janine, thank you for a wonderful time.
I will always remember you,
all my love,
Stan xxx
December 1998

She sat down heavily on the edge of her mother's bed. Who was Stan? Was he her father? Her hands shook so hard the book dropped from her fingers onto the floor. An airmail letter fluttered out; she picked it up carefully. It was postmarked Scotland. She looked closely at the pale blue envelope with the dark blue and red edging; she held it to her nose and sniffed it deeply, as if it held the answers to all the questions about her father she'd pestered her mother with since she was a child.

She carefully unfolded the thin blue paper and took a deep steadying breath before she read the letter.

Stanton Hall,
Stanton Holm,
Scotland.

25th March 1999

Dear Miss Ainsworth,

Be assured my son wants nothing to do with you or your child. How do we know it is even his? I enclose a cheque for £1,000. Do what you must. Do not contact my son or me again.

Yours faithfully,
Lady Isobel Scott

The letter was direct to the point; her father and grandmother wanted nothing to do with her. Was the money to pay for an abortion or towards the cost of bringing up a child? It wasn't clear, but in that moment her world changed forever. As she read its contents her heart hardened into a tight ball. She'd always felt a mixture of anger and frustration with her mother, at her unknown father and at the world in general. Now, she would focus that anger on Stan and Lady Isobel Scott. She resisted tearing the letter into a thousand pieces. No, she would keep it. It was evidence that her Scottish grandmother was a bitch. And, by the sounds of it, a rich bitch at that. She would get to the truth about what happened all those years ago even if she had to go all the way to Scotland to confront her father and grandmother.

Over the next few days Kirsty's thoughts were in turmoil; she'd been looking forward to university life and making new friends but since she'd found the poetry book with the devastating letter, she'd not been able to settle. She phoned her cousin at the sheep station and confided in her.

'Emma, I've found out my mum's big secret. My dad's from Scotland. He is some sort of lord. I'm thinking of going to Scotland to find him. It would be a big step; it would mean giving up my course or at least postponing it. I'm in two minds if I should go, but before I decide I need to find out a bit more about him. She probably met him at the sheep station; it's the only explanation I can think of. Can you do me a big favour and dig about in your dad's old records? See what you find out about him for me?'

'I've got a better idea. Why don't you just ask your mum? Wouldn't that be far easier?'

'No. She's refused to tell me anything about my father all my life, why should I trust her to tell me the truth now? Please Emma, at least look him up for me.'

Emma was three years older than Kirsty. They had grown up together and were more like sisters. Emma was her great-uncle's daughter so they were first cousins once removed. Emma helped out in the family business by doing the farm accounts, so was able to access the farm records. She phoned Kirsty back a couple of days later to update her on her progress.

'Most of the old records were filed away in storage boxes stacked up on shelves in my dad's office. To be truthful they were in a bit of a mess, but funnily enough some of the records for the year you asked about were laid out neatly, as if someone had already been through them. I found what I think you're looking for. I'll scan the pages in and email them to you.'

Kirsty realised she'd been holding her breath in anticipation, and had twiddled a lock of hair round her finger tightly. She let both go.

'Thanks. I appreciate it.'

'It took me ages, so you owe me big time.'

'That's fine. Once I come into money, you'll be first on my list.'

'What? Come off it. Do you really think this Scottish family of yours will pay you off? Anyway, I'm not after money. I'm just worried about you. This is a harebrained scheme, and you damn well know it.'

'Finding my father isn't about money. I've always felt as if part of me was missing, like a lost piece of a jigsaw puzzle, but without a picture on the box to help identify it. Meeting my father will help me know who I am. When I was little, I imagined he was an explorer travelling to some far-flung part of the globe and unable to get to Australia.' She laughed weakly at the thought. 'As I grew older, I thought maybe he was some random one-night stand. Now, I know he didn't care about me and what a bitch my grandmother is, so things have changed. Before, I was curious, now I'm angry.'

'Do be careful. I know what you are like when you get an idea in your head. If you get into trouble in Scotland, your mother won't be able to bail you out.'

'I'll be too busy to get into trouble. I've learnt my lesson after what happened last year. I was lucky to get into university. I don't want to ruin my chances by falling foul of the law again.'

'If you say so, cousin dear,' Emma replied sarcastically. 'I'm not convinced that you've reformed. Once a rebel, always a rebel.'

Swearing Emma to secrecy, Kirsty hatched her plan. Emma traced the original request from an agricultural college in England, who was looking for a placement on behalf of a student called Stanley Scott. Kirsty thought he must have been the 'Stan' who had signed the book of poems she'd found. A quick internet search showed that Lord Stanley Scott was the owner of Stanton Hall, near the village of Stanton Holm, in the Scottish Borders. His mother, Lady Isobel, was still alive. His wife, Fiona, ran an events business from the castle. They weren't super rich, but rich enough. Kirsty rubbed her hands together with delight.

It looked as if she'd hit the jackpot. Although finding her father wasn't about the money, some monetary compensation wouldn't come amiss after all those years of missing out on school trips and what her mother called 'non-essentials' because they simply couldn't afford it.

Kirsty emailed the college in England. They no longer ran exchange schemes with Australia, but put her in touch with the organiser of the Scottish Association of Young Farmers Clubs in Edinburgh. There was a bit of back and forth but it wasn't long before she rang Emma with the good news.

'Bingo,' she shouted down the phone. 'I can't believe my luck. I was offered a placement at a farm in Aberdeen and another near Fife, but both were too far. I've been offered a shepherding job just near Stanton Hall. It's initially for the lambing season but it fits with my plan perfectly.'

'But, Kirsty, you don't even like sheep – well, not the hands-on work, anyway. You say you care about animal welfare and consider yourself to be an animal rights activist, but you moaned all the time you helped my dad out on the sheep station. I can't see you getting up at dawn and doing all the dirty jobs on the farm. If nothing else you'll have to sacrifice your precious nails, never mind compromising your principles.'

'Don't be so negative. You sound just like my miserable-faced mother. Don't try and talk me out of it. I've made my mind up. I'm going. It's a big step for me to put my place at university on hold and take a gap year, but I've given it a lot of thought and if I don't do this now I never will. Farm work is the easiest way I can get work in Scotland, even better because there's suitable accommodation thrown in. If it doesn't work out, even in a rural area, there's bound to be some casual work going. I can always get a job in a bar or something. I'll not rest till I find my father and ask why he didn't want anything to do with me.'

'I think I understand, but promise you'll keep in touch.'

'Yes, but you must promise me something. Don't let my mother know where I am.'

'Okay, I promise,' Emma replied, grudgingly, 'but I don't like deceiving your mum. She's always been good to me.'

Kirsty was on the plane ten days after finding the book.

Chapter 3

Stanton Holm Farm

Wednesday 24th January: Stanton Holm Farmhouse

Next morning when Kirsty opened her eyes she was surrounded by blue and white and at first she wondered if she was still on the plane. She stretched out her limbs and realised she was lying in a bed. A panicked glance at the digital clock radio by the bedside read: 10.59. She'd overslept. Damn it. She'd wanted to make a good impression on her first day; little chance now. She had a warm shower then dressed in the thickest clothes she'd brought with her, pulling on a pair of work jeans and T-shirt over a pair of plain black briefs and matching bra, adding a red and black check work shirt to complete her outfit. Just then her phone, which she'd left plugged in near the window to charge, pinged. It was a text from Emma.

Your mum's been asking me what made you choose to go to Scotland.

I said I didn't know. What will I tell her?

She replied. Nothing.

Grabbing a large envelope from her bag, Kirsty made her way down the stairs to start her new life. Taking a deep breath to steady her nerves, she breezed into the kitchen.

'G'day, Lizzie. Sorry I overslept. I slept like a log.'

She smiled at her host as she placed the envelope on the table.

'Here's a little something for you I picked up at the airport. I forgot to give it to you last night.'

'Thanks very much, lass. It's kind of you.' Lizzie opened the envelope and took out a large pictorial calendar of Australia.

'Oh, this is lovely. My Jim will love it. I expected you'd need the lie-in... so no need to apologise.' She looked her new worker up and down. 'Is that the warmest clothes you've brought with you, lass? Let me find you some thicker ones to wear or you'll freeze to death on the hills. Help yourself to some breakfast while I'll see what I can find. If you'd not been veggie I'd have made you a full Scottish breakfast with all the trimmings,' Lizzie said curtly, then added more softly, 'We'll have to sit down later and we can go through some menus. There's cereal on the table, bread for toast and there's milk, jam and homemade marmalade in the fridge.'

Kirsty helped herself to cereal and toast with a generous spread of the delicious marmalade, which was full of chunky pieces of orange peel. She'd barely finished eating when Lizzie reappeared in the kitchen carrying two large bags of clothes.

An hour later Kirsty was kitted out in a pair of Lizzie's old cord trousers with a hand knitted woolly jumper worn over her cotton t-shirt. She thought Lizzie must have either emptied her wardrobe or found a bag of clothes she was going to give the 'Op Shop,' or whatever the Scottish equivalent was. Lizzie had also found her a spare pair of waterproof over-trousers and a green wax jacket.

'I'm making chicken sangers for lunch. My Jim always enjoys "roast chook," as he calls it.'

Kirsty laughed.

Lizzie added, 'I'll make some egg sandwiches for you, if you're okay with eggs.'

Kirsty nodded.

***

After lunch Jim gave her a tour of the farm, accompanied by Will, his old sheep dog. He ruffled the fur on the dog's head affectionately. 'He's more a pet than a working dog. I can't bear to part with him; we've been together since I was hardly any older than our Euan.'

Kirsty was impressed at the way Jim communicated with his faithful dog, but furrowed her brow as she bent down to pet the dog. 'Wow, I thought dogs only lived to be about twelve years old.'

Jim laughed. 'Well, it feels like we've been together a long time; we're both suffering with our joints from being out in all weathers. Now let me show you around the layout of the fields and introduce you to some of our ewes.'

'Okay. I'll follow you. Everything here is so different to what I'm used to so best pretend I'm a complete newbie.'

'No worries lass. I'm sure once you get started it'll all come back to you.'

Kirsty nodded her agreement, hoping he was right, and that he wouldn't suspect that she'd told Euan a load of lies when she'd applied for the job. She inhaled deeply. The familiar smell of sheep brought back memories of her childhood on her great-uncle's sheep station that she'd tried to submerge, and she had to force herself to concentrate on what Jim told her.

'We've got 400 breeding ewes. The local vet, Tom Malcolm, scanned them a couple of weeks ago. We're delighted with the result. Only thirty-seven ewes weren't carrying any embryos at all and more than half are carrying twins; they're the ones sprayed with blue dye, so we *ken* to feed them with extra supplements. There's a dozen carrying triplets; they're ones with red marks on them.'

Kirsty nodded and tried to remember everything he told her. The farm's fields were the size of postage stamps compared to the many thousand acres of her uncle's sheep station, with its vast flocks of Merino sheep. Jim showed her round the 450 acres of fields and hillsides that made up Holm Farm.

'The sheep in the fields nearest the farmhouse on low lying ground are what we call our *in-bye sheep*. They're known as *mules*; they are a cross between two types of purebred hill sheep. They are less hardy than Cheviot sheep but first to lamb. They are my favourite sheep, because they generally produce twins that mature quickly.'

He smiled and continued. 'We farm the fields right up to the fencing at the top of the hillside. All the ground above there is managed by the Stanton Holm estate gamekeeper.' He pointed to the rough ground stretching towards the horizon. Kirsty looked up in the direction he pointed. She could see two long stretches of woodland and thought she saw a flash of colour as a figure ran through the trees and wondered who it was.

Jim continued, 'The ewes in this field are the purebred Cheviot *hogs* expecting their first lambs, so we need to be extra careful with them. Those in the field above them are what we call the *second shears*; they have lambed twice so are more experienced mothers.'

She nodded again. There was so much to take in that she hoped she could remember all the terms he used. As she looked around, she noticed something that didn't look right. 'Look over there, that sheep there looks as if it has got its head stuck between two strands of wire fencing. It's struggling to free its head.'

She immediately ran towards it, bent down and speaking in what she considered to be a soothing voice, stroked it gently. Its fleece felt warm and soft under her fingers. She carefully parted the wire, releasing the ewe. She couldn't help smiling as she watched its head bobbing up and down as it ran to join the rest of the flock.

Jim caught up with her. 'Thanks lass. I'm not as quick on my feet as I used to be. I'll get our Euan to check the whole of this section of fencing as a priority.'

She noticed Jim was in pain, so slowed her walking pace to match his. She could see the relief on his face when they arrived back at the farmyard, where there was a series of sheep pens laid out next to two large barns. As they walked Jim whistled a catchy tune. She didn't like to ask him what it was.

Jim was clearly proud of his flock of Cheviot sheep, which he told her had won several awards at the annual Highland Show in Edinburgh, in previous years.

'It sounds as if you did well.'

'*Aye* lassie, you're right enough there. I'm *gie* proud of our successes. We've worked hard to build up our flock.'

'You'll have to show me your rosettes.'

'They are pinned up in the boot room. I can show you

when we get back to the house.'

'Ah, so that's what they are. I spotted them when I was putting my boots on and wondered what they were. There were sure a lot of them. You must be very proud.'

'*Aye*, but I can't take all the credit. Some of the rosettes are Euan's and Lizzie has won awards for the baking and crafts.'

She'd warmed to this kindly Scotsman, who clearly cared about his animals, offering them the best standard of care that he could, not like her uncle whom she'd often seen kick pregnant ewes out of the way in a drunken rage.

For their evening meal Lizzie had prepared a thick leek and potato soup served with homemade bread, followed by shepherd's pie brimming with meat for the others and a vegetable pie for Kirsty. There was a bowl of fruit on the table.

'That's really kind of you Lizzie but you shouldn't have gone to the trouble of making something different for me.'

'Okay lass, but it is very cold out and you'll need something to keep you going.'

Euan laughed, turning to Kirsty. 'I should have warned you Ma likes to feed everyone up, meat eater or veggie.'

Chapter 4

Settling in

That evening Kirsty wrapped up warm and sat up in bed to read before attempting to settle down to sleep. She was physically and emotionally exhausted. She'd taken a big risk in uprooting herself and moving to Scotland but was determined to uncover the truth about her birth. There was so much to take in. She had to concentrate hard to understand what her hosts were saying, let alone making sense of all the farming terminology. She hadn't wanted the family to know she had little practical experience of shepherding, so she'd bought a book on sheep husbandry online and read it cover to cover on the plane journey. She picked it up and flicked through the pages half-heartedly, then put it down again. Instead she picked up the red backed poetry book from the bedside table and read through a couple of the poems. The rhythm of the now familiar words lulled her back to sleep.

***

Next morning Euan showed her round the farmyard, introducing her to the working sheep dogs, Ruff and May, who lived in outdoor kennels. Ruff was inquisitive and sniffed excitedly at Kirsty's legs; he nuzzled her hands gently when she patted him. May was more reserved but responded readily to Kirsty stroking the back of her ears.

'Last year May gave birth to eight puppies. We introduced them to the sheep when they were about nine weeks old to see if they had an instinct as sheep dogs. To our delight they passed with flying colours, and we sold all of them, which brought in some extra income, but I'm thinking of keeping two next year to train for ourselves.'

Nearby there were two large barns; one was piled high with bales of silage to feed the sheep over winter. Euan told her that the second barn was used for lambing. Next to the barns were a series of stone storerooms; at the entrance to the first one there were two pallets of red containers labelled 'twin lamb supplement,' that were waiting to be unloaded. Further back were sacks of high energy food supplement.

Euan pointed to the next store. 'Here's where we keep all the chemicals under lock and key. I won't expect you to administer any medications or treatments, but at least you know where they are kept for when we need them.' Then he showed her where the farm's two quad bikes were kept and let her have a go at riding one round the farmyard. She was used to riding all-terrain vehicles round her uncle's sheep station and quickly got used to the feel of the bike.

'Make sure you always put the key somewhere safe. Don't leave it in the quad bike. Thieves have been known to target the farms around here.'

'Perhaps I can try it across the fields tomorrow. It must be a quicker way to round up the sheep rather than on foot.' She'd not wanted to admit her limbs were aching having walked across the fields with Jim.

'*Aye*, you're right enough, lass,' Euan agreed, sounding just like his father.

'If we head to the old barn we passed as we came up the drive, I'll show you my herd of blue grey cattle; they are my pride and joy. They eat taller grass from the sheep so are a good mix. I've been investing my own money to build up the herd. They are hardy so are kept outside most of the year, but these ones are all pregnant so I've brought them down over winter.'

'I've never been around cows before so I'm a little nervous,' Kirsty confessed.

'Don't worry. Did you know that cows can recognise up to eight people? The more time you spend feeding and caring for them, the more they will get to know you, so will be easier to work with.'

Kirsty couldn't help noticing the twinkle in his blue eyes and laughed. 'I think you're pulling my leg, but okay, I'll give it a try.'

***

The weather was cold and dull, or *driech* as Jim had described it; at the end of the day Kirsty was glad to sit by the warmth of the kitchen range. She took a few minutes to look round before Lizzie came into the kitchen, which could best be described as 'homely.' It was nothing like the tiny kitchen in the flat where she grew up where everything had its place and her mother would follow her around picking up after her. The farmhouse kitchen was clean but cluttered; a bundle of half-finished knitting lay on the easy chair by the range, a guitar leaned against the wall and what she thought was a ukulele sat on a shelf beside a stack of sheet music and collection of CDs. There were piles of magazines and a large bookcase filled with a hotchpotch of books. She selected books randomly from the bookcase; there were nature books, books about farming, possibly course work from the agricultural college, which could come in useful. There was some fiction and several books of poetry.

Before she could examine the books more closely, Lizzie breezed into the kitchen.

'Help yourself to anything you fancy to read. My Jim's one for poetry, although I prefer a good romance myself.'

'Thanks. I noticed the guitar and ukulele and wondered who the musicians were.'

'Jim plays the ukulele. Our Euan plays the guitar in a band with a couple of local lads. They are called Bellwether.'

'That's an unusual name. What does it mean?'

'It's an old-fashioned term for a sheep that leads the flock... often with a bell around its neck.'

Kirsty grinned as she imagined Euan leading the other band members onto the stage, wearing a bell around his neck and the tartan Tammie on his head.

That evening Jim went to the Burns Supper at the village hall and Euan went to band practice at the Ogilvie Inn in the village.

The two women sat by the stove finishing the rest of the Lamingtons. Kirsty picked the smallest piece of cake from the plate.

'This is so kind of you to go to this trouble. It makes me feel like I'm at home,' Kirsty lied, not wanting to admit her mother never baked and even if she did, she wouldn't make Lamingtons, because neither of them liked the way that bits of coconut got stuck between their teeth. It was one of the few things the two of them agreed on. She still had crumbs in the pocket of her jeans from the day she'd arrived when she'd hidden her piece of cake when the family weren't looking.

'No worries, lass. We're glad you're here to give us a hand. Jim and I aren't getting any younger. Euan works long hours; as well as the sheep and his cows he's involved with the band, so we'd be stretched at lambing.'

'Have you had Aussies help out before?'

'*Aye.* And some Kiwis an' all.'

Kirsty smiled. There was no point in antagonising her host, so resisted asking which worked harder. 'I'll help you wash up.' She picked up the empty plates and coffee mugs.

'Thanks lass, which reminds me, our Euan tells you've done some waitressing work in Sydney. I help out with various events at Stanton Hall. Thankfully, the pheasant shooting season is about to finish; the last shoot of the season is this Saturday. Lord Scott is expecting a good turnout. If you fancy it, you can help me if you are not needed with the sheep. If you ask me, it's more eating and drinking than shooting.'

'Okay. It sounds very different from the bar work I've done in the past, but I'll give it ago.' Kirsty turned away, and plunged her hands back into the dishwater, hoping her excitement at the possibility of finally meeting her father didn't show.

Lizzie took the washed plate from her. 'That'll be great. I help Lady Fiona with the catering if they're having any events. It's been difficult for her since the accident. I wondered if you'd give me a hand at the Light Show they are running at Stanton Hall, the following weekend. I'll pay you for both. You'll get the chance to hear Bellwether play. It should be a good night out.'

'That'll be great. It'll be a good way to meet people. Eh, if I'm not being too nosey, what happened to Lady Fiona?'

'About eighteen months ago she was out riding over the hills when something, possibly a deer, startled her horse. It bolted and she was thrown off and damaged the base of her spine.'

'Oh, that's terrible. Was she badly injured?'

'Yes, but she was lucky in that her spinal cord wasn't completely severed. She was airlifted to hospital in Edinburgh and then went to a spinal re-hab unit for several months. She is in a wheelchair but has a private physiotherapist called Matt Hill. She can now walk a few steps. She's recently taken delivery of a converted mini-van with hand controls. It has a ramp which comes out so she can drive her powered wheelchair up it. The driver's seat swivels so she can transfer onto it. It's all done by a handheld control pad. It's brilliant and means she can get out and about on her own.'

Of course it's been tough on Stan, especially now, with his mother, Lady Isobel, being ill an' all.'

'Stan?'

'Lord Scott. Jim and I grew up with him. We used to play together round the estate. His mother, Lady Isobel, is getting treatment for cancer, so all in all they are having a tough time. If you give me a hand at the "big house" you'll get to meet them. I'll look out one of my spare black skirts and a white blouse for you. They should fit.'

'Awesome. I'll look forward to it.' Helping at the 'big house,' as Lizzie called it, would be the perfect opportunity to meet her father and put the first part of her revenge plan into action.

Chapter 5

The pheasant shoot

On Saturday morning Kirsty woke with a knot in her stomach. She'd come halfway around the world to find her father; today was the day she would finally meet him. She wondered what he would be like and if he might recognise something familiar in her. She dressed carefully in the clothes Lizzie had lent her. The white blouse was immaculately ironed and smelt strongly of washing power, the lined black skirt looked expensive, but judging by the sheen on the back it had already seen good service. To her dismay it was too loose, so she fastened the waistband with safety pins. All in all she looked reasonably decent.

'You can do this, girly,' she told herself as she looked in the bathroom mirror to apply styling gel to her recently cut hair. A quick dab of plum lipstick and she was ready to meet the Scotts, but first she needed to get Lizzie's approval.

Nervously she went downstairs and into the kitchen where Lizzie was leaving out breakfast for Jim and Euan.

'Lizzie, do I need to remove my nose stud?'

'No lass, it is okay for you to keep it in place, but you mustn't to wear any rings or nail varnish.'

She held out her hands for inspection. 'Do I pass muster?'

'You sure do, now let's get going.'

***

Stanton Hall was not as imposing as Kirsty had expected but it was a substantial three-storey property that, according to Lizzie, had been extended and rebuilt over the hundreds of years since it started life as a fortified dwelling. On the journey from the airport Euan had told her that somewhere in the Scott past there were links with New South Wales, going back hundreds of years. Euan had even joked, 'You never know, perhaps you are related to the Scott family.' She'd carefully avoided the subject of her family background, other than to share that her great-uncle had a sheep station in the Outback.

It was a 7.00 am start and Kirsty was kept busy in the kitchen. They were laying everything out ready to start preparation when a young man with unruly red hair and a thick beard strode briskly into the kitchen.

Lizzie introduced them. 'Kirsty, this is the estate gamekeeper, Ted Dixon, usually known as Dixie.

'Dixie, this is Kirsty, she is staying with us up at the farm.'

'Hi, I'm pleased to meet you, Kirsty, but I don't have time to chat. I've come to check everything is ready before Stan does his "meet and greet", and I do my safety talk.' Turning to Lizzie he said, 'If could you put some food aside for the beaters and picker-uppers as usual. That'll be grand.'

Seeing the puzzled expression on her face, Lizzie smiled broadly. 'You didn't understand a word of what he said, did you?'

'No, can you translate for me?' Kirsty asked laughing.

'Okay. I'll have a go at explaining the set-up of the shoot. Today there will be ten "beaters" to frighten the pheasants out of the woods, five "picker-uppers" to collect the dead birds and one man on the game cart. These helpers don't eat with the paying guests, who pay a lot of money to shoot the birds. We call them the "guns." They will be greeted with coffee or tea and biscuits before the shoot, so we need to get that ready.'

Kirsty laughed. 'That still doesn't mean anything to me, but I'm here to help. If you want, I can prep the vegetables for the leek and potato soup.'

'Thanks lass. I'll get on with cooking sausages and preparing the dips to go with the homemade relishes I made in the autumn. These will be served for elevenses. Once that's out of the way you can set out the cheese board. I made a dozen large steak pies yesterday to be served at lunch, so they just need heating up in the oven. A choice of beer and wine will be served with lunch so we will need to put out the glasses. We serve tea and cakes at the end of the day.'

While they were preparing the food Lizzie went on to tell her, 'Dixie plays in the band with our Euan. His wife Summer looks after Lady Fiona's horses. They live in a lovely *wee* cottage on the estate. You'll get to meet them next week at the Light Show. Dixie's dad owns the garage in the village, as well as running a local bus service, so you are bound to meet him at some point.'

As Kirsty prepared the vegetables, she kept a lookout for Stan, Lord Scott.

'Kirsty, could you start taking these to the dining room for me and set up the tea and coffee?' Lizzie asked her.

'Of course. Just point me in the right direction.'

Just then a middle-aged man with thinning blond hair came into the kitchen and spoke to Lizzie.

'How are things going? Is everything on schedule?'

'Yes, Kirsty, who you haven't met yet, is just going to set up in the dining room. Let me introduce you...'

The man turned to towards her. He was dressed in tweeds and she wondered if he was one of the 'guns', but was initially distracted by the array of bright coloured pheasants strutting across his tie. He smiled at her.

'So, you're the Australian girl staying up at Holm Farm. Jim mentioned you to me. I'm pleased to meet you. I'm Stanley Scott, but folks round here just call me Stan.' He held out his hand.

Trembling, she shook it and hoped he wouldn't hear her heart thundering in her chest. 'Pleased... pleased to meet you... Stan.'

'Sorry, I can't stay and chat, work to do, pheasants to shoot and all that. But I'm sure we will meet again at some point.'

She'd been prepared to take an instant dislike to Stan; after all, he was the father who had abandoned her, but he was charming and she couldn't help liking him. Then, a thought crossed her mind and she wondered if he'd used his considerable charm to seduce her mother. She was kept busy for the rest of the day and didn't have time to dwell on it.

***

The 'guns' arrived in good time for Dixie's talk. They were dressed in what looked like a regulation outfit of tweed trousers with a tweed waistcoat, a matching jacket and brogue shoes. They all sported ties with various pheasant designs, looking as if they all shopped at the same gentlemen's outfitters or ordered clothes from the same catalogue. She smiled, thinking they looked like clones. She watched Stan working the room for all his worth. Later Lizzie explained that he needed to make a good impression, so they'd come back next season.

That evening she emailed her cousin.

Hi Emma,

I helped in the kitchen today for would you believe it – a pheasant shoot. I met Stan. He introduced himself. A real toff but very charming. Not sure what to make of him.. Desperate for money by the sound of things. The farmer and his wife are looking after me well but still not sure about the son. See ya xxx

The next day Emma replied,

Hi Kirsty, your mum keeps pestering me to say where you are. Please contact her. She's getting frantic! She keeps asking me why you decided to go to Scotland. I never told her about your finding the poetry book or that I helped you track down Stan. Once you get to know him he might be fine. Try to keep out of trouble.

Emma x

At the end of the week Kirsty sent her cousin another email.

Hi Em, I'm exhausted. I ache from head to toe. I'd forgotten how much hard work it is looking after sheep or how much I really dislike the smelly things. I still don't like what farming stands for but Jim & Euan are considerate of their animals. I've spent time getting to know my way round the farm, and I'm even turning into a bit of a sheep wrangler. Looking forward to helping at a Light Show at the Hall on Saturday, which will give me another chance to meet Stan. Hope you're right about him. Kxx

Chapter 6

The Light Show

The hoofs of the horses! – Oh witching and sweet
Is the music earth steals from the iron-clad feet:
No whisper of lover, no trilling of bird
Can stir me as hoofs of the horses have stirred.

Hooves of the Horses by Will H. Ogilvie

There were posters all around the village advertising the light show, which according to Lizzie was a favourite winter event in the local community.

LIGHT SHOW
Saturday 3rd February 2018
STANTON HALL
7.00 pm to Midnight
£15 admission includes refreshment

During the afternoon Kirsty was kept busy in the kitchen helping Lizzie prepare the food for the forty guests invited for drinks and refreshments with the family in the main drawing room. The menu was adapted from the one served at the shooting event, so was straightforward to prepare. Lizzie introduced her to Lady Fiona and Kirsty couldn't help liking her. She was a lively woman in her early forties, who was clearly not going to let a broken back stop her from doing whatever she wanted.

When everything was prepared Lizzie suggested, 'You go and have some time to yourself, Fiona and I will be okay here for now. If you go and find our Euan he will show you round and introduce you to some of the other young ones.'

'Thanks, that's great, I'll do that, see ya.'

Kirsty quickly freshened up in the ladies room, changing into her own clothes ready for the evening's entertainment. Under pretence of finding Euan, she slipped off to look for Lady Isobel. She tried several rooms on the ground floor, opening the door of each room as quietly as she could. The first two rooms were empty but she found her in the third room. As soon as she opened the door her breath caught at the back of her throat, as the familiar smell of a sick room with its unpleasant odours masked by copious lavender disinfectant hit her nostrils. In that instant she thought of her great-uncle back in Australia; he was such a cantankerous old sod, she wondered how her mother was coping looking after him.

The elderly woman fast asleep in her bed looked serene. Was this the woman who had wanted to deny her life? Kirsty stared at her for several moments, then looked around the cluttered room. Her eyes were drawn by the gleam of something silver; a silver cross on a long chain was curled up in a dish on the bedside table. She picked it up and let the silver chain slowly unfurl, the cross dropping into the palm of her hand. She visualised the chain lying round Lady Isobel's wrinkled neck, then yanking it tight.

'Oh hell.' As she went to drop the chain and cross back into the dish, she noticed the chain had got tangled up in knots. Would she be able to untangle it? Just then she heard the door open, and a deep voice boomed out, 'Who are you? Wait... I know you... you're the girl staying with the Youngs, I met you last week. What the blazes are you doing in my mother's room?'

As she turned round to face Stan, Kirsty deftly slipped the silver cross into the pocket of her trousers. Stan looked at her furiously; his face reddened and she could feel anger radiating from him. She felt the colour drain from her face, but quickly regained her composure. She smiled sweetly.

'Oh, I'm ever so sorry. I got lost. I've been helping Lizzie Young with the food and was on my way to meet Euan. I must have taken a wrong turn. I got a terrible shock when I saw the old lady. She was so still I thought she was dead. I was just going to call somebody,' she said holding up her mobile phone.

Stan pursed his lips. He spoke calmly but firmly. 'This is my mother, Lady Isobel. She's been very ill and is on strong medication, so she sleeps a lot. Thankfully, she is on the mend.'

'That's good she is getting better. I'm ever so sorry to have disturbed her. My mistake. I'd better go and find Euan.'

'I'll show you the way to the side door,' Stan replied gruffly. 'You will be able to find your way from there. I hope you will enjoy our little *son et lumiere*. We don't try to compete with the large-scale events but it brightens the winter months, and brings in some much needed income.' He opened the door which led outside down a short ramp.

'Thanks, I can see Euan over there by the stage. I'd better catch him before he gets ready for his set. Eh, it was nice to have met you again, Stan. Sorry that I disturbed your mother.' She'd come halfway round the world to meet her father and on their second meeting had alienated him. If that wasn't bad enough she walked off with a piece of her grandmothers' jewellery. It wasn't a promising start. She ran across the grass to meet Euan.

***

Stan ignored the noise and crowds of the Light Show. There was a good turnout but he was confident Fiona could deal with any problems. He was unnerved by the feisty young Australian he'd found in his mother's room. He went back and sat by his mother's bedside for a while watching her sleep. She had what people described as a 'formidable personality', and they had always had a difficult relationship. She was suffering with cancer of the throat. She'd been a heavy smoker and even his father's death from lung cancer hadn't been enough to make her give up. He remembered her words just before Christmas. How could he forget them? After the first bout of chemotherapy she'd been very sick and asked to see him. Dismissing the nurse she told him something, her voice rasping with the effort it took her to speak.

'I don't think I've got long for this earth so I need to tell you the truth. I've been keeping a secret from you for nearly twenty years. Some might call it a death-bed confession. I'm sorry.'

'What are you talking about, Mother? What secret? Anyway, you are not dying; your treatment is going well, so there's no need for confessions.'

‘Don’t patronise me. When I tell you I’m dying you need to listen to me. Do as you are told. Look in the drawer. There’s an airmail letter. Take it. Read it. It’s from a woman in Australia. It says you were going to be a father.’

‘What? If you are joking, Mother, it’s in poor taste. I assure you there is no way on this earth that I fathered a child in Australia.’ Perplexed, he ruffled up his thatch of fair hair just starting to thin on the top. He sighed. ‘Let me look at this letter then.’

He found the airmail letter exactly where his mother had said it would be. He read the letter several times.

26 Murray Place
Sydney
Australia
23rd Feb 1999

Dear Stan,

I don’t expect you thought you would hear from me again but I need to tell you that I am pregnant with your child. I am not asking for anything from you but I thought you should know you are going to be a father. I intend to keep the child and bring him or her up by myself. I treasure the gift of the book of poetry you gave me, just as I treasure the time we spent together.

We did not know each other for long but I will always love you for giving me a child of my own – a child I will cherish for evermore. You are welcome to keep in touch – or not, it is entirely up to you.

Wishing you a happy life,

Yours truly,
Janine Ainsworth

Stan had happy memories of the time he'd spent working on a sheep station in the Australian Outback but didn't recollect a girl called Janine. He was puzzled by the letter and why this girl had thought he was the father of her child. He carefully folded up the letter and placed it in his jacket pocket. From her letter Janine Ainsworth, whoever she was, sounded lovely.

The next day he set off to Holm Farm to have a word with his old friend Jim Young. Perhaps he would know something about the girl who wrote the letter. The two of them were outdoors by the long field on the edge of Holm Farm.

'What's with the subterfuge? Why did you text me to meet you here? It's a damn long walk from the barns. My knees are giving me gyp. On damp days like this I feel as if I'm going on eighty and I'm not even forty.'

'Jim this is serious business, best kept between the two of us. My mother has just given me a letter sent from Australia nearly nineteen years ago to say I'd got this girl pregnant. There was only the two of us staying at the sheep station. Remember that drunken chap. What was his name? Let me think... Archie something. A bit of a tyrant he was. I know for certain it wasn't me who fathered this girl's child. I was already engaged to Fiona before we left and was faithful to her, heaven knows why, because it was my mother who pressured me into it.'

'*Aye*, you'd got your eye on my Lizzie, if I remember rightly.'

'Don't start that again, old chap. I thought all that was long dead and buried. But think back. I reckon you must know something about this girl. Her name's Janine.'

'What are you babbling on about, man?'

'Just read the damn letter, will you.'

Jim sat down heavily on a large boulder at the edge of the field. He read the letter over twice. Then he shook his head.

'Sorry, Stan. Doesn't ring any bells. Are you sure you didn't meet this lass somewhere when we were away?'

'I can't remember anyone called Janine. I was one hundred percent faithful to Fiona.' He paused. 'Well... at least while we were in Oz.'

***

Shaken by being caught in Lady Isobel's room by Stan, Kirsty ran across the grass to meet Euan. A whole series of lights illuminated the house and gardens in a kaleidoscope of ever-changing colours, turning the historic house into a fairytale castle. She smiled. It was a fanciful notion, but she imagined herself as a modern-day Cinderella. The Ladies Isobel and Fiona were the ugly sisters; Euan was Buttons and Stan, the wicked king who would eventually claim her as his daughter. Lizzie was her fairy godmother, dressing her in a wax jacket and other items of country clobber instead of a ball gown. But who would be her Prince Charming?

Her thoughts were interrupted when Euan walked briskly towards her.

'Come and meet my friends. This is Ted Dixon and his wife Summer. They both work on the estate. Dixie's in the band with me.'

Dixie smiled warmly at her. 'Kirsty, isn't it? We met last week before the shoot. Sorry I didn't have time to chat.'

'Yes. It was a bit hectic, but nothing compared to this. It looks like a good crowd.'

Summer asked, 'I don't know if you are interested in riding, but I work with Lady Fiona's horses up at the stables.'

'Yes. I love riding. It's one of my favourite things. There's nothing I like more than the sound of galloping hooves.'

Summer laughed. 'Funny you should say that. Galloping Hooves is a poem and the name of the café in the village. It is also Bellwether's signature song.'

'Oh. Is it a song? I never knew that.'

Summer held out her mobile phone. 'If you put your number in, I'll let you know when you can come across. I'll introduce you round while the boys get ready to play. The Gimmers are up next, they're great.'

'What? I thought gimmers were young female sheep.'

Summer laughed. 'You're correct, but these Gimmers are an all-girl rock band. They are agricultural students from a college outside Edinburgh. They are very good. Now let's get some food before they run out. All the food on these stalls is vegetarian. There's a good selection. What do you fancy? Thai or Indian?'

'Either will do.'

While they were waiting to be served, Kirsty admired the silver ring Summer was wearing. 'That's an unusual ring. I love it.'

Summer held out the little finger on her left hand for Kirsty to get a closer look. It was engraved with a design of two entwined horseshoes.

'Dixie bought it for me at the Edinburgh Festival last year. I love it and never take it off.'

Suddenly loud music blared from the speakers, lights flashed and mayhem erupted on the stage.

‘Gimme, gimmie. Gimmie this. Gimmie that. Who are we? We’re the Gimmers!’

Kirsty was exhausted as she watched the leather-clad girls strut their stuff. She shouted to Summer, ‘This is awesome. I’m super impressed. They’re as good a group of rock chicks as I’ve seen in Sydney or Melbourne.’

She thought Bellwether, a three-piece band, was more pop and rock than folksy. She really enjoyed their set and had nearly choked on her elderflower cordial when Euan ran onto the stage wearing his tartan Tammie. He was the lead guitarist and another local lad, Billy Moffat, played the bass guitar, Dixie was on drums. They soon had the large crowd singing traditional Scottish songs but with an upbeat twist. They finished the set with their version of ‘Galloping Hooves.’ The crowd went wild and there were cries of ‘encore.’

After they had finished their set Euan and Dixie joined them.

‘Are you okay, Summer?’ Dixie asked anxiously. ‘I thought I saw your ex in the crowd. I hope he hasn’t started his old tricks again.’

‘I’ve not seen him; mind you, there are so many people here he could easily get lost in the crowd. Anyway, as far as I know he’s still working in London.’

Later on, Euan confided in Kirsty about Summer’s ex-fiancé, Carl Noble.

‘He gave her a really hard time after she jilted him a couple of days before their wedding, having met Dixie on her hen night, at a Bellwether gig in Newcastle. Apparently, he caused them problems for a long time afterwards. Dixie is still afraid he is going to cause more trouble. I’ve no time for people who burn themselves out plotting revenge.’

'Eh, me neither,' Kirsty assured him, shaking her head emphatically and crossing her fingers behind her back.

Chapter 7

Border Raiders

Last night a wind from Lammermoor came riding up the glen,
With the tramp of trooping horses and the laugh of reckless men
And struck a mailed hand on the gate and cried a rebel glee:
"Come forth. Come forth, my Borderer, and ride the March with me!"

The Raiders by Will H. Ogilvie

It was a cold, bright morning and Kirsty was gradually adjusting to the Scottish weather; for the first time she noticed her suntan had faded. She dressed in the thick clothes Lizzie had lent her and she smiled at the thought that Tahnee and Ash, her best mates from school, wouldn't recognise her. She wrinkled her nose. Even though she washed her hair and scrubbed herself from head to toe every night, the smell of sheep hung about her like the stink of an old bush ranger. She reckoned the smell lingered on the clothing and decided she would invest in some outdoor clothes of her own as soon as she got the opportunity. She'd washed her hair so vigorously it got tangled. It had taken her ages to get all the knots out and her comb was full of hair. The colour was fading so she'd have to find a hairdresser soon. She would ask Lizzie if she was due a day off to go shopping and get her hair done.

She'd been upset the previous day when she'd overheard Euan complaining about her to his father. 'This lass staying with us is a bit of an enigma. When she arrived her nails were *gie* huge; she could 'ave damn near sheared a ewe with 'em. We're looking for a shepherd, not a beauty queen.'

She heard Jim sniggering, then Euan continued, 'She told me she grew up on a sheep station, yet one minute she shies away from the sheep, the next she charges after them, scattering the flock all over the place. She's like an untrained sheep dog.'

'*Aye* an' all puppy dog eyes an' all. I've seen the way you look at her. Perhaps you could write a song about her.'

'Ha, very funny,' Euan replied, playfully cuffing his dad on the arm. 'I'm not in the least bit interested in her like that. All I need is for her to do the job we've taken her on for. She's no use to us as she is.'

Kirsty had been so angry at what she'd heard, she'd nearly burst in on them, but instead she'd let off steam by sending a text to Emma.

You would not believe the arrogance of the man. As if I'd even look at him.

Emma texted her back with one word: Really?

***

When she'd enquired about shepherding jobs, she'd been economical with the truth. She had grown up on the sheep station until she was six years old, then when she was in her teens helped on her great-uncle's sheep station during her school holidays, but not to the extent she'd told

Euan. When it came to lambing, the Merino ewes were left on their own to give birth. It was the only way her uncle and three station hands could manage a flock of several thousand sheep.

So far, she was impressed by the way that Jim and Euan ran the farm; they weren't cruel in the way that her uncle had been. As a child she'd seen him lash out at sheep many times. She remembered dreading the regular shopping trips with her great-aunt to the nearest town. Their final stop of the day was always to the butchers where her aunt stocked up on various cuts of meat plus plenty of bones for soup. One day the butcher noticed she jumped when he'd chopped the bones particularly loudly. 'Sorry little lady, I didn't mean to make you jump.' After that he seemed to delight in chopping the bones as hard as he could; even though she was very young she knew he was doing it deliberately.

By the time she was in her teens her great-uncle was keeping a small herd of cattle as well as pigs, some of which were slaughtered for their own use. A mobile butcher would come every few months to do the necessary business. One time towards the end of the school holidays, she and Emma had been for a ride round the property and were taking the horses back to their stables; she heard the squeals of terrified pigs being herded into to the pens waiting to be stunned before slaughter. Afterwards she saw the carcasses stacked up in the out-house ready to go into their freezer. That night her uncle roasted one of the pigs on an open fire. She refused to eat the meat declaring, 'Emma and I have fed them since they were piglets. I won't eat them.'

Her great-uncle, who'd had a good few beers by then,

shouted, 'Girlie, you forget you are living on a farm. That's what we do; we grow animals for wool or meat. How do you think we could afford to feed and clothe you all these years when your mother palmed you off on us? This is damn good pork. If you won't eat it there's nothing else on offer, so off to bed with you.'

She ran inside in tears and sobbed herself to sleep.

Returning home, she had declared, 'Mum I'm a vegetarian, don't ever put meat on my plate – I won't eat it. It's too cruel.'

She settled into a routine on the farm and was getting familiar with her tasks. Right from the start she told Euan, 'My uncle used different terms and methods so please explain everything to me as we go along.'

She'd learnt a whole new vocabulary and new ways of doing things and had thought everything was going well. However, she was bitterly disappointed when she overheard Euan griping about her a second time. She was just coming into the kitchen for breakfast when she heard a conversation between him and Jim.

'I don't know why I ever agreed to take this girl on. She hasn't a clue. She hardly knows one end of a sheep from the other.'

'Give the lassie time. She'll soon pick it up. Things are totally different in the Outback.'

She clattered through the doorway and they both turned and smiled at her, wishing her good morning.

'G'day. What's all on for today then?' she asked brightly, trying to cover up her anger.

'We've got a big day,' Euan explained. 'One of the important jobs we need to do before lambing is to vaccinate the ewes, to protect the lambs against tetanus as well as other infections. I'll show you how to read the vaccine labels and how to record the date and batch.'

She was amazed at how quick Euan was at injecting the ewes and fascinated by the way he handled them firmly, yet gently. Whenever they were working, she was drawn to watch his hands and soon knew the faint marks across his right hand where he had injured himself playing rugby and the tiny birthmark on the knuckle of his left hand. Willing herself to concentrate, she marked each ewe with a dab of red dye on the top of its head, to make sure they didn't get a double dose, and carefully recorded the relevant information.

Jim whistled to himself while they worked. The tune had a familiar ring to it and it kept running through her head as if it was on a loop; it took her a while before she realised it was 'Galloping Hooves', Bellwether's signature tune.

After each batch of ewes was vaccinated Kirsty helped to round them up and move them back to the fields to graze.

'That's a good day's work done, lass,' Jim said smiling. 'You've been a good help. The next important task we need to do before lambing is shave the ewes under the tail and between the legs to remove any clumps of dirty wool we call "dags", so they don't get in the way when they are lambing.'

'Okay. I've seen my uncle do something similar with the Merino sheep, but never helped.' She shuddered at the thought of it.

A few days later she woke with a knot in her stomach. After a quick breakfast of cereal and toast she reluctantly made her way to the sheep sheds. Jim and Euan were already in the largest shed.

'Hi lass,' Jim called out. 'Watch. You'll see how the job is done.'

Euan looked up at her and smiled. She felt her stomach lurch.

She nodded and watched apprehensively while Euan put the ewes into the correct position and Jim deftly shaved them. She could see they were being as gentle as possible. The cacophony of bleating echoed off the metal roof of the barn; in that instant she was transported back to the sheep station and was six years old again, watching her great-uncle and a team of contractors busy in the shearing shed. They were carrying out a process called *mulesing,* removing the skin round the buttocks and the base of the ewe's tail. She heard the screaming of the terrified sheep as the shears tore away the flesh; she heard the echo of her own sobs, then her uncle's harsh voice yelling, 'Stop your crying, girl. It's a farm, not a bleeding holiday camp. I don't know what your mother is doing palming you off here every damn holiday. Get out of my way before I wallop you.'

***

Fearing she was going to faint, she leaned heavily against the wall of the shed.

Jim looked up. 'Are you all right, lass? You've gone deathly pale.'

'I'm okay. I was just thinking about my family back in Oz.'

'Get yourself back up to the farmhouse. Have a cuppa and some tucker. Lizzie has left a stack of sangers. We'll be along soon.'

'Thanks,' she replied laughing at Jim's attempt at Aussie speak.

Worried that Euan and Jim would realize her lack of experience and terminate her employment before she'd even started on her revenge plan, she was determined to prove herself. After lunch, she made a concerted effort to help with the task. She watched closely as Euan held each ewe in position and Jim carefully shaved it with a pair of sharp clippers; she told herself it was the same as her shaving her friend Ash's head. Euan let go of the sheep and it ran to join the others, totally unconcerned by its ordeal.

'Can I give you a hand to get the sheep in position?'

'*Aye*, lass, that'll be a grand help.' Jim smiled as he watched her and Euan work as a team and finish the job in record time.

'Well done lass,' Jim complimented her, putting his arm round her shoulders.

'I'm impressed. We'll make a Scottish shepherd of you yet.'

'Thanks for having faith in me, Jim.' Kirsty felt warm inside at Jim's praise, but guilty at deceiving him.

***

Next morning it was her turn to do an early check on the sheep. She didn't mind rising at 6.30, especially if the sky was clear and the dawn sun gradually lit up the sky, staining any clouds with delicate wisps of red and pink. Today the dawn sky was streaked with grey; the gathering clouds gradually obliterating the red, forming ominous shadows on the hills. She wanted to get the sheep checked before the rains came tumbling down. By now she could tell the difference between the young rams, known as 'tups', and the 'first crop ewes', the first-time mothers that needed a careful eye on them, and the more experienced two- and three-crop ewes. She knew her way round the fields and which sheep should be in each field, so immediately realised something was wrong.

The field with the thirty-odd barren sheep was half empty; the gate was lying loose. Perhaps a walker had left the gate open and they'd got out. If so, where were they? She skirted all around the fields on the quad bike as fast as she could and looked for the escapees, but there was no sign of them. She headed back to the farmyard where Euan was cleaning out the cowshed. She yelled at him, 'Half the geld sheep are missing.'

She took a deep breath and continued, 'The gate was flapping open. I've searched all round the adjacent fields and can't find them anywhere.'

'That's not good. I wonder if they've been taken during the night. I'll come out with you and check again. We can ill afford to lose livestock.'

They searched all the fields and checked the gullies round the field edges, but still no sign of the missing sheep. It had rained in the night and Euan spotted some unfamiliar tyre marks along the back road near to the field from where the sheep had gone missing. This confirmed his suspicion that they had been stolen. He phoned the police station at Kelso, who told him there had been several sheep rustling incidents locally and they would pass the details onto the Police Scotland's Rural Crime Unit.

Crestfallen, Euan sighed heavily. 'That's the last we'll see of them. They've almost certainly been taken to be slaughtered for meat.'

'What! I can't believe there's sheep rustling in such an idyllic place like this.'

'It's easy money for some unscrupulous folk. Mind you, the Borders has a long and bloody history of cross-border raids. I'll look out some books if you are interested.'

That evening Kirsty e-mailed Emma to tell her what happened.

Hi Em, we had an upset on the farm today. Would you believe we had 15 sheep stolen overnight? Never imagined there would be sheep rustling here. Lizzie and Jim are very upset. Euan was a star and helped me search. Now I'm getting settled I need to make more of an effort to get on with my plans. Kirsty xx

Chapter 8

The Galloping Hooves

It was four weeks since Kirsty had arrived in Scotland. She was frustrated at not having made progress with her plans, other than for leaving a few negative reviews about the Light Show on the estate website. However, a chance meeting in the village shop gave her the opportunity she was looking for. Lizzie asked her to go with her into the village to buy extra supplies while she went to see Dixie's father George, who owned the garage in the village, to arrange an MOT for the Land Rover and didn't know how long she would be.

'George also runs the local bus service. I'll pick up a timetable just in case you ever need it. And be warned, the shop manager, Netta Grieve, is the village busybody. I swear she must have been born with two sets of ears. She knows everyone's business, so don't tell her any secrets unless you want it spread round the village by lunch time.'

'Okay, thanks for the heads up,' Kirsty laughed.

Lizzie dropped her off in Stanton Holm village which comprised a small shop cum post office with an adjoining cafe, a pub, and a garage with a few stone-built houses scattered at intervals either side of its approach roads. She stopped for a few moments to admire one of the houses with a thatched roof, and a charming pocket handkerchief front garden, with a snowdrop filled border. It was enchanting; she's seen nothing like it at home. Turning to face the other direction, she could see the church in the near distance at the end of the village towards of Stanton Hall.

The weather forecast had dire warnings of heavy snow and Lizzie wanted her to stock up the store cupboard with extra provisions, in case they were snowed in. The shop was well stocked, and she soon found all the items on the shopping list: pasta, rice, lentils and other dry ingredients. She was impressed that the shop stocked a range of vegetarian and dairy-free products, and bought some oat milk and some Soya desserts as well as a supply of vegetarian sausages and meat free mince. Several people said hello or nodded to her.

The shop was packed tight with displays of merchandise, and she had to step backwards to avoid colliding with an elderly woman. She made her way round the other side of the shop to look at a display of greeting cards. She was looking at the selection of condolence cards when she felt a sudden pain in her right foot.

'Oh, that hurt,' she screeched.

'I'm sorry, Miss. I didn't mean to stand on your foot.' A man held out his hand to steady her. 'Allow me to introduce myself, Matt Hill. I'm a qualified physiotherapist. Please let me examine your foot to see if it is broken.'

Kirsty recognised the name. He was Lady Fiona's physio. In his 30s, tall and muscular, he was dressed in lightweight jogging gear even in the cold weather. She stammered, 'I don't think it is broken. I just need a minute and I'll be fine.'

'Netta, can we have a chair for this young lady to sit

on?' he asked, flashing her a charming smile with perfect white teeth.

The shopkeeper nodded as she brought out a chair from the side of the counter; heavy red ceramic beads round her neck clacked together like beads on an abacus.

'Sit yourself down, lass. I keep a chair handy in case any of the older folk or pregnant mums need to sit down.'

Kirsty forced a tepid smile, wondering which category this beautifully dressed middle-aged woman with her fair hair, worn in a neat chignon, thought she fitted. Matt carefully examined her foot and ankle, taking longer than was strictly necessary. As he leaned towards her Kirsty detected the strong musky scent of his body odour, and wondered if he'd come straight from a jog. She smiled up at him, wondering if it would nicely mess things up with Fiona Scott if she went after this dark-eyed Adonis.

Looking directly into her eyes he asked, 'If you have finished your shopping perhaps you can join me for a coffee, by way of an apology.' Turning to Netta he added, 'The coffee shop next door has good coffee and excellent cakes, doesn't it?'

'*Aye*, you're right there, Matt. Fresh made today.'

Turning to Kirsty she said, 'I'll keep your messages behind the counter for you, lass.'

'What messages? Has Lizzie Young left a message for me?'

'She means your shopping. You'll need to learn a whole new lingo living here,' Matt explained, doing his best not to laugh.

Netta put the bill for the farm's shopping onto Lizzie's account. Kirsty paid for her own purchases and accepted Netta's offer to keep the bags of shopping behind the counter for Lizzie to collect later. Matt helped her into the coffee shop cum bistro. Once she was safely seated, she sent a text message to Lizzie to let her know to meet her there and asked her to pick up the shopping.

Kirsty looked round the room, entranced; she felt she'd gone back in time. The café had dark wooden beams; the whitewashed walls were decorated with pictures of fox hunting and fishing scenes. The small wooden tables were covered with red gingham tablecloths and a smell of fresh baking pervaded the air. The café was called 'Galloping Hooves.' The name had a familiar ring to it. Feigning ignorance she commented, 'The name of the café is unusual. What does it mean?'

'I believe it is from a poem by a Borders author called Will H Ogilvie. Apparently, he spent some time in Australia years ago and is known as a bush poet. I don't know if you will have heard of him.'

Kirsty shook her head, not wanting to admit he was the author of the book of poems her father had gifted to her mother and the reason she'd ended up in Stanton Holm.

Matt's mobile phone rang. Glowering, he picked it up, glanced at it, frowned then turned it off. The look on his face suggested he wanted to fling it across the room as far away as possible.

Before Kirsty could ask if anything was wrong, he said, 'It's not important. It'll wait. Now tell me all about yourself.' He leaned towards her across the table looked at her directly.

Kirsty felt her heart lurch but forced herself to concentrate.

'I decided I wanted to travel... see a bit of the world before studying, so I've put my place to study physiotherapy at university in Melbourne on hold.'

'A physiotherapist? Well, that's another thing we have in common as well as being outsiders. We outsiders must stick together.'

'Outsiders? Why are we outsiders?'

'Anyone who was not born here is an outsider. You could live here for forty years and still be an outsider. The locals are always suspicious of outsiders, or "in-comers," as they call them. You're an Aussie. I'm a Geordie.'

'A Jordy what?'

Matt laughed. 'It means someone who comes from the area around Tyneside and Newcastle in the Northeast of England.'

The two of them got on well and by the time Lizzie arrived they were exchanging mobile numbers, to make arrangements for Kirsty to visit to him at the gatehouse. Matt helped her into the Land Rover.

'I'm looking forward to showing you round the estate.'

'Me too,' Kirsty agreed, trying to contain her smile.

***

Like most gatehouses, the one at Stanton Hall was in two halves. Matt lived in one half and had set up the other half as a physio cum fitness studio, referred to simply as 'Matt's Gym.' He was employed to give Fiona daily physiotherapy sessions, for which he was provided with free accommodation and received a weekly payment to cover his personal expenses. Their agreement allowed him to provide freelance personal fitness sessions, which brought in a small amount of extra income. He and Fiona had been due to meet up in the gym for lunch before his afternoon appointments. He would be late, and hurried back; he needed to keep her on side. The money lenders were pestering him to pay off his debt and he was running out of options. Meeting the Australian girl had given him some ideas. Risky but potentially profitable.

***

Fiona was waiting for him when he got there and she wasn't in the best of moods. The last thing he wanted was an argument.

'What kept you? I've been twiddling my thumbs till you got here. I thought you'd stood me up.'

'No need to fly into a radgie, woman,' he laughed, lapsing into Geordie slang. 'But actually, I have... well, sort of. I've been having coffee with that Australian girl staying with the Youngs. I've invited her here for a visit. Hope you don't mind.'

'I've met her. She's a pretty girl. Should I be jealous?'

'No, of course not. Anyway, she smells of sheep.'

'What, not horses like me?'

Matt laughed. 'Seriously, you're improving so much that I won't be able to justify my role here much longer. Stan's sure to get suspicious. There are already rumours going round the village about us. I tried to put Netta Grieve off the scent by having coffee with the girl. I'll show her round the estate, give her a coffee and send her on her way. End of story.'

'If you've been eating the generous slices of cake they serve at the Galloping Hooves, you won't be wanting any lunch.'

'Do you think I'm a greedy gannet, woman? Surely not with a figure like mine?' He posed, flexing his biceps and then tried to kiss her but she pushed him away.

Fiona smiled up at him as she opened the two boxes of salad she'd brought with her and unwrapped a piece of Italian flatbread for each of them. Matt reached over and took a bottle of flavoured water from the bag. His mobile phone rang. He turned it off.

'Sorry about that. It's the service provider; they keep pestering me to increase my data. Anyway, did you tell Stan about us?'

She shook her head.

'Look, Fiona, you need to tell him soon that you want a divorce... unless you are planning on us doing a moonlight flit and simply running away together.'

'I need to sort out the divorce settlement, but my legal advisor is away on holiday and I don't trust anyone else. As you know perfectly well, I'm the one with the money, not Stan. With the estate struggling financially I need to make sure he doesn't clean me out.'

'It's all right, don't get worked up,' Matt tried to reassure her. 'Come here and give us a kiss.'

***

Later that afternoon, after his second paying client had left, Matt went through his phone messages. There were three missed calls and several text messages all from the same number, all saying the same thing:

PAY UP OR ELSE – YOU HAVE TILL MONDAY

He checked his bank balance. He'd maxed out all his credit cards and had been blocked out of his usual online gaming accounts. He was under pressure to come up with the money. But he didn't have it. He still owed the casino £6,000. When his gambling debts had spiralled out of control, he'd compounded his problems by borrowing £20,000 from some money lenders, in the expectation of getting money from Fiona Stanton, but his plans were getting nowhere. Now the money lenders were impatient, making threats of violence if he didn't pay back the money. He'd heard rumours of the damage they'd inflicted on others, so knew they weren't empty threats. Adding all his debts and interest payments, he owed nearly £30,000. He was desperate.

He had several ideas of ways to get the much-needed cash but they were risky. He'd gone across to Stanton Hall before Christmas to review Fiona's physio sessions for the holiday period. The door to Lady Isobel's room had been partly open and he'd overheard a conversation between her and Stan about his having an illegitimate child in Australia. He hadn't wanted to stoop to blackmail but it was looking as if he didn't have a choice. If only he could find the letter the old girl had talked about he'd be quids in. He was sure Lady Isobel wouldn't want the shame of an illegitimate grandchild being made public. Even if Stan didn't care about it, perhaps he could use it to pressure Fiona to leave him.

In January, desperate to pay off the money he owed, he'd promised himself one more throw of the dice, and had been to the casino in Newcastle, but his plan had backfired and he was in even more debt. However, the evening hadn't been a complete loss; he'd met an ex-comrade from his army days, who had just started as a doorman at the casino. They had palled up when he'd undertaken his ill-fated trial for the Special Services Unit. At the end of the evening the two of them had chatted briefly about their past and exchanged mobile numbers. Matt was sure he would be a useful contact. It was time he contacted him.

Chapter 9

The Beast from the East

When she'd accepted the job at the Young's farm, Kirsty hadn't realised it was so near to Stanton Hall and that the two families had such close ties. She worried it was only a matter of time before her identity as Stan's illegitimate daughter was revealed. The displays of greeting cards at the village shop gave her the nudge she needed to get her revenge plan underway. All it took were a few keystrokes on her phone, and a tasteful condolence card was on its way. She wondered what the reaction would be at Stanton Hall.

She'd been in Scotland five weeks and the weather was getting cold. She was woken by light pouring through the window; thinking she'd overslept she jumped up in panic. She hastily opened the blind; the green fields were turning pale in front of her. She rubbed her eyes. It was snowing. The hills in the distance were white and a fine covering of snow clung to the trees in the garden. She threw on some warm clothes and hurried downstairs to the kitchen where Lizzie was busy making breakfast.

'Where are Jim and Euan?'

'They were up before first light ready to bring down some more of the Cheviots.'

'It's a pity we never managed to bring them all down

yesterday. I should go and help them.'

'Don't worry, lass, they'll be back soon enough and you can help them move the rest of the sheep off the hill. You've time for something warm to eat before going out. I've made some porridge. You can sweeten it with sugar or honey if you prefer. I expect you're not used to snow like this.'

'I've hardly ever even seen snow. I've certainly never experienced anything like this,' she agreed, peering through the kitchen window at the snow-covered farmyard. According to the weather report on the radio, a cold wind had blown in from Siberia; it was dubbed the 'Beast from the East.' At first it blew in gently purring like a snow leopard waiting to pounce, sugar-coating the hills with a fine dusting of snow. Gradually, the finest of snowflakes lay like white confetti, turning the hills from green to white.

She heard Jim and Euan at the outer door of the boot room banging off the snow from their boots. They looked half-frozen as they burst into the kitchen and light-heartedly jostled each other for the best place to stand in front of the warm stove.

'How've you got on?' I'm sorry I didn't get up early enough to help first thing,' Kirsty apologised, as she finished her breakfast.

'It is okay, the in-bye sheep, the first to lamb, were near the house anyway. We've moved the Cheviots that are due to lamb first to lower ground but will need to bring the rest of the sheep further down to where they'll be more sheltered.'

'Kirsty, you'll be up to giving us a hand, won't you?' Euan asked, looking pointedly at his father.

Kirsty wore several jumpers under the old wax jacket

that Lizzie had found for her. She pulled on the waterproof trousers over her leggings and then, wearing two pairs of wool socks, pushed her feet into a pair of Euan's old Wellingtons. She wound her scarf tight around her neck, and then added the matching beanie hat and a pair of mismatched gloves. She followed Jim and Euan as they made their way outside to gather in the rest of the sheep to lower ground.

Silence hung over the fields. Kirsty stopped and gasped as the cold air hit her lungs. When she breathed out her breath hung like tiny clouds of mist in front of her; her teeth chattered and her nose felt cold but she smiled. The view in itself was breathtaking, which couldn't have been a bigger contrast from the hot sunny weather she'd left behind in Sydney. From her stays at her great-uncle's sheep station in the Outback, she was used to extreme weather conditions – drought, flood, even bush fires – but nothing like this.

Stunning though the view was, she wasn't there to sightsee and needed to catch up with the others. She'd rarely ever walked in snow, so was glad when Lizzie pushed a red plastic shepherd's crook into her hand as she left the farmhouse. Pulling her hat down as far as it would go she leaned forward into the wind and headed across the farmyard, walking cautiously for the first few steps, hoping she wouldn't fall. She felt her feet sink into the partially frozen snow and leaned onto the crook to help keep upright. Gradually, she got her balance and was able to quicken her walking pace from stop start to slow motion. She was relieved to eventually reach the barn where the quad bikes were stored without landing flat on her face.

Euan exchanged a triumphant look with his father, then turned to Kirsty. 'Well done making it this far. It must be about thirty steps.'

'Thanks. I think,' Kirsty agreed, unsure if he was being sarcastic.

'Ah, and there I was betting you'd only make two or three before falling,' Jim laughed.

Jim took the quad bike, accompanied by his old dog, Will. Kirsty and Euan set off together on the other bike as far as they could get, then walked the rest of the way, followed by Ruff and May. Every step in the snow, which was deeper the higher up they went, was an effort for Kirsty but she was determined to keep up with Euan.

Once the sheep had been herded to lower ground and the large round metal containers were set up with bales of silage, they headed back to the farmhouse for a warm and something to eat.

After an early lunch Jim and Lizzie headed out to check on the cows, which were kept in the barns near the house. Kirsty accompanied Euan for one last check on the sheep. The combination of wind and snow together were dangerous for sheep, so Kirsty and Euan needed to be extra vigilant on their rounds to make sure none had got stuck in a snowdrift.

In spite of her aching legs, once all her jobs were done, Kirsty went for a walk round the farmyard before it got too dark. She wanted to get her 'snow feet', so that she would feel more confident the next day. She stopped to look all around her, captivated by the beauty of this frozen world. Drops of snow resembled glittering diamonds, beaded along the top of the fencing surrounding the fields. Snow stalagmites grew slowly along the guttering around the farmhouse. The stream that ran along the bottom of the hillside was already frozen solid. She heard muffled footsteps in the snow behind her.

'Duck!' Euan shouted.

Before Kirsty could ask what he meant, a ball of snow hit her on the top of her head, showering her with clumps of snow.

'What the blazes is going on?'

'You've never had a snowball fight before?' Euan asked, laughing as he pelted her with snowballs. 'Come on lass, give it a go.'

Feeling fury building up inside her, Kirsty bent down and packed handfuls of snow together. The first two missed their mark, hitting the barn wall. Euan couldn't contain his laughter; while he was doubled up in mirth, Kirsty's third attempt hit him squarely on his shoulder. She followed this up with several more hits to his body.

'Okay. I surrender,' he laughed, holding up his hands. 'Come on. It's getting dark. Best get back before Mum and Dad wonder where we've got to.'

***

The Scottish Borders was firmly in the grip of winter, bringing life to a near standstill. By next morning the snow had drifted up several feet round the back door of the farmhouse. Euan got the shovel, kept outside the back door, to dig it out.

'Come on, Kirsty, you can help me with the cattle this morning,' he called out to her as she finished the plate of beans and eggs on toast Lizzie had made for her. The cattle were all in the barn nearest the farmhouse, so the work was warm and dry. Jim used the tractor to take bales of silage up to the sheep on the lower hillside.

Lizzie told her that sometimes the weight of snow brought down the power lines and once it took over a week for power to be restored. 'But don't worry; we have plenty of candles and batteries as well as fuel for the stove in case the electricity goes off.' It was fortunate they had stocked up the store cupboard, so they never went hungry.

It was a strange feeling being cut off from the rest of the world, but Kirsty didn't have time to dwell on it. During daylight hours she was kept busy round the farm; out and about by 7.30 am to get finished with all the outside chores before it got dark round about 5 o'clock. They spent their evenings playing card games and scrabble. Euan and Jim delighted in using as many Scottish words as they could and challenged her to guess their meaning. They all ended up laughing until their faces ached. But the laughter stopped awkwardly when she confessed that she'd not always understood what they were saying.

'*Dinnie* worry, lass, you'll *ken* the words *yesel*, soon enough,' Euan told her trying not to laugh.

'Okay, two can play at that game.' Keeping a straight face she continued, 'but I'll be kind and start with an easy one.' She placed the letters to make the word, '*chook*'.

'Too easy, I know that one, it's chicken,' Euan said, placing the letter s, on the board so that the letters *e,i,l,a* made the word *Sheila*. 'Okay, if I mix up my lingoes I can say that you are a *braw Sheila*.'

'How would you like a *skelp* on the lug?' Kirsty grinned, then playfully clipped him round the ear.

When Jim won, with *sangers, cobber, bludger* and *arvo,* she good-naturedly congratulated him. 'Jim, I'm really impressed at your extensive Aussie vocabulary.'

Jim moved uneasily in his chair.

'Jim are you go—' Lizzie started to ask when he cut her short.

'It's been a fun night, but it's an early start in the morning so I'd better get some kip.' He got up and left the room without saying goodnight.

Another evening Euan and Jim gave an impromptu music recital and she joined in with Lizzie in the choruses. To her surprise she really enjoyed it, belting out the words to 'Galloping Hooves' at the top of her voice.

'Lizzie, you must let me give you a break from the cooking. I'll make a veggie curry tomorrow if you like.'

'Okay, if you insist. It will make a change but don't make it too spicy or Jim will get heartburn.'

Kirsty enjoyed herself making the meal and even found herself humming the tune of Galloping Hooves. She made some flat bread to go with it, but wished she'd been able to buy poppadoms and mango chutney to make it into a more authentic Indian meal. Euan and Jim pretended to turn their noses up when she served it, but they cleared their plates. She felt all warm inside when Euan asked for a second helping.

***

When the thaw came it was rapid; four sheep drowned in the early morning when the stream near the farm that had been frozen solid, providing a bridge between fields, suddenly melted and became a watery grave. Jim had spotted them lying in the water when he had gone out first thing to check everything was okay. He rushed back to the house, clearly upset.

'With having lost sheep to the rustlers, we can ill afford

many more losses. I'll go back and collect them after I've had something to eat.'

'Don't worry. I'll do it,' Euan volunteered.

Kirsty offered to help and, mindful of seeing her great-uncle bury dead sheep, she went to pick up the spade, but Euan shook his head.

'That's no longer allowed due to the risk of spreading disease. There was a big outbreak of foot and mouth disease some years back. Loads of animals had to be slaughtered. It was devastating.'

'Wow, that must have been tough.'

***

Taking the quad bike, they rode through the fast-melting snow to collect the dead animals. They carefully lifted the sodden ewes and placed them in the trailer. Then they took them to a lidded container in the nearest field accessible from the road, ready for collection by the local knackery as soon as the roads were passable. They worked in silence as they completed their grim task.

As Euan turned his back to close the lid, Kirsty grabbed a handful of soft snow and landed a snowball in the centre of his back. Splat.

'Okay then, if you want to play it like that,' he challenged her, grabbing a fistful of snow. 'I dare you.'

They laughed as they pelted each other with marshmallow-soft snowballs.

'Let's make snow angels,' shouted Kirsty excitedly. 'I've seen people make them on TV, but there's hardly any snow back home so have never had chance to try it.'

'You can, but I'm warning you, you'll get soaked.' Euan moved stealthily towards her then pushed her firmly on her shoulder. She fell backward.

'What the hell...?'

'It's easy, just move your arms and legs...' Euan sniggered as he demonstrated the movements, but before he could finish his sentence, Kirsty leaned forward and grabbed his trouser legs, pulling him towards her. His feet shot out from under him. He toppled forward and thrusting his arms out in front of him, managed to prevent himself from falling on top of her. Their eyes met briefly, but both quickly looked away. Euan rolled over so they were both lying on their backs in the snow.

'Let's make the snow angels and then get back. Ma will have tea on the table.' Wondering if he'd gone too far Euan helped Kirsty up. Avoiding each other's gaze they brushed themselves down and headed towards the farmhouse.

***

Later, after they had changed into dry clothes, they went to check on the in-bye sheep in the field nearest the house. The hedges were decorated in the most amazing sculpted snowdrifts worthy of Henry Moore or Barbara Hepworth. Ruff ran ahead of them to where snow had drifted up against a section of the stone dyke, where there was a holly hedge growing in a corner. He started barking excitedly and digging frantically in the snow.

'I wonder what's going on there,' Euan shouted, perplexed. 'We'd better go and check.'

The air was still cold, so Kirsty pulled her hat further down and followed Euan up the incline, followed closely by May. As they got further across the field, May started barking and sped up towards the corner, joining Ruff digging in the snow. By the time Euan got there he heard bleating and a head appeared through the snow. He carefully dug out handfuls of snow to reveal a ewe and her twin lambs huddled in the corner. The lambs were tiny but still alive. He managed to scoop up the lambs.

Kirsty gasped as Euan pushed them into her arms. 'Wow, this is a miracle.'

It took some effort for Euan to heave the ewe out of the snow drift which had compacted around her. 'Let's get them all back into the barn and warm them up. The mother must have been nibbling on the leaves of the holly bush, which kept her hydrated. We'll see how the lambs get on but we probably need to supplement their feed with a bottle till they put on weight.'

That night Kirsty texted her cousin.

Hi Em,

We've been snowed in all week! It went down to minus 7. The sheep are fine but it was hard going bringing them down to lower ground. I love the snow and being out on the hills. We've spent the evenings playing scrabble and card games and Euan and Jim gave an impromptu music recital, I even cooked a veggie curry and they loved it. Today we found a ewe with twin lambs that had been trapped in a snow drift. It was a miracle they survived.

Kxxx

Chapter 10

Trapped

Matt Hill watched from the gatehouse window as the blizzard raged. He felt trapped, like a forlorn icing sugar figure peering out from the window of a log cabin on a Christmas cake. Fiona phoned him after the blizzard hit.

'Matt, the road down from Stanton Hall is completely blocked. There is no way for anyone to get through. Stan will get one of the farm workers to clear it with a tractor as soon as possible.'

'Okay, but make sure you carry out your exercises at least twice a day. I'll phone you every day to check on you and talk you through them if necessary.'

'I promise I will keep them up. I'll be at the gym as soon as the road is clear. Let me know if you need any urgent supplies and I'll see if someone can bring them to you.'

'Thanks for the offer. As long as the snow doesn't last too long I'll be fine.'

Each day Matt dug out the snow between his living quarters and the gym to allow him access to his equipment to work off his excess energy. Because of the bad weather he'd been unable to do anything about raising any cash to pay off the loan sharks, but at least with the roads blocked they physically wouldn't be able to get to him. He was blocked out of all his online accounts so they didn't pose any temptation. However, being trapped indoors was enough to trigger the bad dreams that plagued his sleep whenever he felt under extreme pressure.

'No Dad, don't, he shouted. 'I'm hungry. Don't leave me here all night.' He thumped on the inside of the coal shed door and yelled again. 'Dad, please Dad. I'll be good.' No answer. Then he heard his father's slurred voice.

'Coming, son. If you've pissed your pants again, I've got my belt ready.'

Then the nightmare morphed into something even more sinister, picking up fears that had been lurking in the back of his mind since he had been thrown out of the army. This time he was incarcerated in a military jail.

'Please let me out,' he pleaded with the prison guard who'd placed a plate of food just inside the door of his cell; the food was crawling with maggots. He picked up the metal plate and flung it against the cell door.

'Let me go, let me out,' he shouted. Instead, an officer appeared in his cell, in front of a table laden with food. Matt gnawed on a piece of dry bread, while the officer feasted on roast chicken. Matt's mouth watered as he watched the officer finish off his main course and then devour a large portion of apple pie with custard. A whip rested at the officer's feet which he picked up periodically and lashed out at Matt leaving red, raised welts across his bare flesh.

'Tell me where the rest of your squad are hiding.'

'Sir, I'm sorry, I cannot answer that question.'

'Tell me where the rest of your squad are hiding.'

'No Sir. I'm sorry, I cannot answer that question.'

'Tell me where the rest of your squad are hiding.'

'Hill. 18.07.1984. Sir.'

Leaping up, Matt screamed, 'Let me go, you bastard.' He darted towards the officer, grabbed the remains of the chicken drumstick from the plate and rammed it down the man's throat.

His screams tore through the ice cold of the tiny gatehouse bedroom, waking him from his uneasy sleep. The sheets were damp with sweat and his skin was covered in scratches where he had clawed at his arms and legs in his effort to escape his tormentors. Ravenous, he got up and padded barefoot towards his tiny kitchen to see what food he could find. He pulled out a couple of hardboiled eggs and a protein shake from the fridge. Looking at how little there was in his fridge, he knew he'd have to ration what was left; the last thing he wanted was to have to ask Fiona to send him food.

Being isolated in the gatehouse was giving him too much time to dwell on the past. He'd had a good career as an army physiotherapist, but wanting a challenge, made the fateful decision to try out for the Special Services Unit. He failed the final part of the training due to his own stupidity, and ended up being thrown out of the army. Given a small sum of money to tide him over until he found work, he took the train to London where he booked into a hotel for a couple of nights, planning to go back to Newcastle to look for a job. The lure of the casino was too much; before he could stop himself, he'd gambled through his remaining cash.

Penniless, he spent several weeks living on the streets of London, where he was befriended by an army veteran called Willie. Willie became his mentor, showing him how to survive on the streets; where to bed down for the night without straying onto someone else's patch, where to get food thrown out from shops and cafes, that was only just out of date. One night as Matt made his way back to his sleeping spot under the railway arches, he saw one of the younger guys spraying a can of lighter fuel into Willie's face. Reacting instantly, he dived between them, tackling the assailant to the ground before they could throw a lighted match in the old man's face. Grabbing his water bottle, he threw its contents over Willie to wash off the lighter fluid. As he made to turn his back, the assailant flew at him. From the corner of his eye Matt saw the knife blade glint in the streetlight; he dropped to his knees and flung the man over his head. The man landed heavily but got up cursing and swearing; he ran off stumbling over people lying asleep, expletives echoing through the night.

That night Matt experienced an adrenaline rush as great as, or even greater than, the excitement of the casino and knew he had to get off the streets or he would die there. He ended up squatting in an unoccupied semi-detached house in Walthamstow. The owners were abroad, so if challenged he told people he was their house sitter. He went jogging every morning in the local park, striking up conversations with the local residents, and offering to do any odd jobs. Soon he was cutting people's hedges, mowing lawns, even dog walking. After a couple of weeks he was doing casual labour on a building site, cash in hand. The hardest part was not getting drawn into any card games at the end of the day, so instead he treated himself to a take-away or a fish shop meal. The first Friday night he went home with a fist full of ten-pound notes in his hand, he stopped off at the corner shop to stock up on food. After he had polished off his fish supper, he gorged on a family sized lemon meringue pie. With head over the toilet pan, he was consumed with guilt as he brought it all back. 'Damn it Matt, if you are ever going to get your life back, this HAS TO STOP NOW. Get a grip,' he yelled at himself in the mirror.

He'd left the army with skills which he decided he might as well capitalise on. A search of the homeowner's desk revealed passwords for the computer. He set up a website, complete with fake reviews and testimonials, to advertise for a job as a private therapist. He was hoping a rich widow or two might want to employ him. Within a few days he received a request from a Fiona Scott in the Scottish Borders for a live-in physio. She was willing to pay the substantial fee he asked and to provide accommodation as part of the package. It was too good an offer to turn down. He carefully packed up his things from the house, cleaned his emails off the owner's computer and, with the money he'd saved from working, bought an old Renault car.

When he arrived at Stanton Hall, he discovered Fiona Scott was anything but a rich widow. Rich yes, widowed, no. Her husband was the local landowner and they lived in a large house on a country estate. She was very attractive but lonely and he soon used his considerable charms to seduce her, but his plan to get her money had stalled. He needed a quick injection of cash.

He phoned the ex-army colleague he'd met at the casino in January, who turned out to have several useful connections with ways to raise some quick cash. As an outsider staying on the estate, he would be a prime suspect, so he needed to find a scapegoat to take the blame in case things went wrong. He had just the person in mind.

Chapter 11

Lambing Fever

The snow was still on the ground when the first lambs started to make their appearance. The ewes were brought into the largest barn when they were nearly ready to lamb. Kirsty was anxious ahead of what would be the biggest test of her fledgling shepherding skills. However, she need not have worried. Euan carefully talked her through the signs to look for when a ewe was about to give birth.

'Often, they will separate themselves from the others; look out for a bobbing head and lifting of her tail. Most of the ewes will lamb on their own but some will occasionally need help.'

'Oh!' Kirsty exclaimed with her head full of the descriptions in the sheep husbandry book of all the ways things could go wrong.

'Don't look so alarmed. It isn't as difficult as you might think.' He smiled as he tried to reassure her.

The first dozen or so ewes delivered their lambs without any help. Kirsty watched awestruck, fascinated by the way nature took over, as if a silent hand guided the ewe as she gave birth. Early one morning as she came into the lambing shed, Euan shouted to her, 'You're just in time, this ewe is going to need a hand.'

Kirsty watched in awe as Euan pulled hard on the two

feet poking out of the ewe's backside; the lamb slipped out of its birth sac, all yellow and bloodied. Immediately the ewe bent down to lick it dry.

'Look out for the twin. It should come out on its own.'

They both heaved a sigh of relief as the second lamb slipped unaided into the world. Then Euan showed her how to dip the umbilical cord into a wide-necked jar of iodine to make sure it didn't get infected.

'Next time you can have a go. We'll make a shepherd of you yet.' Euan laughed, as she pulled a face at him.

Her chance to lamb a ewe came a few days later when she spotted a ewe in the corner of the pen which looked in difficulties. Fortunately, Euan was there and helped her guide it into a lambing pen on its own.

'Okay Kirsty. Talk me through what you need to do.'

She closed her eyes and visualised how Euan had done it. She muttered Euan's instruction under her breath. 'Imagine that the lamb is in a diving position, with its head between its front legs. Put your fingers in and feel for the two front feet then pull firmly; the feet and head will slip out.' Taking a deep breath she plunged her hand into the sheep; it felt wet and slippery. Feeling for the feet, she took hold of them and pulled as hard as she could. The lamb slipped out onto the straw. Silence. Something was wrong... it was struggling to breathe.

'Okay,' Euan spoke calmly. 'Now pick up a piece of straw and tickle it up its nostril to make it sneeze. That'll clear its nasal passages and then it will be able to breathe on its own.'

She did as instructed and then held her own breath, until the lamb took its first breath. Its mother nuzzled towards it and started licking it dry. Soon it was suckling on its mother's milk; a few minutes later the lamb was trying to get up on its feet.

'Well done lass. Grand job.'

Before the day was over the barn was full of more newborn lambs waiting to be turned out into the fields. When she got back to the house Kirsty rushed upstairs to change and couldn't resist texting her cousin.

> Hi Em, I'm so excited. I've just delivered my first lamb. I feel like I'm a shepherd after all. It's all go here. I'm needed with the sheep so my revenge plan will have to be put on hold at least till lambing is over. Kxxx

She worked long hours and was exhausted at the end of every day, hardly able to put one foot in front of another. Jim and Euan called it 'lambing fever'. She thought that in many ways caring for the lambs after they were born was harder than the actual lambing itself. When they were a day or two old, she learnt how to attach identification tags to their ears before they were turned out onto the fields. Billy Moffat, who she'd met at the Light Show, came in to do the night shifts, with Jim and Euan taking turns to support him. By the time there was another fall of snow on the 2nd April, which was Easter Monday, she took it all in her stride.

***

She and Lizzie shared the task of bottle feeding the 20-odd pet lambs who were either rejected by their mothers or when the ewe had died. She helped Lizzie mix the milk powder with warm water; each bottle held enough to feed four lambs. The first couple of times she struggled to hold the lambs, which squirmed in her arms, desperate to get to the teat. The bottles were made of soft plastic and she tried not to giggle when she accidentally sprayed Lizzie with milk, which ran through her hair and over her face.

When they were newborn the lambs were fed four times a day: 8 am, 12 noon, 6 pm and midnight, gradually reducing the frequency as they started to eat pelleted food. The lambs were increasingly heavy and she was exhausted by the time she finished. It was feeding on a near industrial scale; a far cry from the romantic image she'd had of sitting with a pet lamb on her lap by the kitchen stove.

Occasionally Euan helped her feed the lambs and the two of them worked well together, getting into a steady rhythm. When they had finished Kirsty brushed her hair from her eyes and looked up to see him smiling at her.

'What are you grinning at?'

'You... you look totally at home with a lamb in your arms... like a born farmer.'

Kirsty laughed. 'Thanks for the compliment... I think.'

Euan was right. She was comfortable with a lamb in her arms. She felt an unexpected feeling of warmth and contentment holding each wriggling bundle of life in her hands. She loved it and wondered what her friends Ash and Tahnee would think if they could see her now. It was if something inside her had shifted. She'd been so horrified by how her uncle treated his animals on the sheep station, that she'd equated any form of animal husbandry as being the same. She still felt some methods were cruel and had no regrets in gluing herself to a wagon transporting live sheep for export. But the way Jim and Euan treated their animals was a revelation to her.

Chapter 12

The Gatehouse

Beneath the green fir branches where doves sit wing to wing
A maid comes up the pathway across the woods of Spring;
Her face is lit with sunshine, her eyes are soft with showers,
Her heart is filled with music and both her hands with flowers.

April by Will H. Ogilvie

It was over a month since Kirsty had met Matt Hill in the village shop. Today's visit to meet him at the gatehouse, delayed due to a combination of the snow and lambing, was the perfect opportunity to snoop round Stanton Hall estate.

When she'd gone to check on the sheep early that morning, the sky was heavily overcast with black clouds, as moody as her mother after a bad day at work. Kirsty loved the smell of the damp air first thing in the morning and wondered if it was a trait of her Scottish genes.

It seemed to her that once the snow had melted, spring had come in a hurry. The leaves on the apple trees in the garden unfurled like green caterpillars, then burst into a haze of pale pink flowers, promising a bumper autumn harvest. A light breeze blew the clouds away and the sun was shining; it was a perfect day for her visit. She could have easily walked to Stanton Hall, but Lizzie was going to meet up with Fiona Scott to plan the weddings and other events booked for the coming season, so insisted on dropping her off at the gatehouse.

As soon as she got out of the car Matt came out of his door; he was dressed in grey jogging gear, with a black and white bandana tied round his head. 'I'll show you round the estate first,' he called out enthusiastically, 'just follow me.' He strode purposefully along the paths round the estate with long lolloping strides and Kirsty had to walk fast to keep up with him.

It all looked so different from when she'd been there for the Light Show; each twist and turn of the main paths revealed another beautiful vista. Everything was green and lush. The air smelt fresh and clean; it was such a contrast to the dry heat she was used to. The grass banks round Stanton Hall were glowing with drifts of crocuses in shades of purples, yellows and oranges. Fat spikes of daffodils peeped through the grass and Kirsty couldn't wait to see them in full bloom.

'Wow. It's so beautiful,' she exclaimed, captivated by the spectacle.

Matt insisted they go for a walk through the woods at the edge of the property, which were filled with swathes of snowdrops. The pretty white flowers were just past their best but still beautiful and she wished she'd seen them a week or two earlier. She couldn't resist snapping a few pictures on her phone.

Matt gushed, 'this whole area will be carpeted in an array of bluebells in a couple of weeks, but before then it's the Spring Open Garden event next Sunday. You will be amazed at the variety of lovely flowers in people's gardens.'

He turned to her, smiled then leaned towards her. For a moment Kirsty thought he was going to kiss her. Her heart beat rapidly... but then he took a sudden step back and pointed to some buildings at the side of the main house. 'That's the stable block. I'll race you.'

He ran off at speed. Kirsty, caught off guard, struggled to catch up with him.

'That was mean of you,' she gasped out of breath as she reached the stables. Matt laughed.

There were two horses stabled in adjacent loose boxes, with an adjoining tack room at right angles. One of the horses was being groomed by Summer Dixon, whom she'd met at the Light Show.

'What magnificent horses. Are they Lady Fiona's?

'Yes, this is Dusty, her prize black horse. I ride her regularly to keep her in good condition until Lady Fiona is well enough to ride.'

She turned to an attractive grey horse, inquisitively looking over the door of the second loose box.

'This is Blaze, she's a young mare. The two horses are great companions.'

Kirsty went over to Blaze and stroked her head gently. The horse lifted up her ears, then responded with a gentle whinny, nuzzling Kirsty's fingers.

'I see you two are going to be great friends. Let me know when you want to come across to ride her. I'll show you round the estate. You can see so much more on horseback.'

Matt was getting restless. Looking directly at Kirsty he declared, 'It's getting nippy so let's get you indoors for a warm. Come on and I'll show you round my little palace.'

As soon as Matt unlocked the front door, Kirsty smelt

the aroma of fresh coffee. 'Wow, I never expected anything like this,' she gasped looking round.

'The gatehouse is tiny but it has everything I need,' Matt said proudly. 'There's a galley kitchen, a shower room and a bedroom. But come through into the sitting room and get yourself warm. I left a pot of coffee to percolate while we were out, so it won't take me a moment to pour.'

Through an open door into what she assumed was his bedroom, she saw a tiny alcove with all his clothes hung neatly. Somewhat incongruently there was a stack of what looked like neatly ironed underpants set out like a concertina on the mantelpiece above an old fireplace. There was a motto hung on the wall: 'A place for everything, everything in its place.'

Kirsty settled into a worn Parker Knoll armchair and relaxed in front of the tiny wood burning stove. The small room was dominated by a mahogany, glass-fronted corner cabinet. She guessed the décor was country house style and wondered how much of the furnishings belonged to the estate and how much were his own. Matt carried in two china mugs of steaming coffee on a large tray with some fresh scones from the village shop, which he served on a plate with a white doily, accompanied by a pot of strawberry jam.

'I'm impressed, Matt. This really is charming. There's nothing like this back home. I love your display cabinet. You have some really nice things. Are they antique?'

'Most of them belonged to my grandmother,' he replied wrinkling his brow. He opened the cabinet and took out some pieces of green Wedgwood pottery and some blue and green enamelled Art Deco jewellery.

'Oh, these are lovely. Can I try them on?' Kirsty asked,

enchanted by the colours of a pair of earrings and matching brooch; the blues and greens shimmered in the light.

'Of course,' Matt agreed, 'but do be careful with them, they are of great sentimental value.'

'Are you kept busy working with Lady Fiona? I met her on the evening of the Light Show. She seemed very nice. From what Lizzie Young has told me it sounds as if Lady Fiona is improving.'

'Indeed, she is. She's very nice, a real Lady,' Matt admitted.

'That's good news. If you need to move on, I'm sure she will give you a good reference. Are there many opportunities for physiotherapists round here?'

'There is bound to be, but I don't want to tempt fate by looking too soon.'

'Fair enough,' Kirsty laughed. 'You never know what happens. I suppose I am hoping there will be plenty of work for me back home after I qualify... but that will be a few years away.'

'Let me know if I can do anything to help? Maybe I can lend you some books if you want to do some preliminary reading.'

'Thanks, but I want to concentrate on the job in hand.'

'But let's keep in touch. Perhaps we can go for a jog together when you have finished lambing. I can show you the best runs through the hills.'

***

While Kirsty was with Matt Hill, Lizzie and Fiona were planning the up-coming wedding season. Lizzie couldn't help notice Fiona looked downhearted as she poured their coffee.

'What's wrong?'

'We've had several bad reviews about the Light Show. Stan's livid. We can't afford for such a big event to get a bad reputation. We need income early in the year to fund advertising of the wedding packages. Look...' Fiona took out her mobile and showed the comments to Lizzie.

What a rip off- Light show was a real waste of money – the lights were second- rate – a real disappointment. As a family of four it cost us a fortune – the only thing my teenagers enjoyed was The Gimmers – the all girl band.

Went to light Show at Stanton Hall. Won't bother next year - if they have the cheek to do it again.

Poor showing: I took my girlfriend to the light show planning to propose to her, thinking it would be the perfect setting and look good on Instagram, but so bad I kept the ring in my pocket.

Lizzie thought for a few moments before responding. 'At first glance they look damning but actually the one about the families has given me an idea. We could offer an Early Bird Family booking, with heavier discounted family tickets, if people booked say by the middle of December. People could buy them as Christmas presents. It could bring in more families.'

'Great idea. In fact I'm surprised we've never thought about that before. I'll put in a response thanking them for their helpful comments.'

By the time they had finished their second coffee

Lizzie was full of ideas. 'The lights were much better than previous years so I think that particular comment was unfair and we should ignore it, but the comment about the engagement photo has given me another idea. How about we set up viewing points to take photos? We could even link it to our wedding event packages, giving a discount to couples who get engaged at the Light Show. We could call it a Diamond Package.'

'What a sparkling idea,' Fiona agreed laughing. 'Talk about turning a negative into a positive.'

'Well, I'm sure there will only be positive reviews about next week's Open Garden Event,' Lizzie said as she picked up a copy of the poster from a pile on the table.

STANTON HOLM ESTATE
SPRING OPEN GARDEN EVENT
Sunday 15th April
10.00 to 3.30
Lady Fiona Scott
will judge the gardens.
Prizes to be given out at 3.00pm in the marquee.

'Do you want me to put up some more posters round the village? I've another idea; Euan is going to the agricultural merchant in Kelso tomorrow. If Kirsty went with him she could put some posters round the town. It will be a good way for her to get to know her way round.'

***

Kirsty enjoyed the unexpected trip to Kelso. It was an attractive market town with lots of independent shops; Euan dropped her off at one of the two main shopping streets while he did his errands. It didn't take Kirsty long to hand out the posters; she found a chemist where she stocked up on toiletries, delighted to find her favourite brand of plum hair dye, saving her an expensive trip to the hairdressers. Thrilled to find a sizable branch of a well-known clothes store, she bought some tops and a couple of pairs of jeans.

She arranged to meet Euan in the town square at 11.30. Running late, she saw him from across the square waiting by the Land Rover. Her heart beat fast as she ran towards him.

He smiled. 'Do you mind if we go to the garden centre? It isn't far. Mum gave me a list of seeds to buy for the garden.'

The garden centre was larger than Kirsty had expected for a small town. It didn't take them long to purchase the seeds. Kirsty chose a peace lily, with a profusion of white flowers, as a gift for Lizzie, to thank her for being so welcoming and understanding about her being vegetarian.

Purchases paid for, Euan suggested, 'We could eat at the garden centre café but as it's a lovely day we could get some sandwiches and go for a walk by the River Tweed. Which would you prefer? You choose.'

'A walk please.'

As they strolled side by side along the river bank, Kirsty was acutely aware of Euan next to her. Resisting the desire to hold his hand she took out her mobile phone. 'This is just lovely, the river is so calming. I must take some photos to send back to Australia.' She clicked away, then stopped suddenly, pointing to the opposite riverbank. 'What's that tall grey bird, poised like a statue at the water's edge?'

'It's a heron. I expect it's his regular fishing spot.

Beautiful though it is, we will need to be getting back to the farm soon. I promised to finish checking the rest of the fencing.'

As they drove out of Kelso, Euan turned and pointed out Springwood Park to her. 'That's where the Spring Fling is going to be held in May. It'll be a *gie braw* do.'

Kirsty smiled hoping he would invite her.

***

Kirsty was looking forward to the Open Garden Event; she and Euan had arranged to meet up with Dixie and Summer. Lady Fiona greeted people at the front of Stanton Hall with a map of the woods round the house and the location of the six gardens that were open on the estate. Kirsty enjoyed herself. It was good to be able to relax away from the farm for a while. It occurred to her she wasn't a bit homesick at all. There was no sign of Stan, and she wondered where he was, but decided not to waste time brooding about her revenge plot.

She was captivated by the colours of the spring flowers and the way people had made the most of even the tiniest cottage gardens; several even had miniature ponds with waterlilies or water features. They spent couple of hours looking round before it suddenly started to shower.

'Here, come under my brolly,' Summer shouted to Kirsty. Together they made a beeline for the refreshments marquee, which was crowded as people took shelter from the rain. Netta Grieve and her sister were helping Lizzie to serve refreshments. Kirsty and Summer joined the queue, while Euan and Dixie Dixon found a table in the corner of the marquee. Twenty minutes later Kirsty made her way through the crowd to the table. She carried a plate piled high with a selection of pastries and scones, followed by Summer, balancing a tray of hot drinks.

'Wow, that was some queue. You two got the easy job,' Summer moaned to Dixie, as she placed the steaming mugs of coffee on the table. 'I overheard the judging of the gardens has had to be postponed due to the heavy rain.'

'We've been planning our programme for the Spring Fling in Kelso next month. It will be here before we know it.'

'Does that mean more practising?' Summer asked coldly. 'I'm fed up of spending my evenings alone.'

Euan turned to Kirsty. 'Once the rain eases off a bit more, Dixie and I are going to have to head off and spend a couple of hours at band practice. Do you want to stay here with Summer?'

'Oh, yes please do,' Summer replied, 'I'll show you round the stables first then you can come back to the cottage for coffee.'

'Okay. I'll pick you up from there when I drop Dixie off.'

Before they left the marquee Kirsty headed back to the bar to return their empty plates and mugs. Netta was talking to an attractive dark-skinned girl with jet black hair woven in braids, coiled round her head. The girl moved away just before Kirsty got there.

'Kirsty that was Sia Laidlaw I was just chatting to, she's about your age or maybe a little older. She a wonderful musician and plays the guitar. I'm surprised Euan and Dixie haven't asked her to join Bellwether. I think the two of you will get on famously. I must introduce you sometime.'

'I'll look forward to it. I promise to call in the shop but don't know when it will be, we're still busy with the last of the lambing.'

***

It was a long time since Kirsty had been around horses and she was thrilled with the idea of riding again. She hadn't seen Matt Hill at the garden tour but saw him jogging past the cottage on his way to the gatehouse. He gave her and Summer a cheery wave and she hoped they would be able to meet up for a jog when lambing had finished.

Kirsty settled herself on the settee while Summer made coffee in the tiny kitchen.

'The cottage is a bit on the small side, but there's just the two of us, so it will do for now.' Kirsty thought she heard a hint of wistfulness in her new friend's voice.

Looking round Kirsty said, 'You've certainly given it a modern touch with the navy cord suite and gold accessories. I really like it.'

'Thanks.' Summer carried two oversized white mugs, with outlines of horses' heads on them, and placed them on the gilt-edged glass coffee table that stood in front of a small wood burning stove.

'I like the gilt-framed mirror above the fireplace, it's a great way to bring extra light into the room,' Kirsty commented admiringly. Photos of Dixie and Summer in gilt photo frames were displayed on the mantlepiece.

'Is that a photo album I spy?' Kirsty pointed to a navy photo album, with gold tassel, sitting on the corner of the coffee table. 'Do you have any photos of your sister in Melbourne?'

Summer picked up the album, and then sat next to Kirsty on the settee, pointing out her sister Faye, who looked to be several years older. A good-looking Black man, about her sister's age, appeared in a lot of the snaps and Kirsty wondered who he was. 'Wow, is that your sister's boyfriend? He is such a hunk; just look at those muscles, he looks as if he spends most of his time surfing. Is he Australian?'

Summer shook her head and sighed deeply. 'No... that's Carl Noble, my ex-fiancé. I didn't realise I'd left so many photos of him in the album. He came out with me to Australia for a couple of weeks, a few years ago. He was in the army catering corps and he had just finished a long tour of Afghanistan.' She sighed. 'I expect you've heard the gossip.'

'Euan mentioned in passing that you and Dixie met at one of their gigs. It seemed a bit rock and roll to me.'

Summer laughed. 'You make me sound like a 1960s groupie. I was on my hen night, but I had been having doubts. We had a blazing row just before I left. Carl said, "Honey," he always called me that, "don't cop off with any other blokes while you're away." He made me feel so cheap.' She pulled out a slim envelope from inside the cover of the album and handed her a couple of photos. 'Look at these.'

Kirsty had to look twice to realise the short skirted, bleached blond girl was Summer.

'Wow, you look stunning. You made a perfect couple.'

'Perfect, is the right word. Physical looks meant a lot to him. He always wanted me to have the shortest skirts, the longest eyelashes, and blondest hair of any of his mates' girlfriends. He was always immaculately groomed and obsessively self-conscious about a scar above his right eyebrow. It must have initially been a tiny cut but because of the way his skin healed, it formed a bigger area of scar tissue, which he thought spoiled his looks. I kept telling him it was hardly visible.'

'Your hair is gorgeous as it is now. Is it your natural colour?"

'Yes. For some unknown reason Carl hated red hair. If I didn't agree with anything he said or wanted to do, he'd call me a "ginger whinger", or even worse a "ginger minger".'

'He sounds very controlling.'

'You're right; he was very controlling and treated me like a living doll, with no opinions of my own.

'When I saw Dixie leaping onto the stage with his long red hair flying behind him, something clicked in my head. I got talking to him after the show and knew if I married Carl, I was walking into the biggest mistake of my life. Dixie gave me his phone number and I telephoned him as soon as I got back home and arranged to meet him. I knew even if nothing developed between us, I could never marry Carl. The upshot was Carl blamed Dixie for splitting us up and made our life miserable for a while. He seemed so bent on revenge that I'm always worried he is going to reappear and make our lives miserable again.'

Kirsty leaned forward and gave Summer a hug. 'Don't worry. I'm sure his thirst for revenge will have burnt itself out by now. These things usually do once the person has got their anger out of their system.'

Chapter 13
What's going on?

Just before the Beast from the East descended, Stan had been troubled. One morning when he had gone through the post, he'd put the brown envelopes to one side to open them later in his study. Fiona always complained he never remembered important dates so when he spotted a plain blue envelope he wondered if he had missed a birthday or anniversary. He opened it and took out a card. He gasped in shock. It was an unsigned condolence card.

'Wishing you every sympathy on the death of your mother'

Thankfully, his mother was responding to treatment, but he was perturbed. Who would do such a terrible thing? The postmark was smudged so there was no knowing where it had been posted. He had kept the information about the condolence card to himself, but Fiona was with him when a week after the thaw, a funeral wreath of white lilies was delivered. The card was unsigned.

To the Scott family.
Sorry for your loss.

'This is terrible, Stan. Why on earth didn't you tell me about the condolence card straight away?' Fiona moaned at him as she searched the card and envelope for clues of its sender. 'I'll check in the village shop, but I don't think the card is a brand they stock.'

Several phone calls to the florists in the area didn't reveal who had sent the wreath either. They realised the card and flowers were probably ordered over the internet and it would be impossible to trace who had sent them. It was a mystery. A troubling one at that.

Stan was relieved his mother had continued to improve, getting up out of bed for a few hours each morning. The following week he heard shouts coming from her bedroom and went to investigate. His mother and her nurse were in the midst of an argument.

'What's all the shouting about? Mother, what's going on?'

'I am feeling much brighter today and wanted to get dressed and join you and Fiona in the dining room for lunch.' She pointed angrily at the nurse. 'I asked her to pass me my silver cross from my bedside table. But it was gone.'

Stan turned to the nurse who looked agitated. 'I searched on the bedside table. It wasn't there. I looked to see if it had fallen on the floor.'

Stan could hear the familiar tut-tutting sound his mother made when her wishes weren't carried out immediately.

'Mother, please let the woman finish explaining what happened.'

'Sir,' the nurse explained, 'this might be presumptuous of me, but when I realised the silver cross was missing,

I checked your mother's jewellery box and noticed that several pieces of her collection of Art Deco jewellery were also missing.'

Stan managed to dissuade his mother from sacking the nurse on the spot. Good nurses were hard to come by, especially ones who could put up with his mother's moods. There was something going on; first the condolence card, then the wreath, and now the missing jewellery. It couldn't just be a coincidence. There had to be more to it.

***

Stan confided his fears in Jim Young when they met up at the edge of the long field. 'With so much funny business going on at the house I'm thinking of hiring a private detective.'

'What's wrong with notifying the police?'

'Nothing, I suppose. But I want discretion. This all started after that girl came from Oz. What do you know about her? Did you get references before offering her the job?'

'To be honest I'm not sure. At the time I had various appointments at the hospital about my knees, so Euan dealt with all the arrangements. As far as I know she's on a gap year before starting a course in physiotherapy at university. I think she lives in Sydney; the family have a sheep station in the Outback and she helped there during her school holidays.'

'Jim, the Outback's a damn big place. Do you know whereabouts it is or the name of it? Do you know who in her family has the sheep station?'

'No. But why are you getting so agitated about this?'

'Maybe I'm being paranoid, but I wondered if it is the

same place we stayed at. How old did you say she was? Do you know what her family name is?'

'Erm I... I'm not sure...' Jim hesitated as he tried to remember what Euan had told him about the girl.

'Surely you should know all this,' Stan snapped at him impatiently.

'I think her last name begins with an A... possibly Armstrong. But to be truthful I don't know. I didn't think to ask but she must be about eighteen or nineteen, about the same age as our Euan. Do you think she has something to do with it? Surely it must be a coincidence.'

'I found her in my mother's room the night of the Light Show. She could have taken the silver cross. She was acting suspiciously. Do you know if she's short of money?'

'I don't know. Look, I'll get Lizzie to have a quiet word with her. She's better at that sort of thing than me.'

'Jim, I don't think it is a coincidence. Don't think I didn't notice you sneaking off with the station owner's niece when we were in Oz. She's sure as hell not my daughter but she might well be yours. You need to be careful about her and Euan. If my hunch is correct they could be half-brother and sister.'

'What?' Jim pulled a horrified face at him.

'Don't look at me like that, this is serious. Let me know how you get on. I've got to get going. I've got a meeting with Hamish Braverman. You've met the fellow and know how persistent he is. He's been pressing me for a while to go over the estate accounts with him. Things aren't looking too good.'

'Wait a minute. Don't turn round. I think someone is watching us from the trees partway up the hill.'

Stan turned round. 'I can't see anyone. Who's sounding

paranoid now? I really must be off.'

***

Lizzie was perturbed when Jim asked her to speak to Kirsty about Lady Isobel's missing jewellery and to find out more about the girl's background. She'd heard the gossip in the 'big house' about Stan being sent a condolence card and then a funeral wreath for Lady Isobel, and was surprised Jim knew about it. She sensed there was more to his request than he had let on, but they had been married long enough for her to know he would tell her in his own time.

'Surely the wee lassie wouldn't have anything to do with it.'

'That's what I told Stan, but he was insistent. We don't want him going to the police. Best speak to the lassie. While you're at it try to find out why she chose our particular farm to work at.'

'Okay, okay, I'll speak to her at breakfast.'

***

Next morning when Lizzie called Kirsty for breakfast Jim and Euan had already set off on their early morning rounds.

'Are you sure you won't have a cooked breakfast, lass? I can do you a couple of eggs and a veggie sausage if you like.'

'No thanks, Lizzie. Cereal and some of that oat milk I get at the shop, with a piece of toast and some of the vegemite I brought with me will be ample.'

'I need to ask you something, lass, but I'm not sure how to approach it, so I'll get straight to the point. There are a few things amiss at the "big house". I'm not accusing you, but do you know anything about who could have sent a condolence card or funeral flowers to Lady Isobel? She's been very poorly but is getting better. And now her silver cross has gone missing.'

'Oh hell. I think I've got the silver cross. I got lost after I'd helped you at the light show. I... I ended up in Lady Isobel's room by mistake. I was admiring the silver cross when Lord Scott came in her room and must have put it into my trouser pocket without thinking, the silver chain got tangled when I picked it up. I was going to undo the knots and return it when I got the chance, but I have been so busy with the sheep I forgot about it. I don't know anything about the other things you mentioned. I'll run up to my room and fetch it. It's bound to still be there.'

Kirsty ran upstairs and looked for the offending item, which she'd hidden in a sock in the drawer in the bedside table. Damn. Which sock was it? She wrenched out the drawer and tipped the contents on the bed. She hadn't brought that many socks with her so it couldn't be far. She checked every pair but couldn't find it. Then she spotted a single striped red and yellow sock lying on the floor by the washing basket. She picked it up and felt something in the toe. Halleluiah! She gave a sigh of relief and wondered why she'd pocketed the silver cross in the first place. She was still furious at Stan and his mother for abandoning her as a baby, but Lizzie and Jim were so kind to her she was experiencing some feelings of guilt about her revenge plan. But there was no point in her confessing to Lizzie about sending the condolence and funeral flowers until she'd revealed her identity to the Scotts.

She ran back to the kitchen out of breath and placed

the silver cross and chain onto the table. Near to tears she blurted out, 'Please tell the Scotts, I'm ever so sorry. I had forgotten all about it. I don't want them to think I'm a thief.'

'It's okay, lass, don't you worry. I'll speak to them for you,' Lizzie reassured her, putting her hand over hers. 'You must miss your family in Australia. Do you live with your mother? Do you have any brothers or sisters?'

'Just me and my mum, she's a schoolteacher,' Kirsty replied, wondering why Lizzie was asking her all the questions.

'Actually I wondered what make you choose this part of Scotland to stay?'

'No particular reason. It was just a contact through the Young Farmers...'

Just then, Euan opened the door from the boot room, popped his head round the door and shouted, 'Come on Kirsty, hurry up. I've not got all day; we've work to do.'

***

A few days later Lizzie was at the table in the kitchen doing the farm accounts when the front doorbell rang. Most people came to the back door, so she wondered who it could be. Opening the door she was surprised to see two police officers standing on the doorstep. The young female officer took a couple of steps backwards when a message came over her radio so the police sergeant did the talking.

'Sorry to disturb you, Mrs Young, we need to speak to a young lady you have staying here.'

'Do you mean Kirsty Ainsworth?'

'*Aye*, that'll be her. Is she around?'

'No, she is out with my husband rounding up the sheep

in the top field. Can I be of any help?'

'When will they be back?'

'Lunch time. Around 1 o'clock.'

'Okay, we will come back later.'

Puzzled, Lizzie waited till they had gone, then set off to find Kirsty. Perhaps something was wrong with her family in Australia.

'Kirsty, I need to speak to you urgently,' she shouted to her as she saw her and Jim in the far field. 'It's the police. They want a word with you, lass. They didn't say why but will be coming back around lunchtime.'

There wasn't a mobile signal on the outer reaches of the farm, so it wasn't till she got back home that Lizzie found the message from Stan, warning her that his mother had insisted he go to the police. On finding out about the condolence card and funeral flowers Lady Isobel been distressed, but the missing silver cross and Art Deco jewellery had been the final straw. She'd flown into a rage at him and insisted he called the police.

***

Lunch was so tense that it was a relief when the doorbell finally rang. Lizzie showed the officers into the kitchen. They introduced themselves.

'I'm Sergeant Tom Elliot and this is PC Sia Laidlaw.'

Kirsty kept her head down while being questioned. She was furious, especially as Lizzie had promised she would speak to the Scotts and smooth things over. Now she was made to feel like a common criminal. The cross had been a genuine mistake – she had been intending to smuggle it back, and then forgotten about it. She didn't consider sending the condolence card and flowers as a 'crime,' more like an making a nuisance of herself, although she regretted it now she realised how much upset she'd caused.

'But as I told Mrs Young, it was a mistake. I'd never been in such a swanky house before; all the doors looked the same and I got lost. I explained this to Lord Scott at the time. I hadn't intended to take the cross. I'd never met a lord before and was nervous...' she stuttered, head bent low. 'I don't know anything about a card or funeral flowers or know anything about other missing pieces of jewellery.'

After the police had left, Lizzie was full of apologies.

'Kirsty, my dear, I'm so sorry about that. I'm so annoyed with the Scotts. Once I'd returned the silver cross to Stan, with your heartfelt apologies to Lady Isobel, I had not expected it to go any further. Apparently, it was Lady Isobel who insisted on calling the police.'

Kirsty struggled to hold back her tears.

'Look lass, why don't you take some time for yourself.'

'Thanks. I'll go for a walk. It will help me clear my head.' As she crossed the farmyard she turned and waved to Lizzie, muttering under her breath, 'Trust it to be that bitch, Lady blooming high-and-mighty Isobel Scott, to cause trouble. I'd been feeling guilty about my revenge plan, but not anymore. Well, wait to see what I've got in store for her and her arrogant son. She's seen nothing yet.'

Chapter 14

The Comfort of the Hills

Heart! If you've a sorrow
Take it to the hills!
Where pity crowns the silence
And love the loneness fills!
Bury it in bracken
Waving green and high:
O'er it let the heather's
Peaceful purple lie!
Trust it to the healing
Heaven itself distils:
Heart! If you've a sorrow
Take it to the hills!

The Comfort of the Hills by Will H. Ogilvie

Kirsty was furious. So there so much swirling round her head, it felt like the fierce Scottish snowstorm she'd experienced in February. She was humiliated at being questioned by the police. The sight of the uniformed officers instantly brought back memories of the trauma she'd suffered the previous year, at the heavy-handed treatment at the hands of the police in Australia. She hoped the local officers wouldn't go as far as checking her record with the police force in Sydney.

She'd taken part in an animal rights demonstration at a large cosmetic research laboratory, with a group of friends from school. More people turned up than had been expected; the large crowd turned from boisterous to rowdy, with some people charging the lab gates. When the police arrived someone started throwing plastic water bottles; before she knew what had happened, she was dragged across the pavement by her hair, manhandled into a police van and held overnight in a cramped police holding cell with twenty other protesters. She was relieved to be freed the following morning with a caution.

Her mother had come to pick her up and was incandescent with rage, yelling at her in front of her friends. Her mother complained all the way home, how she'd let herself down and that her stupidity had ruined her chances of a university place. When they got home she'd retaliated.

'Mum, didn't you do impulsive things when you were a teenager? Like getting pregnant by some random bloke the minute you finished school. I bet you didn't even know who he was. That's why you can't tell me anything about him.'

Her mother went quiet, suddenly lifted her hand and slapped her across the cheek.

'Oh, that stung!' Kirsty exclaimed, more in shock than in pain.

'I'm sorry, my darling, I shouldn't have done that.'

'Too right you shouldn't. Stay away from me.'

'Please forgive me. I don't know what came over me.'

The two of them never spoke for days. The tension between them in their tiny flat was so bad that Kirsty was tempted to phone her cousin Emma and ask if she could stay at the sheep station for a while, but she had exams coming up so had to stay in Sydney.

***

Kirsty hoped a walk would help her calm down. She skirted across the hills intending to follow the old stone dyke back to Holm Farm. As she headed over the hills, she remembered trying on some Art Deco jewellery at Matt Hill's house. They had met up a few times for a jog round the estate, but since he'd shown her round the gatehouse she'd never been back inside. She decided she would seek Matt out and ask him about it. Fighting back tears, she changed direction and headed across the fields to Stanton Hall. As she passed above a stand of trees overlooking the long field, she saw Matt standing behind a large conifer, as if he were hiding. She waved to him but he was looking towards the edge of the field so never saw her. Then she spotted Jim and Stan in an animated conversation and wondered why Matt was watching them so furtively.

As she made her way up the hill, she stopped at a section above where the dyke dropped down towards a stream. The view was stunning. She breathed in deeply, smelling the freshness of the spring air all around her. Overhead she heard the now familiar mewing of buzzards: keey ya, keey ya, they called as they effortlessly soared upwards on the thermal currents. Suddenly it was if her worries were lifted off her shoulders, soaring high into the sky, flying away with the shrieking buzzards. She stood awhile enjoying the view, absentmindedly fingering the keys of the quad bike in her pocket, then she followed the wall upwards towards the summit of the hill.

She stopped and gazed down at Stanton Hall in the valley below. It looked idyllic and she wondered what it would have been like to have grown up there. It would have been unimaginably different from growing up in a crowded inner-city suburb, with a single parent, struggling to make ends meet. Her mother worked school hours, but left her with neighbours when she had to stay late for parents' evenings or to attend courses. She was resentful at being packed off to her great-uncle's sheep station every school holiday, and bitter she'd never had a father to spoil her, or call her 'my little princess'. She wondered what sort of father Stan would have been.

While she was in deep thought she hadn't noticed dark clouds building up. Large drops of rain landed with a plop on her jacket. Within minutes the rain lashed down, forming rivulets of brown water gushing down the hillside. It was getting dark, so instead of risking cutting over the fields back to the farm, she headed for a footpath leading to the village. Glad to leave the rain-drenched hillside, head bent down, she hurried along the road. Beads of sweat glistened on her brow despite the chill. By the time she got to the village she was soaked so decided to treat herself to coffee and a comforting piece of cake at the Galloping Hooves, before heading home.

She nipped into the ladies and dried her hair as best she could by putting her head under the hand dryer. She ran her hands through her hair, which was damp but at least it wouldn't drip into her coffee. She came out of the ladies, phone in hand and carrying her wet coat over her arm and nearly collided with Netta Grieve.

'G'day Netta. I didn't know you worked here. I've got soaked. Is there somewhere I can put my coat to dry while

I'll have a coffee and a piece of the wonderful carrot cake?'

'I'm covering for my sister Peggy who works here; she's got a bad dose of the flu. You're looking a bit *peely-wally* yourself. I hope you're not coming down with it.'

'*Peely -what*?' Kirsty asked puzzled.

'It means, you're looking pale. You *ken*, a bit off-colour, except in your case you're flushed. Are you sure you've not got a temperature?'

Kirsty forced a smile. 'I'm not crook. I've been for a long walk in the hills, and got soaked, so I'm wet and windblown. And I've just tried to dry my hair under the dryer, which might be why I'm looking flushed.'

'Wet and windblown? More like a spit-roasted drowned rat,' Netta said, laughing. 'Here, let me dry your coat and hat in the kitchen. I'll put them near the oven to dry.'

A few minutes later Netta placed a cup of coffee and a generous slice of carrot cake in front of her. The hot coffee soon revived her. Netta sat down at the table and the two of them chatted like old friends, exchanging juicy gossip.

Netta told her proudly, 'It was such a good turnout, the Open Garden event. It raised over £1,000 for the village hall.'

'What do you know about the girl you were speaking to?'

'Sia Laidlaw, you mean?'

'You never said she was a police constable.'

'*Aye*, she completed her police training last year. Her dad is local and her mother is from Tanzania. They met when he worked over there, something to do with gold mining, I think. There was some sort of accident and he came back, got a job with George Dixon, driving the local bus and rented a cottage on the estate. His wife and Sia turned up a couple of months later. Sia was just a toddler. Her mum manages a hairdressing salon in Kelso.'

'I met Sia in her official capacity today. She questioned me about something going missing from the "big house".'

'Oh dear. That sounds bad, but I'm sure you've done nothing wrong, so don't worry about it. I'll keep my ears to the ground.'

'Thanks Netta, that's kind of you.'

'Actually my dear, I'm not having a good day myself. A couple of my friends, who rent estate property in the outskirts of the village, have just got letters from the Stanton Holm Estate Office offering them the opportunity to buy their cottages.'

'That's a good thing.... isn't it?'

'Well, it would be if they could afford it. They get told it's a good price for sitting tenants but it's way beyond what they can afford. A couple of months ago the Paterson family, further up the valley, were given six weeks' notice to move out. They'd lived in there for over forty years; brought up three kids there, an' all. They were heartbroken losing all those memories. They moved into a flat in Hawick to be near their eldest son. They were here last week for coffee. They said it wasn't the same living in a flat in the town.'

'I grew up in a flat in Sydney. The area had a tough reputation; there was always plenty going on, but I love it here with the hills and wide-open spaces.'

'Even in the rain?'

'Even in the rain. I love it. But why did Lord Scott make them move out?'

'I can tell you in one word. Money. The estate is on its uppers and he'll be worried about the future impact on farming with all this climate change stuff.'

Then, Netta leaned forward and said conspiratorially, 'I wouldn't be surprised if his Lordship wanted to sell the Youngs' farmhouse. He'd get a good price for it. Then he'd plant up all the hills with trees paid for with a generous forestry grant. Trees are supposed to be good for this global warming malarkey.' She paused. 'Are you all right, lass? You've gone pale. I'll get you a top-up for your coffee. And I'm sure you can manage another slice of cake on the house.'

Kirsty had always considered tree planting as a good thing, but the farmhouse was Jim and Lizzie's home. Jim had told her his family had lived there for six generations; it was the land Euan expected to farm and where he would bring up his own family. She was an ardent supporter of green issues but had never thought of its impact on peoples' lives, especially for people she cared about. Kirsty was shocked at the thought of her father evicting people from their homes. It just went to prove he was a nasty person. She'd been right all along. She was more determined than ever to get her revenge. She'd been distracted. She'd come to Scotland to find and punish her father and grandmother. She needed to focus. It was time to put the next part of her plan into action, but before that she needed to get home.

She picked up her phone and called Euan. 'Hi, is there any chance you could pick me up from the village? I'm at the Galloping Hooves.'

'Okay, but you'll need to be ready sharp. Ma's about to serve dinner.'

Euan arrived twenty minutes later and rushed her out of the door. It was only later she realised she'd left her coat and hat behind.

Chapter 15

The missing quad bike

Next morning Euan went out at 5.30 to check on the cows, several of which were due to calf any day. Even in the dark, as soon he approached the barns, he knew something was wrong. The quad bike that Kirsty used wasn't in its usual place. He ran indoors and shouted up the stairs to Kirsty.

'Kirsty. Can you come down? I can't find your quad bike. Did you park it somewhere else?'

Kirsty came running down the stairs, hastily pulling her sweater over her T-shirt. Her hair was uncombed and she looked half asleep.

'What's the panic?'

'I can't find the quad bike. Did you leave the key in the ignition by any chance?'

'I don't think so. I'm so used to the job now that I tend to do things automatically. I was in a rush because Jim called me over to help with one of the lambs that had a sore foot. I'll check all my pockets. I'll get my jacket from the boot room. Oh hell, I remember, I left my jacket at the café yesterday. I'll have to pick it up later.'

'You can borrow one of my spare coats for now,' Euan offered. 'Look in the boot room and see what you can find.'

A search of the farmyard and the fields near the house showed no sign of the quad bike. Euan phoned Kelso

Police Station as soon as it opened at 8 o'clock and came back with worrying news.

'There have been several thefts on local farms. We need to be extra vigilant with all our other equipment. It seems we aren't the only ones to lose stuff.'

'It'll be covered by insurance, won't it?'

'*Aye*. But it could put up the next premiums. The sergeant said he'll put feelers out to see if it turns up, but apparently there have been a number of farm thefts across the area.'

***

Later Kirsty called into the village shop to pick up some supplies, intending to go into the café afterwards for her jacket. As she packed her shopping Netta commented, 'I see you got your jacket back then.'

'No. Euan lent me an old one of his. I was just going next door to pick it up.'

'That's funny. I asked my sister about it, she said she never saw it so I assumed you must have come back for it. I wonder what's happened to it.'

'I only realised I didn't have it this morning when Euan called me to help look for the quad bike that had gone missing... oh hell.'

'What's wrong, you have gone pale as a sheet of frozen puff pastry.'

'I think I might have left the quad bike keys in the pocket.'

An extensive search of the café as well as the house and farm came up blank. Euan phoned the police station to say the keys to the quad bike might have been in the jacket that had gone missing from the café kitchen.

***

Kirsty didn't get much time off because they were still busy with lambing, but she managed to get a couple of Sunday afternoon sessions riding with Summer Dixon at the stables. Summer rode Fiona's horse, Dusty, and Kirsty rode Blaze, the young grey mare. She'd learnt to ride during her school holidays, and it was one of the few positive things about spending time at the sheep station. She loved it. There was so much land to cover it was easier on horseback. She and Emma must have ridden thousands of miles across the Outback during their teenage years. In some ways Summer reminded Kirsty of Emma and she enjoyed her company. Summer had been to Australia a couple of times to visit her older sister, Faye, in Melbourne so it was good to talk to someone who knew the country.

The first time out on the horse she followed Summer up a well-worn track leading from the estate and onto the hills above it. Riding over the wind-swept hills was invigorating. The sound of the galloping hooves of the horses on the hillside made her think of the song Euan and his group, Bellwether, sang at the Light Show. It was written by the same poet who had written the book her father had given her mother all those years ago. Her father could never have imagined that in the future his daughter would be riding over the hills of his beloved Borders.

Summer slowed down and stopped by a cluster of trees growing by a wall. She dismounted and waited for Kirsty to join her.

'Look, that's a badger sett by the wall. You can see the holes where they go in and out. There'll be a whole network of tunnels under the ground.'

'Wow, I've never seen a badger except in pictures.'

Kirsty looked in awe at the way the ground was humped up around the base of an old tree growing by the wall.

'If we sit still, will we be able to see them?'

Summer laughed. 'Not unless you camp out at night. They're nocturnal. Dixie is proud to have them on Stanton Holm land and sometimes comes out at night to check on them to make sure there are no foxes after them.'

Kirsty was fascinated by the badger sett and when she went out riding on her own the following Sunday afternoon, she stopped to look at it. She tethered her horse to a tree and sat on the grass imagining the black and white badgers going about their business in the dark.

Something glistened in the grass. She bent down to take a closer look. It was a piece of twisted wire in the shape of a noose; the end of the wire was twisted round a piece of twig. Wondering if it was a snare, she took out her phone and took a photo of it.

Just as she was back in the saddle, she heard Dixie shooting rooks in the woods round the estate. She shuddered at the thought of dead birds falling from the trees. Euan had told her the birds went for the eyes of young lambs so perhaps it was a necessary part of farm life.

Later that night she sent a text message to her cousin.

> Hi Emma, I found an animal snare up in the hills today when I was out riding. I suspect it's illegal. My new friend Summer's husband is the estate gamekeeper – he should be all over anything like that. I'll keep my eyes peeled. Kxx

The next time she was in the village Kirsty asked Netta Grieve if she knew anything about snares being used on the hills and if they were legal.

Netta whispered, 'Some kinds are allowed. But I recently overheard a walker outside the café phoning to report a dead goshawk on the hills. I hope Dixie doesn't get in bother. He does a grand job looking after the game birds on the estate. I'm sure he wouldn't resort to trapping or shooting wild birds.'

'I'm sure Dixie isn't up to anything untoward, but I'll keep my eyes open.'

Chapter 16

Fire, fire

It was a bright spring morning. Matt was out for his regular early morning jog, when as he neared the vicinity of the stables he smelt smoke; a heavy acrid smell hung in the air. He grabbed his mobile phone, hit speed dial and alerted Fiona, then ran pell-mell towards the loose boxes. As he got nearer he heard the shrill whinny of the panicked horses and the sound of their flailing hooves beating frantically against the wooden doors. Beneath the sound of the horses he heard a muffled cry come from the tack room. 'Help! help!' Even though it was barely audible, he recognised Summer's voice. He had to get her out before she suffocated.

He pulled the bandana from round his head, took a deep breath and hastily tied it round his mouth. He opened the door cautiously, unsure of the impact of letting oxygen into the confined space. Smoke was rising from some bales of straw stored in the far corner of the room; plumes of grey smoke drifted towards the ceiling. Looking round he spotted Summer lying on the floor next to a fire extinguisher; he crawled across the floor, below the level of the smoke, to reach her.

'Summer? It's Matt. Can you hear me?'

She nodded and lifted her hand as if she were going

to pull down the wet scarf tied round her mouth. 'No, no don't do that. Let me check you over first. Does anything hurt?' Summer pointed to her left foot. Following his first aid training, he felt her pulse before checking her neck and spine for any damage, then made sure there were no obvious broken limbs.

'Can you stand?'

Summer tried to get up but winced with pain when she tried to put pressure on her foot. Matt mumbled through his bandana. 'I think maybe you've broken something in your foot, but we need to get you out of here.' He reached up and grabbed a quilted horse blanket from a shelf. 'Can you help me get this under you?'

The smoke had got thicker and had dropped down towards the ground, making visibility increasingly difficult. They both struggled to breathe but knew they had to get out as fast as they could. Breathing heavily, but with Summer's help, Matt carefully rolled her onto the horse blanket, took hold of two corners and slowly dragged her towards the door. To his relief he heard Stan and Dixie's voices outside the tack room. Pulling down the corner of his bandana he called out, 'I've got Summer. She's hurt. Help me get her out.'

Matt hauled himself upright using the sides of the door frame then flung open the door. Whipping off his bandana, he gasped for breath. Stan and Dixie helped him drag Summer well away from the building.

Dixie leaned over to comfort his wife. 'I'll stay here with Summer to wait for the ambulance. You two need to help Fiona get the horses out as quick as you can. I've opened the gate of the field downwind of the smoke. If you open the stalls, Fiona can lead them and you bring up the rear.'

With hardly any time to catch his breath, Matt ran with Stan towards the loose boxes, where Fiona waited at a safe distance. She shouted over the commotion of the horses, 'Be careful. You'll need to get them both of them out at the same time... they won't leave without each other. Be careful when you open the doors... a horse weighs the same as a Sherman tank... if they knock you down you'll know about it.'

Matt would rather have faced close combat with an armed enemy than approach the horses that were so panicked the whites of their eyes were prominent and their nostrils flared. The horses were frantically clattering on the doors of their loose boxes with their hooves in a desperate effort to escape the smoke.

Stan shouted, 'I'll get Dusty, you get Blaze.'

'Okay ready now.' In unison they opened the stable doors. Freed at last, the horses whinnied loudly and followed Fiona as she spoke calmly to them and headed towards the open gate. Stan and Matt nervously followed.

Both horses were distressed and covered in dust and flecks of soot. Speaking softly, Fiona ran her hands down the necks of her frightened horses. 'It's okay, Dusty, steady now. Hush Blaze, you're safe now.'

Summer was propped up against a tree, still struggling to get her breath.

Dixie impatiently paced up and down. Eventually two fire engines arrived, closely followed by an ambulance. The paramedics checked them all over and insisted that Summer and Matt should go to the hospital to make sure there was no damage to their lungs.

The firemen quickly dealt with the blaze. Fiona was distressed at the damage to the stables but relieved there was no one was seriously hurt. Tom Malcolm, the vet, assured her that with care the horses would recover from the effects of the smoke inhalation. She phoned round her equine contacts and managed to find alternative stabling for the horses.

Just as the firemen were leaving one of them picked up a brightly coloured scarf lying by the path behind the stables.

'Hey, I recognise that. It belongs to the Australian girl staying at the farm. She must have dropped it when she came for a ride.' Fiona held out her hands to take it.

'No. I'll have to hand it in. It might be evidence.'

'Evidence?' Stan asked, alarmed. 'You don't think it was deliberate? Surely not!'

***

Kirsty and Euan were busy with the sheep. It was getting towards the end of lambing and they were still working long hours. They were up on the hills checking on the flock when Euan had stopped suddenly.

'Look down there. I can see smoke billowing from the direction of Stanton Hall. There's no reason for anyone to light a bonfire at this time of year. Something must be wrong.'

'You're right; I can smell smoke in the air.'

'We are nearly finished. Let's get back and find out what's happening. They may need help.'

By the time they arrived back to the farmhouse, Stan had already been in touch with Lizzie to let her know that the fire was under control. The house was untouched but stinking of smoke. He told her that Summer had broken a bone in her foot, and was waiting to have it plastered. She would be kept in the hospital overnight to be monitored for any damage to her lungs from the smoke inhalation. The doctors at the hospital pronounced Matt fit enough to go home even though he'd inhaled a lot of smoke.

***

When Matt eventually returned to the gatehouse he found a buff envelope pushed under his door. He picked it up. There was no name on it. He wafted it under his nose and sniffed. Even though he stank of smoke from the fire he could detect a whiff of burning. His hands trembled as he yanked open the envelope and pulled out a sheet of white paper. It said in large typing,

This is your LAST warning. Pay up or else.
It WILL be worse next time.

A spent match was attached to the bottom of the paper.

Matt froze. Good god! The loan sharks were responsible for starting the fire. His mind could hardly process this piece of information. He was so exhausted from his exertions in rescuing Summer and the horses, he could hardly take it in. He didn't know how long he stood rooted to the spot but eventually loosened his grip on the piece of paper and sank to the floor, sobbing for the first time in years.

His efforts to raise money had hardly put a dent in his debt. All the time the loan sharks kept raising the amount he owed; he had felt as if he was chasing a running man, always ten paces ahead of him. He'd been so desperate he'd contacted his old army comrade he'd met at the casino in January and taken some reckless steps to raise money – but it still wasn't enough. He wondered how he was going to get out of his predicament.

Exhausted, he got ready for bed. As he pulled the covers back, to his horror he saw a large butcher's knife with another buff envelope attached to the handle. He carefully lifted the knife and ripped open the envelope and pulled out a sheet of paper and read it in horror.

Do you have the balls not to pass out when we remove your manhood?
This is a final warning. Pay up or else.

Christ! Someone must have been in the house while he was fighting the blaze and left it there. The bastards had some nerve. He was wide awake now.

That night he hardly slept. His throat felt sore from the smoke and every now and then he went into spasms of coughing and had to get up to take sips of water. Although he was teetotal, he kept a half bottle of brandy for medicinal purposes. If ever he needed it, it was now. He took a few sips along with the water, to relieve his cough. He ignored the messages on his phone but eventually he gave into temptation and read the text messages. He listened to the voice messages in the forlorn hope they might have offered him a way out. He thought perhaps they might have been asking him to do jobs for them such as collecting money from some other poor sod that had got into difficulty. He drew the line at drug running or violence, but was desperate. Each message was more threatening.

He went back to bed in the hope he could get a few hours' sleep, but the threats were buzzing round his brain.

In his dreams the voices were American-Italian, as

if Tony Soprano was mumbling in his ear, *'give us the mullah, we want our dosh, pay up now or else.'*

Even after drinking a fair amount of brandy with the water his nerves were still on edge. It was useless attempting to sleep so he spent the rest of the night trying to think of ways of raising the money. The warning letter with the spent match, and the knife in his bed, meant these guys meant business; setting fire to the stables was serious. Summer could have died if he'd not got there in time. It occurred to him that maybe the loan sharks had been watching him and knew his routine. Surely even they couldn't be so callous as to have risked her life. He was worried about Fiona's safety. They were bound to know she was a wealthy woman. He would not put it past them to kidnap her.

His previous attempt to find the money had failed badly. He had taken a risk in taking Kirsty Ainsworth's wax jacket, with the quad bike keys in the pocket, from the kitchen at the Galloping Hooves. He had taken an even bigger risk creeping into the farmyard at night to steal the bike; the sheep dogs could have easily woken up the household. Jim Young was bound to own a shotgun for taking out any foxes.

He was disappointed the quad bike he'd sold to a friend of a friend had only brought him in £1,500. He had gone to the Casino in Newcastle and used the cash as seed money to play roulette. He ended the night £4,000 better off; it wasn't much, but he'd hoped it would help to keep the money lenders off his back for a while. But to his horror, when he came to cash in his chips, the cashier looked up at him and smirked.

'Mr Hill, I see you have had a good evening. I've been

instructed by the management that any winnings go to pay off your debt to the casino. You still owed £6,000, adjusting the amount for interest that leaves you with still £2,750 to pay off.'

'Damnit, man. You could have warned me.'

'Sir, you must surely have known the house rules of this establishment by now.'

Furious that the cashier had had the last word, Matt had driven back home in record time, relieved he never got stopped for speeding. The money he owed the casino was only part of his debt; he owed the money lenders £30, 000.

He wished he'd never got involved with them. If he was desperate then, he was even more desperate now. He would need to take drastic measures.

So far, Fiona hadn't come up with any cash, but he was still hopeful. His nightmare reverberated in his ears; he needed money, mullah, dough, dosh, cash... whatever he called it... he needed a lot of it, and he needed it fast. He jotted down some ideas to raise money, each becoming more unpalatable.

> *apply for more credit cards – worth a try, look for schemes to help pay off the debt – too late now – wouldn't help pay off money lenders – so go further away for housebreaking, sell off gym equipment but Fiona had bought it and would notice it gone – but could steal more farm equipment – risky & prices rock bottom, blackmail Stan – worth a try, (pretend) to kidnap Fiona – last resort – so try all above first...*

Chapter 17

Aftermath of the fire

The day after the fire Lizzie went to Stanton Hall to see if Fiona needed any help to clear up the smoke damage, while Jim went to the agricultural merchant to pick up some supplies. Kirsty and Euan were in the kitchen eating egg sandwiches Lizzie had left for lunch. Euan looked at her across the table, 'Kirsty, there's something I keep meaning to ask you.'

Thinking he'd rumbled her ruse and that he was going to mention Stan, Kirsty felt her face going red. and nervously twisted a strand of hair round her finger.

Just then the door doorbell rang. Kirsty smiled thinking she was being saved by the bell. Euan opened the door to Sergeant Tom Elliot and PC Sia Laidlaw.

'You've found it then?'

'Found what?

'The missing quad bike.'

'Eh, no, we are actually here to have a word with Ms Ainsworth?'

'Come in. I think you *ken* the way.'

When the two officers were seated in the kitchen, Kirsty asked,

'What's this about?' She'd thought the matter of the missing piece of Lady Isobel's jewellery was finished with.

Sergeant Elliot cleared his throat. 'We're making some enquiries and need to ask where you were yesterday.'

'I was with Euan rounding up the sheep and helping with the lambing all day. Why?'

'Mr Young. Can you confirm that?'

'*Aye.* I can, because Kirsty's quad bike was stolen so we both used mine. We were together the whole day. In fact, I thought you had come to tell us you had found it. What's this all about?'

'Is this yours, Ms Ainsworth?' Sergeant Elliot asked holding up a photograph of a red and yellow scarf.

'It looks like mine. My cousin Emma bought it for me as a going away present. Where did you find it?'

'It was behind the stable block at Stanton Hall. Any idea of how it got there?'

'Yes. I was there on Sunday. I went riding with Summer Dixon. She'll confirm that. I must have dropped it.' She paused for a second; then her voice rose in anger. 'Hang on, surely you don't think I had anything to do with the fire?'

Euan got up abruptly from his chair. 'Sergeant, Kirsty was with me all yesterday. She'd legitimate reason to be up at the stables on Sunday. After the business with the jewellery, suggesting she'd anything to do with the fire is amounting to harassment. Please leave. I'll see you to the door.'

'It's okay,' PC Laidlaw replied getting up from her seat. 'Ms Ainsworth, you've answered everything we wanted to know. We were just making some initial enquiries. We'll return your scarf in due course, although you might want to give it a soak. It reeks of smoke.'

Euan showed them out and then went back to the kitchen to find Kirsty in tears. She looked up and rubbed her eyes with the back of her hand.

'Euan, I can't thank you enough for your support. I can't believe they would think I had anything to do with the fire. I'm totally shocked.' Her voice broke with suppressed emotion.

'Come here. I think you need a hug... and a cup of tea... in that order.'

Euan went to put his arms round her, but Kirsty impulsively moved towards him and gently kissed him on the cheek. Euan hesitated for a split second then responded with a kiss on the lips. They heard Jim's vehicle in the yard and they both quickly pulled away.

'About that cuppa, I'll put the kettle on... my *faither* will be here in a moment. He'll be gasping for drink.'

He moved away, but after a few seconds Kirsty caught him looking at her strangely, as though wondering what had just happened between them.

***

After their kiss in the kitchen, Kirsty couldn't get Euan from her head. Apart from the fact Euan was a farmer and she had sworn never to get involved with one, she was conflicted by her attraction to Matt. Since she had first been to the gatehouse the two of them had been jogging together a couple of times but never on a date, as such. She was grateful for Euan's backup when questioned by the police but the last thing she needed was getting too close to him. She didn't want him asking too many questions about her background. Her revenge plan hadn't made much progress and she didn't want her plans thwarted, but nevertheless she couldn't help be drawn towards him.

***

A couple of days after the fire, Matt was invited to Stanton Hall for drinks. He was self-conscious about the hollows under his eyes after several sleepless nights in a row, and uncomfortable at the prospect of being in a social setting with Fiona and her husband. Stan welcomed him into the lounge and offered him a drink.

'Just tonic water for me, please. My throat is still sore from the smoke.'

'Matt, we can't thank you enough for what you did in rescuing Summer and helping to save the horses. Is there anything we can do to repay you?'

Matt was tempted to ask for a bonus but thought it would look too mercenary.

'I just reacted in the heat of the moment. I'm just glad no one was hurt. What about the smoke damage. Will you be able to claim on the insurance?'

Stan and Fiona exchanged glances. Stan answered, 'We have only just downloaded the forms and the fire investigator still has to do his investigation.'

'Surely they don't think it was arson?'

'What makes you say that?'

'No reason. Just hope you won't be out of pocket. It must cost a lot to stable the horses elsewhere.'

'Insurance claims are never rushed. We're just relieved that Summer's recovering well. And don't worry about the horses,' Fiona said reassuringly. 'They're fine where they are till we can get the stables repaired, although the tack room is such a mess it might be easier to knock it down and build a new one.'

Matt spotted the horrified look Stan shot at Fiona. He suspected Stan would want her to sell the horses and to save the cost of stabling them elsewhere.

***

A week later, Fiona visited Summer at her cottage. 'I'm so glad you're making a good recovery. You gave us such a fright. We really appreciate what you did to try to put out the blaze, but you were foolhardy to risk your life.'

'When I came to the stables I smelt smoke and automatically grabbed the fire extinguisher. There was much more smoke than I expected, I couldn't see where I was going and tripped, dropping the fire extinguisher on my foot, breaking the bone. It could have been much worse.'

'I really appreciate what you tried to do.' Fiona hesitated and looked down at her fingers, then continued, 'I'm truly sorry but once your sick pay ends, I can't keep you on now the horses are stabled elsewhere. I've asked around to see if anyone needs a groom but got no luck unless you were willing to move from the area.'

'Thanks Fiona, I understand. Dixie loves his job as gamekeeper and all his family are here, so I wouldn't expect him to move.' She pointed to the plaster cast on her foot propped up on a stool. 'This walking plaster they put on has to stay on for four weeks, then I get some physio, but I won't be fit enough for stable work for a while yet anyway. I've done bar work in the past and I've heard that the barmaid at the Ogilvie Inn is leaving, so I might try there once my ankle is better.'

'That's a good idea, but you're a damn good groom and I hope you'll come back once things are sorted with the stables.'

***

After the fire there was so much to see to at the hall that it was a while before Stan and Jim met up at the long field.

'Are you okay, Stan? You're looking worried. Is it to do with the fire? Any word about the insurance claim yet?'

'You know, Matt Hill was very quick to ask if the fire in the stables was arson. He looked shifty when I challenged him about it.'

'I can't say I *ken* the bloke. Summer Dixon's husband plays in the band with our Euan. He's seen Summer flirting with Matt and made out he was worried about his friend, but I think he's sweet on our Aussie worker. She's been spending time with Matt up at the estate and I think he's jealous. If you're right about her I hate to think of the consequences of her and my lad getting together.'

Stan groaned. 'I sincerely hope nothing is going on there. You need to challenge the girl and warn Euan to keep his distance. It's not legal if they are half-brother and sister. Matt Hill's definitely a ladies' man. He flirts with any woman. I've seen him wrap Netta Grieve round his little finger. I've never said anything before, but I've been concerned about the amount of time he and Fiona spend together. I'm not convinced it's all physiotherapy. I had actually thought he was seeing Kirsty. According to Fiona, he's shown her round the estate and entertained her at the gatehouse.'

'I think Lizzie mentioned something about it. I think he lent her some books. They have a common interest; the lassie is hoping for a career as a physiotherapist. Mind you, what she's doing working as a shepherd during her gap year is beyond me. But to my surprise, after a shaky start, she's turning out to be a dab hand with the ewes.'

Chapter 18

The dead Goshawk

Fiona was looking out of her bedroom window when she saw a vehicle with the distinctive paw logo of the Scottish Society for Prevention of Cruelty to Animals pull up in front of Stanton Hall. She wondered why they were up at the house so headed outside by the side door and wheeled her chair down the ramp at the side to meet them at the front door.

A man walked towards her and introduced himself. 'Hello there. I'm Inspector Steve Knight, and this is my colleague Tara Browning. We are part of the Scottish SPCA special investigations unit. We are looking for Lord Stanley Scott and his gamekeeper, Edward Dixon.'

'I'm Lady Scott. Can I be of help?'

'Do you know where we can find them?'

'My husband is at a meeting in Kelso, and I think our keeper is out checking his traps on another part of the estate. What's this about?'

'We are investigating a report from a member of the public of illegal snares being used. We have found a dead goshawk on your land. It is a protected species; we have reason to believe it has been poisoned, so are taking it for forensic examination. Furthermore, we have authority to search the storage area used by your gamekeeper to look for any illegal traps or poisons.'

'Wow, I'm totally shocked by your accusations. I can't imagine Dixie would do anything like that. He's very conscientious. I'm sure you will find nothing untoward. Oh, wait. I can see his Land Rover coming up the drive.'

Dixie was taken for questioning at Jedburgh police station then charged under the Wildlife and Countryside Act 1981, with setting illegal snares and laying down poison. The bird found on the edge of the estate was held as evidence.

'I don't understand,' he told Summer indignantly when he arrived home from questioning. 'I never, ever use poison, you know that. The snares they found are old ones, probably left lying about by the previous keeper. Mind you I admit I should have cleared them all by now. I don't know who could have reported me. But I'll tell you this. Someone's gone to a hell of a lot of trouble to set me up. You've gone quiet. What are you thinking? Do you have any suspicions? You don't think it would be your crazy ex, Carl Noble, up to his tricks again?'

'No, no, nothing like that. I doubt he's even in the country. But I'll keep an ear out.'

Summer kept her thoughts to herself until she could prove it. If she was wrong, there was no point upsetting Dixie unnecessarily. Besides if she shared her concerns about Kirsty Ainsworth, he was likely to tell Euan and the whole thing would get blown out of proportion. The next morning when she saw Matt out for his early morning jog she waved to him and he stopped to speak to her.

'What do you know about this Australian girl staying at the Youngs'?'

'Kirsty Ainsworth? I thought you two were friends.

Why are you asking?'

'No real reason but I'm not sure about her. Things don't add up.'

'Such as?'

'Well, if she wants to be a physio, why is she working on a sheep farm?'

'But why not? It's one way to see another country.'

'Someone has made complaints about Dixie to the wildlife people. I think it's her.'

'Whatever makes you think that? Have you any proof?'

'No proof. Just a gut feeling. But I'll find one way or another.'

While Dixie was up at Stanton Hall meeting with Stan to discuss the situation, Summer emailed her sister in Melbourne.

> Hi Faye,
> Could you check some info for me? I told you about the Aussie lass working as a shepherd on the farm near us. She's called Kirsty Ainsworth. She lived in Sydney till recently before taking a gap year. I suspect she's causing trouble for us. Could you find out if anyone knows anything about her?
> Many thanks & lots of love,
> Summer x

A few days later Faye replied with information that fuelled Summer's suspicions. That evening, when she was at the Ogilvie Inn while Dixie was at band practice, Matt came in and she couldn't wait to get a few quiet minutes with him and share what she'd found out.

'That's very interesting indeed,' he commented, his brain full of possibilities of how he could use this information to his advantage.

***

Bellwether met at the back room of the pub for band practice. Euan and Dixie chatted while they waited for Billy Moffat to join them to go over their set for their upcoming gig at the Young Farmer's Spring Fling at the end of the month.

'I can't wait for Summer to start her new job. I'm hoping with tips on top of her basic wage she'll be bringing in more than she was earning as a groom.' Dixie sighed heavily. 'I'm worried about losing my job so we'll need to save any extra money. The wildlife team have scrutinised everything with a fine toothcomb, but they're keeping quiet of the possible outcome. I don't *ken* how I'd cope without Summer's support. She's been brilliant. Anyway, what about you and Kirsty? Have you told her how you feel?'

Euan shook his head. 'What's the point, she'll be going back to Australia in a couple of months' time. Long distance romances never work and you can't get much longer distance than Oz.'

Dixie nodded his agreement. 'When she first arrived she sounded like a real city girl, but from what I've seen of her, she's settling down to country life no bother.'

Euan hesitated before replying, '*Aye*, but every time I think we're getting close she becomes distant. I'm not sure about her feelings for Matt Hill. I think they've been meeting up. I've seen her check her phone a couple times as if she's got something to hide.'

'But there's no reason she shouldn't see him so why should she hide it?'

‘Exactly.’

‘Sounds as if the green-eyed monster is taking over. Just tell her how you feel. What have you to lose?’

Euan shrugged his shoulders and picked up his guitar to tune it before Billy Moffat arrived.

***

It was several weeks after the fire and Fiona still wasn’t sleeping well. She was having frequent nightmares about her horses being trapped and being unable to rescue them. The initial report from the fire investigation said there was no evidence of an accelerant being used to start the fire, so the probability was some cleaning fluid kept in the tack room had overheated and had started the fire.

After her riding accident she’d initially given up on her ability to ever be able to ride again and had considered putting her horses up for sale. However, riding was her life blood; she’d grown up around horses and couldn’t be without them. Giving up her horses would be an admission she was giving up on life. During her period of hospitalization, Summer Dixon had made sure they were exercised and well cared for. Once the physio sessions had started to pay off, she’d had a high ramp installed, enabling her to wheel up it in her wheelchair. With support from Matt and Summer she was able to mount her horse, and with Summer leading the horse, she was able to manage a slow trot round the fields.

Physically, along with her wheelchair, horses were a substitute for her limbs but emotionally they meant so much more. While riding, she could forget her limbs wouldn’t work anymore. She hoped in time to be able to ride at speed over the hills, no longer Lady Fiona, the landowner's crippled wife, but Fiona Macdonald, the energetic girl of her youth.

She always rose early to give herself time to get ready for her physio sessions with Matt; she felt tired but would hopefully feel energised after a refreshing shower. Stan had thoughtfully arranged for adaptations to be made to her bathroom before she came home from rehab so she could be independent as possible. She transferred out of bed into her wheelchair. She looked around, then cried out in alarm.

'Come quick, Stan, someone's been in here. My dressing table drawers have all been pulled out. Everything's a mess.'

Still half-asleep, Stan came running in to her room, almost tripping over an open jewellery box lying on the floor. Underwear and nightgowns were scattered about. Fiona fought back tears. 'I hate to think someone was in here while I was asleep.'

He placed his hand lightly on her shoulder to try to reassure her. 'Okay, darling. There's no one here now. Let's see what's missing?'

'Do you think we should leave everything as it is to show to the police?'

'I don't know, darling. Best not touch anything just in case.'

As far as they could tell several pieces of silverware and most of Fiona's jewellery, as well as his mother's, were missing.

Stan checked his jacket pockets; the letter from Australia his mother had given him was still there. A search round the outside of the house showed a number of footsteps in the flower bed; a window of one of the downstairs rooms looked as if it had been forced open. Stan phoned the police who said someone would come out from Hawick Police Station as soon as possible, but it might be a day or two as there had been a spate of incidents in the area.

Chapter 19

The Road to Roberton

The hill road to Roberton's a steep road to climb,
But where your foot has crushed it you can smell the scented thyme,
And if your heart's a border heart, look down on Harden Glen,
And hear the blue hills ringing with the restless hoofs again.

The Hill Road to Roberton by Will H. Ogilvie

At Hawick police station Sergeant Elliot and PC Laidlaw were busy investigating the spate of burglaries in the village and the outlying areas of Stanton Holm. At the daily briefing they updated the senior officer, Inspector Derek Thompson, on their progress.

'In addition to the break in at Stanton Hall, there have been six other housebreaking incidents in the last two weeks. They are all similar with various small, but valuable items being taken. Someone has been very busy,' Sergeant Elliot said, as he pinned the locations on a map of the village.

'You know, Sarge, there's something familiar about the way they're clustered round Stanton Holm estate,' Sia Laidlaw said excitedly. 'I went to the Spring Open Garden event on 15th April. I'm sure all these properties were on a map that Lady Fiona Scott handed out. Remember the Australian girl, Kirsty Ainsworth, staying up with the Youngs at Holm farm. We previously interviewed her about some items belonging to Lady Isobel Scott that were stolen from up at the hall and then about the fire at the stables. I'm sure I saw her and Euan Young at the Open Garden Day. I was trying to get a shot on my phone of the wonderful display of candelabra primroses round the pond at The Shielings, when it started to pour down. I accidentally took pictures of some of the crowd who walked into view; I might still have them on my phone.' She got out her mobile and searched for the pictures.

'Look, there they are: Euan and Ted Dixon; there's Kirsty Ainsworth. You can just see her under the red umbrella. I think it must be Summer Dixon holding the brolly, but she is just out of the shot, so I'm not sure.'

Just then they were interrupted by the duty sergeant. 'Boss, there's something just come in from Crimestoppers about a report from a pawn shop in Newcastle that you really need to see.'

***

Lizzie opened the front door of the farmhouse to see the two police officers again.

'Mrs Young, we are here to speak to Kirsty Ainsworth.'

Lizzie showed them into the kitchen where Kirsty was eating breakfast having been out early checking on the sheep. She looked up from her breakfast apprehensively as Sia Laidlaw spoke.

'Ms Ainsworth, you will remember us, Sergeant Tom Elliot and PC Sia Laidlaw. We are here to speak with you. You're being arrested on suspicion of the theft of items of jewellery from Stanton Hall, belonging to Lady Fiona Scott and Lady Isobel Scott. We have evidence to link you to the crime.'

'What are you talking about?' Kirsty got up from the table and looked at the police officer in shock.

'PC Elliot will read you your rights. You do not need to say anything other than giving your date and place of birth and your nationality. You need to come with us to the police station in Hawick.'

Kirsty was bewildered. She'd already answered questions about the missing jewellery. There was nothing more she could tell them. Still protesting her innocence, she was put into a police car and taken to the police station in Hawick. The journey took a while, travelling through places she'd never been to before. If it wasn't for the circumstances, she'd have enjoyed the view as green fields full of grazing sheep gave way to an array of heather-clad hills.

The two police officers chatted amongst themselves. She didn't pay much attention to their conversation until her ears picked up some words that sounded familiar.

Sia Laidlaw told the Sergeant about a cycle run she had done at the weekend. 'I cycled along the road to Roberton from Hawick to Harden Glen.'

'*Aye*, I bet it's a steep road to climb,' Sergeant Elliot quipped.

There was something very familiar about the place name; words of a poem kept trying to form in her mind – something about the *hill road to Roberton, being a steep hill to climb.* Of course, it was one of the poems in the book by Will Ogilvie, that Stan had given her mother. She recited the words under her breath to try to keep herself calm. She was in a foreign country and did not know how things worked and was worried about what type of treatment she would receive; she needed to have her wits about her. Somehow the familiar words comforted her.

It was pouring down by the time they arrived in Hawick and she was glad she'd worn the old wax raincoat Lizzie had given her. Euan's jacket had swamped her and she'd been relieved when original jacket had turned up in the boot room.

At the police station, an unassuming two storey building, PC Laidlaw showed her into a small interview room with peeling paintwork.

'Take a seat. The custody officer will come and explain your rights.'

Kirsty felt so stressed her legs could hardly hold her upright; grabbing hold of the corner of the table she plonked herself on the nearest chair.

'Are you okay, Ms Ainsworth? You look pale. Would you like a tea or a coffee while you wait?'

'I'm just nervous. But a coffee would be good, thank you.'

The custody sergeant was a burly man with a strong Borders accent; she could imagine him being a worthy opponent on the rugby field. She listened intently, straining her ears to follow his accent. He explained the charges again and that she was entitled to legal representation.

'But I haven't done anything wrong. Why would I need a solicitor?'

'There is evidence to link you to a serious crime, so we would encourage you have the support of a solicitor. Especially as you may not be familiar with the way the legal system works here in Scotland.'

Kirsty wondered if they had checked up on her record

with the police in Sydney. She tentatively took a sip of the cold coffee that Sia Laidlaw brought her. It was disgusting. Sighing deeply, she replied, 'The duty solicitor, please. I don't have access to much money of my own and I certainly don't want to put the Youngs to any expense.'

'Very well. Mrs Young is in reception, she has offered to get a solicitor for you but I'll let her know you'll wait to speak to the duty solicitor. I'll see what they advise.'

The custody sergeant continued, 'I'm not sure who is on duty today but I will give them a phone call and you can talk to them. You can explain your situation and take it from there.'

Kirsty was reassured; the woman's voice on the phone was clear, without a strong accent. 'Miss Ainsworth, my name is Sandra Maltman, I'm the duty solicitor. From what I've been informed you are facing the charge of handling stolen goods, some of which belong to Lady Isobel Scott and her daughter-in-law. I think under the circumstances it would be best for me to come across to Hawick Police Station and meet with you. Are you in agreement?'

'Yes please. I'm not sure what's going on but I didn't do it.'

'Okay. We can discuss it properly face to face.'

***

At Stanton Hall, Stan was deep in thought when their daily cleaner knocked on his study door. 'Excuse me, sir, but I found this note on the door mat. I'm not sure when it came.' It was a typed white envelope addressed to 'Lord Scott.' Stan had the feeling it wouldn't be anything good. He opened it carefully, and then read the letter open-mouthed.

I know about your illegitimate child. I can prove it. I know who she is and where she is living. Pay £30,000 cash by tomorrow or I will go to the press. Leave the money in cash in a sports bag outside the door to the gym.

Stan almost laughed at the pathetic attempt to blackmail him. There was nothing to stop him waiting in the gym to see who collected the money. He couldn't pay up anyway. His bank wouldn't let him take out that amount of money at such short notice and he could hardly ask Fiona for the cash. Perhaps he should just tell her the truth and be done with; he had nothing to hide. He was innocent, but he needed to consider all the people who would be hurt by the truth coming out. He sent an urgent text message to Jim asking him to meet him.

'Stan, we can't keep meeting like this, people will wonder what's going on.'

'Damn it, man. This is serious. I've had a blackmail letter.'

'A what?'

Jim read the letter thoughtfully. 'Do you think this is connected to the burglary? The person sounds pretty sure about an illegitimate child.'

'But the letter is still in my jacket pocket.'

'It doesn't mean anything these days. I've seen our Euan photograph things on his mobile phone.'

'Good god. You're right. I've never thought of that. First my mother's jewellery was stolen; then there was the fire in the stables when poor Summer Dixon could have died. We've been burgled, and then all the trouble with Dixie;

now blackmail. How much worse can things get?' Stan slumped against the nearby dyke.

'Look Stan, I think you should go to the police. You don't really think the Australian lass is behind it, do you?'

'Jesus, Jim. Why the hell would she cause all this trouble?'

'Well, if she thinks you are her father. Maybe she's after your money. She won't know you're broke, or so you keep telling me.'

'Jim, stop burying your head in the sand. You've been preoccupied since I told you about the letter from Oz. Are you sure she's not your daughter? Look, Jim, we both need to deal with this. I'm going straight back up to the Hall to speak to Fiona, then the police. But you must promise to speak to Lizzie and the girl today.'

***

Kirsty was stressed at having to wait for her solicitor to arrive, and was relieved when she finally turned up nearly two hours after their telephone conversation. Sandra Maltman was immaculately dressed in a navy suit worn over a stunning emerald-green blouse; she didn't have a strong Scottish accent, so Kirsty didn't have to concentrate so hard to understand her, so was able to relax a little.

'I always advise my clients to put their comments in writing, so let's go through what happened step by step in your own words. Take your time.'

Kirsty admitted to taking the silver cross by mistake but denied all knowledge of the other stolen items.

Sandra explained, 'At this stage of questioning it is best to co-operate, and I strongly advise against saying "no comment", as it might make you look guilty, but if you think are going to incriminate yourself during questioning then go ahead and say it.'

Kirsty nodded and hoped the questioning would be straightforward.

Ninety minutes later, Kirsty was taken into another interview room which was as bleak and soulless as the first one. Sandra Maltman sat next to her. Kirsty could smell her expensive perfume and somehow felt reassured.

Sergeant Tom Elliot and PC Sia Laidlaw interviewed her. Sergeant Elliot did the questioning, painstakingly writing down her responses neatly in his police-issue notebook. Sia Laidlaw watched her silently. Kirsty felt unnerved; it was as if she were studying her body language, waiting for her to give herself away in a lie; in case a twitch, a raised eyebrow or something as simple as brushing her hair from her eyes was seen as an admission of guilt.

The officers prodded and probed at her to confess something she'd no idea about.

'Is this correct? You have previously been questioned about items belonging to Lady Isobel Scott. You have admitted taking her silver cross from her bedside table, which I understand you returned. Is that correct?'

'Yes. I have already explained that was a mistake and I asked Mrs Young to return it with my apologies.'

'Can you tell us about these items?' They laid out photographs of some Art Deco jewellery and a piece of Wedgwood pottery in front of her.

'I've never seen them before.'

'Are you sure about that?'

'Oh, wait. Lady Fiona's physiotherapist, Matt Hill, showed me some similar ones when I went to visit him at the gatehouse a bit ago. I'm not sure if they are the exact same ones, but I tried on some earrings. He said they were his grandmother's.'

Sergeant Elliot explained, 'We had an anonymous tip-off made to the Crimestoppers phone number, regarding the pieces of Lady Isobel's missing jewellery, and other items that had been pawned in a shop in Newcastle. The owner says they were pawned recently by a girl answering your description. She had red hair, was wearing a waterproof, of a similar description to the one you are wearing this morning. The young woman wore a distinctive bright coloured beanie hat. We compared the description of the hat with the photo of your scarf found at the scene of the fire at Stanton Hall stables. It is very similar.'

Kirsty felt despair and a huge sense of frustration at not being believed, but tried not to show it. Taking a deep breath, she spoke.

'The only time that I've been to Newcastle was when I arrived at the airport in January. I've never even been into the city. Since then, I've been busy on the farm, except for going to a few things around the village. The Youngs will vouch for me.' She paused then asked, 'Does the pawn shop have CCTV cameras? They would show it wasn't me.'

'Unfortunately, the shop's cameras are out of action. They are waiting for them to be repaired. Did one of those things you did round the village include attending the Spring Open Garden Event?'

Puzzled, Kirsty answered. 'Well, yes. I went with Euan Young, Ted Dixon and his wife Summer, who works at the stables on the estate.'

'Did you get a map of the village?'

'Yes. But I don't know where it is now.'

The officers exchanged glances. 'You are familiar

then, with the properties on the Stanton Holm estate. Do you know: The Meadows, The Keeper's Lodge and The Shielings?'

'Ehm, I looked round various gardens but can't remember any of their names. Why?' She glanced at Sandra Maltman who looked concerned.

'Some items that were stolen from these properties have also been found at the same pawn shop.'

The interview was interrupted by another officer who passed an evidence bag to the sergeant. It contained a letter.

Sergeant Elliot read it carefully.

'Do you know Lord Stanley Scott at Stanton Hall, and his wife Lady Fiona?'

'Yes, but I've only met them briefly.'

'Do you hold a grudge against Lord Scott?'

Kirsty shifted her position on the hard seat. She answered, 'No comment.'

Sandra Maltman raised an eyebrow.

'Have you seen this before? It was sent to Lord Scott,' the sergeant asked, holding up the evidence bag for her to read.

I know about your illegitimate child. I can prove it. I know who she is and where she is living. Pay £30,000 cash by tomorrow or I will go to the press. Leave the money in cash in a sports bag outside the door to the gym.

'No, absolutely not. I've never seen it before.' She shook her head and tried to suppress her rage. Her face turned puce, almost matching the colour of her hair.

Sergeant Elliot looked through the papers in front of him, frowned then said, 'Kirsty Ainsworth, you are being detained in connection of the theft of items belonging to Lady Isobel Scott. In addition, you will be investigated for housebreaking in relation to several properties on the Stanton Holm estate, fire raising and blackmail of Lord Scott. There will be a delay while we investigate these matters further before we can make a report to the Procurator Fiscal's office, then you will receive a summons with a date to appear in court.'

'Make a report to the what?' Kirsty shook her head at the unfamiliar term.

'It's simply the name for the prosecution service in Scotland. I'll explain later.' Sandra Maltman looked alarmed at the list of potential charges her client was facing. She turned to Sergeant Elliot.

'I'll need some time with my client to explain how the Scottish Legal system works. We will be a while. Some fresh coffees would be appreciated.'

***

Ms Maltman explained to Kirsty she would have her fingerprints and palm prints taken by an electronic device called a *Livescan* machine, which would also be able to tell if her prints were already in the system. When the formalities had been completed, PC Laidlaw asked her to empty her pockets. She went through each pocket in her jacket methodically, pulling out a red and orange hat and laying it on the table, then removing a packet of vegan candy from another pocket.

'What's this?' PC Laidlaw asked, holding up a receipt from a pawnshop in Newcastle pulled from an inside pocket.

Kirsty protested, 'I've never seen this before. I didn't even know there was another pocket.' She was taken to another room to wait for her fingerprints to be checked against the pawn ticket, the recovered items from the pawn shop and the blackmail letter. She paced up and down the room for what felt like ages. She knew she was innocent so was shocked when a serious-looking Sergeant Elliot eventually returned.

'Ms Ainsworth, your fingerprints were found on the jewellery taken from Lady Isobel's rooms at Stanton Hall. The pawn ticket and blackmail letter don't have any fingerprints, but you could have handled them with gloves. You are being charged with housebreaking and attempting to pawn several items belonging to Lady Isobel Scott.'

'What?!' Kirsty interrupted, aghast.

The sergeant added, 'We are continuing our investigations into the incidents of housebreaking at Stanton Hall and at various properties on the estate. There will be an investigation into the blackmail attempt on Lord Scott. Furthermore, the investigation into the fire in the Scotts' stables will be reopened. Because of the serious nature of these crimes, Inspector Derek Thompson will lead the investigation pending arrival from the Major Investigation Team (MIT) in Edinburgh. Please confirm that you understand everything I have said.'

Kirsty nodded feebly. 'I understand.'

Chapter 20

Who is Gillespie?

When Kirsty was finally free to leave the police station Lizzie was waiting for her in the car park. She threw her arms round her.

'Come on, lass, let's get you home.'

'I'm sorry for all the trouble I've caused you,' Kirsty murmured. 'I didn't do it. I promise I didn't do it. Honest.'

'It's okay. Come, let's get going. You'll feel better once you're home.'

Kirsty sobbed quietly all the way back to Holm Farm. When they arrived she rushed up the stairs and ripped off her clothes, which stank of the police station. She showered and changed into a comfy pair of jogging bottoms, sweatshirt and trainers.

Lizzie knocked gently on her door.

'Come on, lass, you can't stay in your room all day. I've heated up some soup and made some sandwiches. Please come downstairs.'

'Are Euan or Jim there?'

'No, they are still out with the ewes, getting some of the gimmers ready to go to market in Longtown tomorrow. Please come down.'

Kirsty followed Lizzie down the stairs. Over the meal she continued to protest her innocence.

'I just don't understand what's going on,' Kirsty confessed. She stirred the bowl of tomato soup Lizzie had placed in front of her and drank a few sips. She took a couple of bites of the cheese sandwich then put it back on the plate and pushed it away from her.

'You've been so kind to me and gone to all this trouble, Lizzie, but I really have no appetite.'

'Don't worry, lass; I can keep it for later. I think you should phone your mother.'

'No. I can't face speaking to her. Anyway, it will be in the middle of the night at home.'

'You are in shock, so maybe another time. You can use the house phone.'

'Does Euan know?'

'*Aye.* I told him. He knows you're innocent.'

'Thanks for being so understanding. I think I'll go and rest, if that's okay.'

'*Aye.* No bother, lass. You go and rest. It's been a trying day.'

In her bedroom, Kirsty rattled off a text message to her cousin.

> Em, I've been arrested for something I DID NOT DO. It's like someone is doing the things on my revenge list. It's not me. I still have it here. I think someone is setting me up. Surely someone here couldn't have read it? Could it be Euan or Lizzie? Can I trust them? Help. I don't know what to do. Whatever you do don't tell my mum. She'll think I'm guilty.

A while later she got a text message from Emma.

> Sorry to hear your news. I'm sure no one in the house would have read through your things. It will come right in the end. I've

got some important news. I found some more info. Check your emails. Emma xxx

Kirsty opened her emails and read what Emma had to say with interest.

Hi Kirsty,
I snapped my favourite bracelet, the one with the blue and green agate beads you always admired. The beads tumbled all over the office floor. Some of them rolled under the old filing cabinet. I had to get one of the station hands to help me lift it and lo and behold I found something underneath that may be of interest. It looks as if it had been there a long time and possibly missed from the original file. I've sent a copy as an attachment. Part of the letter was damaged under the cabinet so some of the letters are missing. Also, I checked through the file again. When I first looked at it I thought Stan was being paid a lot of pocket money. Now I think it would have been for two of them.
Emma x

Kirsty carefully read the letter that Emma sent her.

The Royal Agricultural University, Gloucestershire, England. August 1998

The student due to travel with Stanley Scott has dropped out and we are requesting a place for Gillespie ------------------

I understand the young man comes from a well-established farming family and is studying at B------ Agricultural College in Scotland.

According to the letter, and by the amount of pocket money being paid out, there could have been two young men in Australia working at her uncle's sheep station at the end of 1998. But who was Gillespie and did it make any difference? Her father was Stan.

Hi Em,
Wow. I wonder who this Gillespie is and how he knows Stan. It looks like the letter is a request for him to go to Australia with Stan, but does not say if he actually went. Never mind that, I've got bigger things to worry about. I'm furious about being arrested and don't know who to trust anymore. I'll let you know how I get on.
Kirsty xxx

She sighed heavily and flopped spread-eagled on the bed, then curled up into a ball and sobbed. Despite all her plans, her new world had come crashing round about her.

***

At Stanton Hall, Stan was going over the estate accounts for the umpteenth time. He was having difficulty concentrating after the shock of the pathetic attempt to blackmail him. After speaking to Fiona, he'd reluctantly handed in the blackmail letter to the police. The money raised from the sale of the estate cottages had only temporarily filled a gap in the finances. He was desperate. It was increasingly clear there was only one viable option that would raise the amount of money needed to prevent insolvency. He would need to speak to Jim and Lizzie urgently and explain things to them. His thoughts were interrupted when the phone rang.

'Hello. Lord Scott speaking.'

'This is Sergeant Elliot, Lothian and Borders Police. You will be pleased to know we have made an arrest for the theft of your mother's and wife's jewellery.'

'Oh, that's progress. Who is it?'

'A young woman called Kirsty Ainsworth. I think you may know her.'

'I know who she is but I had thought that had been cleared up.'

'We have evidence linking her to the theft and several other house-breaking incidents.'

'What?' Stan gasped. 'Surely not.' This was the last thing he had expected.

The sergeant continued. 'So far we can't connect her to the blackmail attempt but we are re-opening the investigation into the fire at the stable. Please let us know if there are any further incidents or if you hear again from the blackmailer.'

***

Later that afternoon Sergeant Elliot was surprised to get a phone call from the pawn shop in Newcastle. 'Our CCTV has been fixed. I can email you some photos of the girl who pawned the stolen jewellery and the other items. They are a bit grainy but may help in identifying her.'

When the photos came through, he didn't recognise the girl in the photo; she certainly wasn't Kirsty Ainsworth. He looked at the photo closely; the woman pawning the jewellery was signing the receipt for the cash with her left hand and was wearing a distinctive horseshoe ring on her little finger.

***

Kirsty was apprehensive when asked to report to the police station the following day. She sat nervously in the interview room expecting Sandra Maltman to join her. The door opened and Sergeant Elliot entered with Sia Laidlaw.

'Where's my solicitor? Ms Maltman told me not to be interviewed on my own.'

The two police officers sat opposite her. 'Don't worry, Ms Ainsworth; we have some good news for you. You are no longer a suspect regarding pawning the missing jewellery.'

'Thank heavens,' she replied, issuing a long sigh of relief. 'But why?'

'It is still an ongoing enquiry so we can't divulge that information. However, at present we can't rule you out of the other crimes. But I would like to ask you some more questions as a witness.'

Sia Laidlaw showed Kirsty a photograph taken at the open garden event. She was wearing the red and orange scarf that Emma bought her.

'Is this the same scarf that was found at the stables after the fire? Did you drop it there or did you lose it somewhere else?'

'I had it after the garden event. I might have worn it when I went riding on the Sunday before the fire.'

'Can you confirm who this is with you holding the red umbrella at this side of the shot?'

'Hm... yes... it's Summer Dixon. You can see the horseshoe ring on her left hand. She always wears it. Her husband bought it for her. The four of us went together. We'd seen most of the gardens when it started to rain. We ran for shelter, then Euan and Dixie went to band practice, and I went to Summer's cottage for coffee.'

'Tell us about the waterproof. Did you lend it to anyone?

Or could someone have taken it?'

'It's an old one that Lizzie Young lent me when I first arrived. I remember wearing it the day you both came to ask me about Lady Isobel's missing items. I went for a walk on the hill and got soaked, so I went to the café in the village. Netta Grieve put it in the kitchen to dry and I went home without it. I asked at the café the next day and it wasn't there. I looked everywhere it could have been at the farm. I'm not absolutely sure, but I think I'd left the keys to the quad bike in it... the one that got stolen. Sometime later, I found the waterproof hung on a peg in the boot room at the farmhouse under some old jackets. I don't know how long it had been there... or how it got there. It's a mystery.'

'Okay. That's all our questions for today. Could you please sign here to confirm our discussion?'

Kirsty picked up the pen in her right hand and signed the form.

Sergeant Elliot nodded and smiled at her.

'One more thing before you go. Could you tell me about your relationship with Matt Hill?'

'I met him at the village shop. Actually it was funny how we met. He accidentally stood on my foot. He checked it over and we ended up having coffee at the Galloping Hooves. We got on well. He said we were both outsiders. He invited me back to the gatehouse at Stanton Hall a few weeks later.'

'Are you sure he stood on your foot accidentally?'

'What? Do you think he did it on purpose?'

'Not sure. Tell me what happened when you visited him.'

Kirsty furrowed her brow as she tried to remember

what happened that day. 'We had a walk round the estate, chatted to Summer Dixon, then went to the gatehouse for coffee.'

'Did you touch anything?'

Kirsty was puzzled by the sergeant's questions. 'Let me think. Oh, yes, I admired some of the things he had in a display cabinet. Then he took them and showed me them.'

'Okay. Can you remember what they were?'

She closed her eyes and tried to visualise what happened. 'There was a piece of green Wedgwood pottery and some lovely blue and green enamelled Art Deco jewellery which I tried on. I think I mentioned it to you when you questioned me the first time.'

'Thank you, Ms Ainsworth. You have been very helpful. We will be back in touch.'

***

Kirsty was glad Lizzie had brought her to the police station; they had left home early, and planned to have lunch in a café, then have a look round Hawick. Lizzie had been looking forward to the shopping trip.

'I want to have a look round the woollen mills. Some of them sell cashmere sweaters at less than half price.' She laughed. 'Otherwise we couldn't afford them.'

After she left the police station, Kirsty rushed up to the car excited to tell Lizzie her piece of good news. Lizzie was talking intently on her mobile and as she opened the car door Kirsty heard the end of the conversation.

'It's okay, Jim. Don't worry. We will be home soon.'

'What's wrong? It sounds serious.'

'*Aye* lass. It is. Euan found half a dozen lambs attacked with puncture wounds to their necks. He thinks it's the fox. Sorry about lunch out but I think we had better head back straightaway. It'll be another worry for Jim on top of the losses we have already sustained this year. Anyway, how did you get on? You can tell me what happened with the police on the way.'

Chapter 21

The Barefoot Girl

Oh Scotland! Bonny Scotland! In your purple robe arrayed,
You're my laughing barefoot lover and my tattered gypsy maid,
And I'll give my chance of fortune if the fates will let us meet
With the billows of the heather on your brown bare feet.

The Barefoot Maid by Will H. Ogilvie

Jim was exhausted when he finally got to bed having been out on the hills with Euan looking for signs of the fox. He couldn't sleep; he tried sleeping on his back, then on either side; he plumped up his pillows and somehow got tangled in the duvet. His painkillers hardly numbed the pain in his knees. It was getting harder to do his jobs on the farm; it would only be a matter of time before he would have to take a step back, putting extra pressure on Euan. If that wasn't enough, he was tormented about the possibility that he had a daughter asleep in the attic bedroom. He got up as quietly as he could; straightened the duvet, then carefully covered Lizzie up and went downstairs to make himself a cup of cocoa.

He hadn't wanted to wake Lizzie; she knew him well enough to know it wasn't just the pain in his knees that was keeping him awake. He couldn't face a barrage of questions about why he couldn't sleep. He didn't know what Euan had said to Kirsty on the phone before she came, and had never asked him about it, so assumed he hadn't told her he had spent time in Australia. He'd consciously avoided mentioning he had worked at a sheep station in the Outback, to avoid any questions about where he'd stayed and when. He'd not exactly lied but had been avoiding the truth. He felt guilt in case he'd inadvertently drawn Lizzie and Euan into his deception. His brain was in total turmoil.

When he switched on the kitchen light his attention was immediately caught by the calendar that Kirsty had brought them. Taking it from the hook, he slowly turned the pages while he drank his cocoa. January showed the firework display over Sydney Harbour Bridge and he smiled at how he and Stan complained they were a year and two weeks too early to celebrate the millennium in Oz. He and Lizzie had watched it on the television while Euan slept in his carrycot. He slowly turned the pages till he got to November, which showed a picture of the Outback. He stared at the reds and browns in the photo of a dry creek, with a single gum tree clinging to life. He traced his fingers over the forlorn tree and was instantly transported back to Australia, and the smell of the bush. He remembered lying on his back listening to the sound of insects in the grass, the feel of the dry air on his skin.

The picture prompted vivid memories of the time he spent with the farmer's niece; he was ashamed that at first, he hadn't remembered her. He went across to the bookcase and picked up the 1992 copy of Border Poems of W.H. Ogilvie that he'd bought to replace the red first-edition copy he'd given her. He stroked the cream cover with the outline of border hills drawn in red. He poured a tot of whisky into his cocoa, then sat at the kitchen table with his head in his hands and remembered the conversation with Stan.

'Hi Jim, It's me, Stan. How do you fancy a six-week trip to Oz? All board and lodging paid for. One of the other students at Uni has dropped out. I want you to have first refusal for the place.'

'What's the catch?'

'No catch. We just help out at a sheep station in the Outback.'

'Oh,' Jim heard his voice sink, 'so we're cheap labour then. Anyhow, I can't afford the fare.'

'Come on, Jim. It won't be a free holiday but it's the Aussie summer and we will get a break from our studies. I'm sure you can apply to the agricultural college for a bursary. It will fit in with your course.'

November 1998: Migaloo Sheep Station, New South Wales

They both loved being outdoors in the Australian summer, which was a far cry from the cold Scottish winters that they were used to. Migaloo sheep station was isolated and landlocked; they laughed when the station hands told them that in Aboriginal language, Migaloo meant 'white fella', and was the name of a large albino humpback whale, referring to the shape of an isolated whale-shaped rock formation on the property. The distances were enormous, and led to a completely different way of farming than they were used to. They enjoyed rounding up the huge flocks of Merino sheep on the farm buggies or on horseback. They spent what felt like an inordinate amount of time helping the station hands repair miles of fencing, which marched in a never-ending line across the parched landscape, reaching towards the distant horizon. Their skin burnt in the strong Australian sun, even though they avoided the heat of the midday sun; they found muscles they never knew they had and had never felt fitter.

They were too busy to miss home, but both reacted very differently when, one week, the mail delivery brought them unexpected airmail letters from their girlfriends back home. Stan roughly shoved his letter from wealthy heiress Fiona Macdonald, who he'd got engaged to two months before they'd left for Australia, into his backpack unopened. 'I'll read it before we go home. There's no point in reading it now, I'm too busy to write back.'

Jim carefully read his letter from Lizzie, eagerly waiting for news from home.

'How is she?' Stan asked as he fastened his boots.

'Ugh, as if I'd tell you. She still doesn't want anything to do with you, the way you treated her, dumping her for that Macdonald girl, you selfish bastard.'

One night after they'd had a few drinks with the station hands, avoiding looking his friend in the eye, Stan confided, 'I suspect my mother encouraged me to apply for the placement at Migaloo.' Taking another swig of the beer, he continued, 'To make sure everything was finally over between me and Lizzie.'

His own tongue, loosened by the beers, blurted out, 'Stan, you should damn well look shame-faced. The three of us were friends since we were kids. I was so angry and disappointed in you... you knew full well Lizzie and I were childhood sweethearts. You came home from university, took one look at her all grown up and swept her off her feet.

You betrayed our friendship. I'd not have come with you on this trip but my folks pressured me into it, convincing me it would be a good way to extend my farming experience.'

'But the two of you are back together again, aren't you?'

'Yes, but we're taking it slowly. I was deeply hurt by both of you when she told me you'd asked her to marry you. You should have damn well known your parents would never have agreed.'

'I know you won't believe me, but I was naive where girls were concerned and I fell under Lizzie's spell – call it lust or call it love, I'm not sure now.'

'Then you dropped her like a hot brick after your father died.'

'I don't expect you to understand. Father's death left a huge inheritance tax bill to pay. It was impossible to raise the money. For all her arrogance, my mother does care about her workers and wanted to keep the estate intact; that's why she set up the match with Fiona. It protects everyone on the estate... including your parents... and Lizzie's. So what could I do but go along with my mother's plan.'

'So you're going to marry for money, then?'

Stan shrugged his shoulders. 'I don't have any choice, do I? Otherwise we'll all be out on our ears.'

They were nearing the end of their time working at the sheep station when the station owner, Archie Ainsworth, whom they christened AA, short for alcoholics anonymous, gave them the time off to go to a dance in the local town.

'Wow, who is that?' he'd asked one of the station hands as he saw a striking blond-haired girl appear late in the afternoon. She arrived with the weekly mail run, along with the post and the regular supply of groceries. She carried a small blue suitcase and a bulging holdall. Archie's wife Mabel came out to greet her followed by her two-year-old daughter.

He was smitten from the minute he saw her.

'That's Miss Janine, the boss's niece. She's just finished secondary school. She's come to stay at the farm for the summer holidays. She'll probably be going to the dance in town this evening.'

Later, in their shared room in the shearers' quarters, Jim complained to Stan. 'She'll never look at me twice. She looks like a sophisticated "Sydneysider", as the station hands would say. I never even brought a proper jacket with me. Go on, lend me one of yours.'

'But what about Lizzie?'

'Damn you, Stan. After how you treated her – don't you dare judge me! It's only a bit of fun.'

'The weather's warm. You don't even need a jacket. A fresh shirt and a clean pair of trousers is all you need.'

'Go on, Stan. Lend me your linen jacket as you aren't going to wear it. I want to make a good impression. I promise I won't get any amber liquid down the front of it if I have a beer or two.'

'It's my college jacket. It's too big for you anyway. Besides, you don't speak as if you attended Eton. You won't be able to carry it off. The minute you open your mouth, she will know you're a phoney.'

'Stan, don't be such a snob.' Taking some Australian money from his wallet, he held it up. 'I bet you twenty dollars I'll be able to impress the young lady.' He put on the cream jacket and walked round the room, straight-backed as if on parade. Then he took off the jacket and pretended to shake out any creases and carefully put it over the back of a chair.

Stan laughed. 'Okay, it's a bet then. Jolly easy money.'

'You bet?' Jim bent down and picked up the dirty pair of socks he had just taken off and threw them at Stan.

Stan ducked. 'Oy, you filthy brute.' He grabbed hold of the book of poems Jim kept by his bed and flung it at him.

'Hey, don't do that, you'll damage it, you ignorant poetry-hating Philistine.'

'Who's the snob now?'

The two of them tussled half-heartedly, then the punches got harder. Jim's fist made contact with Stan's eye.

'Cut it out, Jim, I don't want to go to this shindig with a black eye.'

Having finally got his anger out of his system, Jim lay on his back on the floor breathing heavily.

'Come mate, let's get ready.' Stan offered him his hand and pulled him up.

Archie's niece waited by the sheep station's battered Ute. She was wearing a short, blue, cotton sleeveless dress, with white sandals and matching clutch bag. She had a blue and white spotted kerchief tied round her neck. To Jim she looked every inch the sophisticated Sydneysider he had imagined her to be. She stepped forward and greeted them with a smile.

'G'day. I'm Janine. I believe we're getting a lift together into town.'

Stan gave a little nod and held open the door for her next to the driver.

'Hi there, bonnie lass,' he replied in a strong Scottish accent. 'I'm Jim and this 'ere is me mate, Stan.'

Jim nearly choked trying not to laugh but pulled himself together quickly and after taking a deep breath mimicked Stan's public school accent.

'Good afternoon, Miss Janine.' He held out his right hand. Janine went to shake it, but he took hold of her hand and gently kissed the back of it.

'Bonjour mademoiselle. Enchanté. I'm pleased to meet you. You look very Parisian with that neck scarf. It suits you.'

Janine giggled. Turning to 'Jim,' she said, 'It's okay but I'll sit in the back with your friend.'

The driver, one of the station hands, muttered, 'I thought your mate was shy. Never knew he could charm the Sheilas.'

Afterwards Stan confessed to Jim he was amused, thinking it was worth losing the twenty-dollar bet just to see his old friend, usually so awkward around girls, impersonate him with such panache.

Jim never knew if it was the jacket, or the phoney accent, which he gradually dropped, but he and Janine got on a treat. They danced together most of the evening and arranged to meet up at the sheep station the next day. In the few days left before he had to leave for home, they met up when he could get away from his jobs and without risking Stan finding out; he'd not wanted to risk Stan telling tales to Lizzie when they got home.

Janine knew plenty of places they could sneak off to where they wouldn't be disturbed. Jim always took the red-covered book of poetry, by his favourite poet, Will H. Ogilvie, with him. Janine would look up at him with her wide blue eyes, listening intently while he read his favourite verses. To his surprise she knew some of the poems by heart.

'We studied Will Ogilvie in literature class. He is more famous as an Australian bush poet, but I always preferred the Scottish poems. Did you know he stayed at a sheep station called Belalie? It's not that far from here, as far as Australian distances go. It's a pity you can't stay longer, then we could have checked it out. Maybe we could stay over for a couple of nights,' she added suggestively.

'That sounds brilliant, but I'm due to go back to Scotland the day after next.'

On their last night together, they arranged to meet up by a dry creek at the back of the woolshed. Janine packed a picnic and brought a tartan rug to sit on. They sat under the shade of three old gum trees that had survived through drought and floods. The air was dry and still except for the buzzing and chirps of insects.

'Now give me the book,' Janine commanded grabbing his copy of *The Border Poems* from his hands.

'Hey, don't damage it.'

She carefully placed the book on the ground out of his reach, then took off her shoes and wriggled closer to him. Jim chuckled, thinking of the poem 'Barefoot maid,' with her brown bare feet. He could smell her perfume and moved towards her; the poetry book lay forgotten as their kisses became more ardent. She lay down next to him and started to undo the buttons of his thin shirt. Jim grabbed her hand to stop her.

'What if your uncle finds us? I know he has a shotgun. I've seen the gun safe.'

'Don't worry. They are all out for the evening. Don't look so nervous.' She paused, seeing the startled expression on his face. 'Oh, wait. It's your first time, isn't it?'

He nodded.

'Here, let me take your hand...'

***

When it was time to return to Scotland, Jim wanted to give Janine a keepsake; unable to get to the shops before they left, he gave her a gift of his precious book of poems. At school he had been mocked for his love of poetry; he'd travelled to the other side of the world and found someone who shared his passion. He'd have liked nothing more than to stay on in Australia and explore the Outback with this wonderful girl, especially as it turned out poetry wasn't the only thing she was well-versed in. In spite of the time they had spent together and the passion they'd shared, Jim knew Janine, the beautiful Sydneysider, was out of his league. She had a good career ahead of her; he was a simple farmhand. Her life was literally a world away from his.

***

When he and Stan arrived back at Stanton Hall, Lizzie and Fiona were waiting on the steps to meet them. Lady Isobel had sent her driver to the airport to pick them up. The driver took out Stan's luggage and waited by the car.

Stan kissed Fiona hesitantly on her cheek. Lizzie ran down the steps, threw her arms round Jim and kissed him firmly on the mouth. 'Oh Jim, darling, I've missed you so much.'

Looking towards them, Stan said, 'Okay, you lovebirds. Jim, if you want a lift home, you'd better be quick about it. Mother is going out this afternoon so will want her driver back sharp. '

'Thanks. It's been a great trip. I've loved it but I'm glad to be *hame*.'

He and Lizzie got engaged at Hogmanay and invited all their friends and family round to Lizzie's house to celebrate. There were plenty of turkey sandwiches, sausages, cheeses and Christmas cake to go round.

A few weeks later Lizzie came to his house. 'Ma stuffed the fridge with so many leftovers from Christmas dinner, I'm not sure it kept the food cold enough, so I when I kept being sick, I thought it was food poisoning, and went to the doctor's. He did some tests. It's early days but it turns out I'm pregnant.'

He paled and was about to protest that they had only done 'it' once, but as a farmer he knew once was enough. He took a deep breath. 'That's wonderful news. You'll make a great mother. We'll manage somehow.'

They married in the village church on a cold day in February, surrounded by family and friends, followed by a small reception in the village hall. At the time he worried Lizzie had married him on the rebound. They moved into Holm Farm with his parents, and they had been there ever since. Euan made an early appearance at the beginning of August. He had a low birth weight but quickly put on weight and they were relieved he was healthy. Their lives were determined by the seasons and the never-ending cycle of farming tasks. Their social life revolved round events in the village. They were content with each other and their lives.

***

Jim sat in the kitchen deep in thought. It was possible that Stan was right and he was the girl's father. He wondered how Lizzie would take it knowing he'd had a secret love child, one who had been living under their own roof. He needed to lay out his thoughts in the hope it would enable him to sleep. He went to the drawer where Lizzie kept a pad of writing paper and envelopes. The few prizes he'd won during his schooldays were for penmanship; he lifted out the precious Parker pen set he'd won in the last year of school, checked it was full of ink and started to write. He found the movement of the pen strokes across the page soothing; by the time morning approached he'd emptied his deepest thoughts onto paper. Sighing, he crept back to bed to catch a couple of hours' sleep.

***

Next morning, he texted Stan to ask him to meet him urgently.

'It all came back to me last night. The girl in the blue dress. The farmer's niece. Remember, you lent me your posh jacket. I bet you twenty dollars I could get off with her.'

'Good god, yes. I'd forgotten about that.'

'I'm so ashamed. I didn't want to hurt Lizzie. I must have pushed it right to the back of my mind. I don't know if this lass staying with us is my daughter. But if she is, you must promise never to tell her, or her mother, that we'd had a bet. It would be too cruel. She's a good lass and I loved her mother, if only for a *wee* while. She was my barefoot girl, but I don't want Lizzie to think she's second best, because I've loved her since we were kids.'

'Look. This is eating you up. Why don't you do a DNA test? Take a hair from her hairbrush. I think it needs be one with a hair follicle. That way you'll know the truth.

You can do it without hurting her or Lizzie. Then if she's not your daughter no one need know.'

'Hm. Worth thinking about. I've written the lassie a letter. Here, please hang on to it for me until I'm sure. Lizzie's threatening to get Kirsty to help her do a spring clean. I don't want to risk either of them finding it till I know the truth.'

'Okay,' Stan promised, reluctantly taking hold of the envelope. 'Now, something has come up about the estate I need to warn to you about. It's really important and will have far reaching consequences.'

Chapter 22

Spring Fling

Young Farmers
Annual Spring Fling
Friday 25th May
7.30 – 11.30 pm
Springwood Park
Kelso

The Young Farmers' Spring Fling was a popular annual event in the local Young Farmers calendar. After the humiliation of her arrest, Kirsty hadn't wanted to venture out in public, but Euan persuaded her that if she didn't go to the dance, it would look like an admission of guilt.

'Kirsty, you are innocent so you should hold your head up proudly. Anyway, after what you've been though, you need a good night out. It'll do you a world of good. Besides, I need someone to support Bellwether. These farmer types can be a hostile crowd,' he added laughing.

'But I've nothing to wear. When I packed, I wasn't expecting to be going out dancing.'

'Don't worry about that,' Lizzie assured her. 'I've got the perfect gown in the wardrobe.'

Kirsty felt apprehensive as she got ready for the dance.

She wondered if Matt Hill would be there and if the police had already interviewed him. Would he know that she'd mentioned his name to them? She was increasingly unsure about him but hoped he had been telling the truth and the Art Deco jewellery he showed her really had belonged to his grandmother.

The deep lilac dress Lizzie found for her wasn't what she would have chosen, but it fitted her perfectly. It was a simple design, beautifully cut with thin shoulder straps. It looked expensive and she wondered if it was another of Lady Fiona's cast-offs. The fitted style showed off her slim figure, and she grudgingly accepted it suited her. She slipped on the pair of silver sandals Lizzie had lent her and popped a lipstick, phone and some money into the matching clutch bag and made her way downstairs.

'Wow, you look beautiful,' gasped Euan. 'I won't wolf whistle. I've just combed my hair, and I don't want a clip round the head, but you look absolutely stunning.'

'Thanks for the compliment, but the outfit is your mum's choice.'

Lizzie handed her a short black jacket to wear over the dress. 'It will be cool when you come home so you will need this.'

'Thank you, Lizzie, it's kind of you to lend me these beautiful clothes.'

Turning to Euan she said laughing, 'I hope people don't think you're taking your mum to the dance.'

'No way, you look absolutely stunning,' Euan assured her, unable to take his eyes off her.

Before they left Euan turned to his parents and asked, 'Will you both be okay?' Kirsty heard the concern in his voice and knew if it hadn't been that Bellwether was playing at the dance, he would have stayed at home.

'No worries, lad. You two go off and have a good time. Your *faither* and I'll be just fine.' Lizzie patted Euan on his arm, and hurried them out the door.

Jim had received a letter in the post that morning from Stanton Hall estate with some appalling news. They were being given the opportunity to buy the farm at a reduced rate for sitting tenants; if they didn't agree to the buy-out they would have to sell up and move out. There was no way on earth they could have afforded even a fraction of the price the estate was asking.

***

When they got to Kelso, Euan followed the road by the River Tweed, crossed the old bridge and turned into Springwood Park. Kirsty was entranced by the venue, which was set in attractive parkland. Euan parked the car and she followed after him as he hurried to the Pavilion, a modern single story building where the dance was being held.

Euan showed her where they could leave their coats and pointed out the main function room. The walls were draped with curtains, dividing the space from a larger area. Tables and chairs were arranged along the sides. A few couples and a group of girls were up dancing in the middle of the floor. The stage was at the far end of the long room. Billy Moffat waved to them, beckoning Euan to join him.

'Will you be okay while I go and set up with Dixie and Billy?'

'Yes, I'll be fine, you go on.'

She looked round and saw Matt Hill striding purposefully towards her. Dressed in a formal navy suit, with a white shirt and navy tie, he looked devastatingly handsome. Her heart lurched; inwardly she felt a maelstrom of emotions. She was inexplicably drawn towards him, even though part of her suspected he was the one who had set her up. She'd had several restless nights debating in her head whether she should confront him.

Matt beamed. He looked her slowly up and down. 'Wow, Kirsty, you look fabulous. That colour is perfect on you. I was hoping you would be here. It's a while since I've seen you.' He turned to Euan, and gave him a broad smile.

'I'll take care of her. You go do your stuff. The DJ's not up to much so everyone needs Bellwether up on stage to get the party going.'

Matt took Kirsty by her arm and led her on to the dance floor. After the first few dances, he said, 'I've built up quite a thirst. Let's go to the bar for a drink.'

It was crowded by the bar. Kirsty spotted Summer Dixon talking with a group of other young women and tried to attract her attention, but Summer turned away to face in the opposite direction. Kirsty wondered if it was her she was avoiding or Matt. It was warm in the bar and Matt suggested, 'It's stuffy. Let's take our drinks outside and get a bit of fresh air.'

He found a bench just outside the main hall doorway.

Sitting close to him on the bench Kirsty took a slow sip of her elderflower wine. 'Matt, can I ask about when I visited you at the gatehouse?'

'Sure. What about it?'

'The earrings and stuff I tried on. Whose were they?'

'What do you mean?'

'You told me they were your grandmother's. I don't know if you heard but I was arrested and charged with pawning Lady Isobel's jewellery. I didn't do it. I've never been to Newcastle since I arrived at the airport in January. It occurred to me the description of the items was similar to the ones I tried on at the gatehouse. You said they were your grandmother's.'

Matt moved away from her on the bench, his body tense. He turned his head and stared at her angrily, raising his voice. 'Wait, are you suggesting I had something to do with it? Come on, Kirsty, you know me better than that. I'm shocked by your accusations. That style of jewellery was popular in those days. Lots of women wore them.'

'Well, I didn't do it. It's the only explanation I can think of.'

'I am very disappointed in you, Kirsty.' Matt shook his head. 'I really thought you and I were friends.' He leaned in closer and gently stroked her cheek, then tilting her head towards him, he kissed her roughly on the lips.

'What the hell do you think you are playing at?' Kirsty shouted, pulling away from him and standing up abruptly.

A couple standing not far away from them turned to look at them. For a brief second Matt sat frozen, then stood up and turned to face Kirsty. His eyes glinted angrily in the reflected light from the bulb above the hall doorway.

'Oh, don't be like that. Pretending to be little Miss Innocent. You're been leading me on for weeks.'

'What – leading you on?' Kirsty shrieked incredulously.

'I know the game you're playing. I know you're Stan's illegitimate daughter and you are here to exhort money from him.'

Stunned by Matt's accusations she stared at him, wondering how he knew about Stan.

'Well, your silence says everything. You are not denying

it then?'

'Denying what? Leading you on or being Stan's daughter?'

'Either? Both? Take your pick,' Matt replied sarcastically.

'What makes you think I'm Stan's daughter, anyway?'

'I overheard his mother telling him about it just before Christmas.'

Kirsty's heart skipped a couple of beats and she swayed towards Matt, who instinctively put his arm out to steady her.

'Look Kirsty, I'm so sorry. I don't know what came over me before. I didn't mean any of it. I shouldn't have said those things. It was uncalled for.'

'Too right. But now you've told me about Stan and what Lady Isobel told him, I'm grateful. It confirms what I thought.'

'Ah, so you are his daughter then?'

'I think so. I haven't confronted him yet.'

'Hm, I think Stan might have his hands full so maybe hold off for a while. Which reminds me, I better get going. I've somewhere to be. Good luck.'

He turned and walked away briskly without a backward glance. Fighting back tears, Kirsty wandered back into the hall to look for Euan.

***

It was 9.15pm when Matt left the dance, wound up by his argument with Kirsty. He knew he had handled the situation badly, but at least if anyone asked about him, he had made his presence there known. He'd been thrown when he saw Kirsty walking towards him wearing one of

Fiona's dresses. Her scent clung tenaciously to the fabric of the dress, filling his head with so many erotic memories that he'd gone and made a clumsy pass at the girl. How could he have been so stupid? Trust the girl to realise the jewellery didn't belong to his grandmother. If he'd had any valuables they'd have been pawned long ago. He'd taken a risk and crept into Lady Isobel's room while she was in the hospital, banking on the fact she wouldn't be wearing them for a while. He'd invited Kirsty to the gatehouse in order to get her fingerprints on the jewellery.

He waited in the car for a few minutes for his anger to cool, before he checked his mobile phone. He swore, threw it onto the back seat then sped off in the direction of Stanton Hall, gravel flying up behind the car.

***

Bellwether's first set went down well. From the stage Euan had watched Kirsty dancing with Matt Hill and struggled to concentrate on the music. The DJ took over while the band had a break so he went outside for a breath of air. He sighed and went back into the hall to find Kirsty. He was surprised to find her sitting by herself in the corner of the room. Her shoulders were hunched up and at first glance she looked near to tears.

'Are you okay? Where's Matt?'

'We had a row.'

'Oh, what about?'

'I'll tell you about it later, but he's gone off in a temper.'

Euan felt perturbed. He put one arm behind his back, gave a formal bow and asked, 'Miss Kirsty Ainsworth, will you do me the pleasure of this dance?'

Kirsty suppressed a giggle and dipping a curtsy replied,

'It will be my pleasure, kind sir.'

The DJ played some 80s music and they let rip, leaving their problems behind, at least while the music transported them to another era.

Bellwether took to the stage for their last set of the evening. Euan had arranged to meet Kirsty outside the main entrance when he'd finished to give her a lift home. The crowd of dancers had thinned out; the shepherds and cowmen who couldn't get cover for the morning stint had already left. The DJ slowed down the tempo of the music. Outside, Euan breathed in the cool night air. Where was Kirsty? If she wanted a lift back to the house, she needed to be quick, he'd promised he wouldn't be back late and it was already after 10.30. He hoped Matt hadn't turned up again. He didn't trust him. There was something 'off' about him. The man seemed to exert a hold over her, but he didn't have time to be jealous, he'd promised his dad he would come back in time to help check on the sheep.

Kirsty came running towards him. 'Sorry, I had to queue up for my coat.'

'I was worried Matt had come back.'

'I had a horrible row with him. It was really nasty. He tried to fob me off with a load of lies.'

Euan put his hand protectively on the small of her back. 'Forget him. Let's get back to Holm Farm, Ma and my *faither* will be waiting for us.'

Chapter 23

On the Hillside

Jim paced the floor impatiently, anxious to check up on the flock. In spite of Lizzie's protestations, he hadn't wanted to wait till Euan came home.

'I'll not be long. We've lost so many ewes, we can't afford to risk losing any more.'

'Are you sure? Our Euan promised he wouldn't be home late, so why not wait another half hour?'

Jim shook his head. 'Don't fret, lass. I'll be home before you know it.'

He unlocked the gun safe and rejected the boxlock 12 bore shotgun. He'd no time for modern guns with their safety catches that pressed on/off like a light switch; the sound made a click, so as soon the fox heard it, he would turn tail and run off. This fox was an old animal who had evaded their many attempts to kill him, so he didn't want to make him suspicious. Instead, he took out his grandfather's old hammer gun and a box of ammunition.

He dressed in a dark green windproof jacket, shouted goodbye to Lizzie, pulled the boot room door shut and strode across the hillside with his old dog running behind him. There was a sudden breeze, and he felt the cold air fresh against his skin. He breathed in deeply. He loved this land no matter the weather. He knew and loved every hill, every valley, every tussock of the land and all the animals, in fact everything about his farming life. A memory came suddenly into his mind of his childhood...

He, Lizzie and Stan were playing in a field on the estate, laughing and chasing each other, like young lambs. He and Stan were the same height although Stan was about twelve; he and Lizzie were both ten. Lizzie's long fair hair was loosely plaited in two unkempt pigtails; her jeans were worn and caked in mud, looking every inch a tomboy.

He remembered shouting, 'Hey Stan, bet I can beat you t' top of the dyke.'

'Okay. Last one's a dunce,' Stan shouted back.

'I bet I can beat both of you,' Lizzie challenged them, hands on her hips.

Stan was having none of her sass. 'Boys are stronger, and we've got longer legs, so one of us will win, won't we, Jim?'

They lined up and readied themselves.

Stan shouted, 'On your marks, ready, steady, go.'

As they neared the old dry-stone dyke, Lizzie gained speed and dived towards the wall touching it first. The two boys were neck and neck behind her.

'I beat you, Stan,' he shouted. 'You tell him, Lizzie.'

'That's poppycock. It was me. I beat you. You tell him, Liz,' Stan shouted even louder. She grinned and watched the two boys tussle on the ground still arguing about which one of them had won the bet.

'Stop your fighting. You both came second. It was a draw. I'll race you down to t' woods.'

He and Stan jumped up and ran after her.

Then he remembered the other bet; the one between him and Stan in Australia, which led to his romance with Janine.

If Stan's theory was true, even if he had to own up to being Kirsty's father, she and her mother must never know the truth about the bet.

In a moment of clarity, and in spite of the momentous changes undoubtedly coming, he realised that overall, he was content with his life and had so much to look forward to. He was sure enough of Lizzie's love to trust her to accept Kirsty, if she was indeed his daughter.

When he got to the brow of the hill, he hunkered down behind the stone dyke overlooking the forest. He waited with his dog obediently at his side. He was glad of the warmth from the dog's body close to him and gently stroked its fur with its familiar smell of sheep and outdoors. Holding his grandfather's gun carefully in his hands, his mind dwelt on the letter from the estate. Stan had promised they wouldn't be put out of a home or left without some land to farm, but it simply wouldn't be the same. Generation after generation of Youngs had farmed this land; he didn't want to be the last one.

Knowing he needed to be fully alert to outwit the fox, he pushed the thought to the back of his mind.

Despite his taking his maximum dose of painkillers his knees were stiff and throbbed with pain; he really needed to stand and stretch his muscles but gritted his teeth and decided to wait a while longer. If the fox didn't make an appearance soon, he'd give up and head back home to Lizzie and the warmth of their bed.

After another half hour he sensed the ewes becoming agitated. The moon suddenly came out from behind the clouds; he saw a large fox purposefully heading towards the flock, head down tracking the smell of the ewes. As he stood up to take aim he felt his dog move between his feet. His knees buckled. The gun went off...

***

Euan was glad to leave the dance, reassured that Kirsty was with him. They hardly spoke, both deep in their own thoughts, but no doubt she would tell him what had happened with Matt Hill in her own time. He knew his parents were in bits after the letter they had received that morning on official Stanton Holm Estate paper, signed Lord Stanley Scott. Recently, he had noticed his father was quieter than usual and worried about something. Even though he had sensed something was wrong, the letter offering them the opportunity to buy the farmhouse at a reduced rate for sitting tenants came as a complete shock. There was no way they could afford to buy it and Stan knew it. Euan's dislike of the man turned to hatred.

It was dark as he drove through the back roads to Holm Farm. Suddenly the clouds parted and the moon appeared. Silver-coloured, it shimmered above the trees that lined the edge of the road, giving them an ethereal quality. He shivered. It was as if someone had walked over his grave. As he neared the lane to the farmhouse, he spotted the old Land Rover parked by a gate. He hoped his father wasn't out already checking on the sheep.

'I wonder what's going on here. Kirsty, I'll drop you off at the house and double back.'

***

Euan parked his car and headed across the field. A fox had probably been after the sheep again. They'd lost a dozen a few weeks ago and they had been checking them every night. He had promised his *faither* he'd go with him when he got back from the dance.

'*Faither*, where are you?' he called out.

A bark answered, cutting through the silence of the night. Will, his *faither*'s old sheepdog, ran towards him barking furiously; the dog turned back to run across the field. Running, Euan followed the dog; his heart beat even faster when saw his father leaning against the stone wall.

As he got near to him nothing could have prepared him for what he saw. His father was slumped over the stone dyke gasping for breath. Even in the dark he could see there was a pool of blood spreading on the ground.

'Hold on, *Faither*, I'll get some help.'

He dialled 999, relieved he could get a signal.

'It's my *faither*.' He hesitated and struggled to get the next words out. 'I... I've just found him slumped over a dry-stone wall. He must have accidentally shot himself in the foot. He looks like he has lost a lot of blood.'

He carefully helped his father to lie down on the ground. While he waited on the phone, the call handler talked him through what to do.

'Do you have anything you can use as a tourniquet?'

'*Aye*. I can use my tie.'

'Good, tie it as tight as you can, then if at all possible elevate his limb so it is higher than his heart... blood can't flow upwards... and stay on the line...'

Euan swiftly removed his tie, and tied it tight round his father's leg above the ankle to try to stem the flow of blood. Even in the dark he could see the section of the wall where his father had been leaning was loose; gathering his strength he pushed off the top row of stones, which landed with a heavy thud on the other side. He carefully manoeuvred his father towards the wall and lifted the injured leg onto the remaining stones, then cradled his father in his arms while they waited for the ambulance. All the time he murmured,

'It's okay, *Faither*, help will be here soon. Just keep talking to me.'

Jim lay in his son's arms. His breathing gradually became more laboured, and he took short gasps of breath, but as the life ebbed out of him he found the strength to whisper, 'I'm so sorry, son. Tell your dear mother... and... and... the wee lassie, I'm sorry. I love you all... I'm so so sorry... I...'

Euan held his father in his arms and rocked him to and fro. Tears rolled down his cheeks.

Chapter 24

Where's Jim

Kirsty walked up the drive, tottering on the uncomfortable heeled sandals that Lizzie had lent her. The cool night air had helped clear her thoughts. She was pleased she'd confronted Matt but had been totally unprepared for his reaction. How could she have been so naive? But at least he had confirmed her parentage.

She entered the house through the boot room to be greeted by Lizzie, anxiously waiting up for her and Euan.

'Where's our Euan? Is he not with you?'

'He's gone to find Jim.'

'He's been a while. I wonder what's kept him. I begged him not to go after the fox but wait for Euan.'

'I'm sure they won't be long.'

'Anyway, how did you enjoy the dance? Tell me all about it. Do you want a cup of tea or anything while we wait for them?'

'No thanks to the tea. Let's just say it was an eventful night. I'll go and change out of this dress and come back down when the others are back.'

***

Lizzie fell into a shallow sleep in the armchair and woke up with a jolt when she heard sirens. They were getting closer. Too close. The sound of the sirens stopped. Nothing happened. Then a while later she heard a noise and looked out of the back door. Euan, followed by Jim's old sheep dog, came running across the farmyard. Euan stumbled into her arms; his clothes were covered in blood.

'My god, son, what's happened?'

'I'm so sorry but it's *Faither...*' He hesitated, breathed in hard, then let out a long breath, and the words gushed out of him; 'There was nothing I could do... it was too late. He was in a bad way by the time I got there. He must have shot himself in the foot. I tried to stop the bleeding but there was nothing I could do to save him. I'm so sorry, Ma.'

'No, that's not right. It's all lies. All lies. Your *faither*'s just gone to check on the sheep. He'll be back soon,' she screamed, beating him in his chest with her fists. Sobbing, she sank to the floor.

***

Kirsty had been in the shower and never heard the sirens but flew down the stairs two at a time when she heard Lizzie's screams. One look at Euan's blood-soaked clothes told her all she needed to know. She sat on the floor next to Lizzie, who cried inconsolably. She tried to pacify her, holding her in her arms. Eventually, the GP came and gave Lizzie a sedative.

Kirsty turned to an ashen-faced Euan. 'You take some time for yourself. Get changed. Do whatever you need to do and I'll see she gets to bed and stay with her till she falls asleep.'

Euan nodded and then made his way upstairs as if in a trance.

A while later, having settled Lizzie in bed, Kirsty came back downstairs into the kitchen. It was all in darkness except the range was still burning; the stove door was open wide, throwing light and a welcome warmth into the room. There was an eerie silence; then a strange sobbing noise emerged from the darkness, a primeval sound like a ewe wailing for her dead lamb. She could just make out a shape of someone in the easy chair by the stove. The old sheepdog, curled up in his basket at the side of the chair, stirred in his sleep.

'Euan? You startled me. Why are you sat in the dark? What's the noise I just heard? Was it you crying? Can I get you anything? A whisky?' Then she spotted the empty glass and bottle lying on its side on the floor. 'Or perhaps a coffee?'

'No. Nothing more to drink. Just hold me.'

Without hesitation, Kirsty crossed the kitchen floor and took Euan in her arms. He sobbed as if he'd never stop. Then a kiss, then another... Kirsty pulled away.

'Stop, Euan. I've wanted you ever since I saw you at the airport wearing that ridiculous Tammie, but now is not the right time. You're in shock.'

'Now is the perfect time. My *faither*'s dead. I'll never forget the sight of him lying slumped over the dyke. I felt so helpless holding him in my arms watching him die.' He sobbed. 'I want to forget, even for a little while. Let's just pretend I've just brought you back from the dance, as if nothing bad had happened. Please Kirsty, I just need to feel that I'm still alive, that I'm real and not in the middle of this dreadful nightmare.'

She nodded then silently folded him back into her arms and gave into the feelings she'd long submerged.

***

By morning the news about Jim Young's death was all over the village. It was the only thing people in the village shop could talk about.

'It's a bad show,' Netta Grieve commented for the umpteenth time.

'Right enough. It's poor Lizzie and Euan I feel sorry for,' agreed Dixie, packing milk, rolls, cheese, ham and a selection of snacks into a shopping bag. 'I am on my way up to Holm Farm now. Summer suggested I take them some fresh groceries. I'll see if Euan needs any help with the animals. I've sent a text message, but he hasn't replied. He's probably still in shock.'

Netta continued speaking. 'Jim Young was a local worthy. He'll be sorely missed. I don't know what his Lordship will do with the farm now. Heard he'd been speaking to the forestry about planting up the hills with trees. No need for sheep then. If they put the farmhouse up for sale the London boys will be all over it like a shot. It'll bring in well over a million, but that'll be peanuts to them. I wonder if Jim had got wind of it...'

'Oy, Netta, watch your tongue. I'm not sure what you are suggesting, but that's how rumours start, so keep your thoughts to yourself,' Dixie snapped at her.

'Sorry, I didn't mean any harm. But I reckon I won't be the only one thinking it.'

Dixie let the door slam on his way out.

***

Euan paced the kitchen floor. He didn't know what to think. He needed someone to blame. Lord Stanley Scott, bloody high and mighty, his dad's so-called best friend, had signed the bombshell letter that had arrived yesterday morning, offering them the opportunity to buy the farmhouse at a reduced rate. They couldn't even afford a fraction of the money and his bloody Lordship would have known that. Had his father decided to end his life because of it? Was this what his father was saying sorry for? Euan tried to make sense of what had happened. No, it was too slow a death to be deliberate, but it was probably preying on his mind. He heard his mother moving about in the bedroom and wondered if she even remembered much of what had happened the previous night. She came into the kitchen in her dressing gown, still half asleep.

'Euan, what time is it? Where's your *faither*? Surely, he's not been out with the sheep all night?'

'Come sit down, Ma.'

'No, not till I see my Jim.'

'Ma, remember last night? There was a terrible accident. I'm so sorry but he's gone. He's not coming back. An ambulance came to take him away. He's at the hospital – in the mortuary. We can go and see him if you want to. I'll ring and make an appointment when you feel ready.'

'What? I don't believe you. What kind of son are you to say these terrible lies?'

'Ma, last night when I told you what had happened, you never believed me. You were hysterical so the doctor gave you a sedative. I'm very sorry but it is true. I wish it wasn't... but it is.'

'No, no. It can't be true. I need him.'

***

Kirsty came in from checking on the sheep; as she'd hung her jacket in the boot room she heard Lizzie shouting angrily at Euan. She heard the despair in his voice as he tried to get her to accept what had happened.

Kirsty was closely followed into the kitchen by Dixie, who put a bag of groceries on the table. Neither spoke. Lizzie abruptly stopped her ranting. Silence was suspended in the air, the moment laden with possibilities like the dawn of a new spring day.

Lizzie looked from one to the other; their downcast expressions instantly dispelled any hope. She turned to look properly at Euan, whose sagging shoulders and red-rimmed eyes told her he was telling the truth, louder than any words. Lizzie grabbed the corner of the kitchen table to steady herself. As her knees buckled, Dixie darted forward and caught her before she fell and gently guided her into the armchair.

'I'm so sorry for your loss. Both of you. Jim was a good man,' Dixie mumbled, unsure of what else to say.

Euan threw his arms round his mother, and they wept, their tears merging in their grief.

***

Kirsty was shocked by the news and felt an unexpected sense of grief. She'd taken to Euan's dad and in many ways wished he was her father, not Stan. Accidents with guns happened in the Outback, but never to people she knew. Jim was a decent, level-headed chap, surely not one to take his own life. But then, you never knew what was going through someone's mind. She had stayed with Euan till it was just light, then changed into her working clothes and went to check on the sheep nearest the farmhouse. She'd not been able to go to where the accident had taken place; her feet simply wouldn't let her. It was all cordoned off, anyway. She was emotionally and physically exhausted and grateful that Dixie had offered to check on the rest of the flock and help as long as needed.

Chapter 25

Kidnap

Sunday morning Stan headed into the kitchen where Fiona had just finished her breakfast. She looked up at him concerned.

'Are you okay? Did you get any sleep? I hardly slept a wink last night. I couldn't get poor Jim out of my mind.' She added, 'There's coffee in the pot if you want some.'

'Thanks.' Stan poured himself a coffee and pulled up a chair next to her. 'Thanks for phoning the farmhouse yesterday. I picked up the phone to call Holm Farm several times yesterday but then put it down again, deciding it might have been seen as insensitive.'

Fiona sighed. 'When I spoke to Euan, to pass on our condolences and offer any support, he said his mother was too distressed to talk to anyone. It sounds like Dixie and the Australian girl are looking after the animals.'

'I can hardly believe the news myself. Did you know Jim and I went to the same local primary school until my parents took me out and sent me to prep school in Edinburgh? I hated it and always felt my life went downhill afterwards.' He sighed heavily. 'We even travelled to Australia together, where he fell for the farmer's niece. We had a big row about it recently.'

'Oh, so that's what the tension between you two has

been about, and not to do with selling the farm?'

Just then Stan's mobile bleeped. He picked up the phone, read the message and the colour drained from his face.

'Are you okay? Not more bad news, I hope.'

'Hamish just sent me a text message to say he'd already sent Jim the letter about selling the farmhouse. He most likely got it on Friday morning. I had forewarned Jim about it but never expected it to have been sent out so soon. Damn. I had intended to go up to Holm Farm to warn Lizzie, but with all the drama going on at the hall with my mother I'd forgotten about it – it's unforgivable.'

'Stan, with business being so bad, what choice do you have? Jim would surely have understood the rent from the tenants, even with the pheasant shooting and social events, don't bring in enough to cover the costs of running the estate. I know you're worried about the potential impact of leaving the European Union.'

'It's not just that – there's the long-term pressures of climate change on farming. There is no way to predict its impact. I never wanted to put my old friends out of their home, but the estate's teetering on the verge of bankruptcy. Selling off some of the smaller properties brought in some much needed cash, giving us a temporary reprieve, but Stanton Holm Farm would bring in the best return. We should be able to get a good price for the farmhouse and the forestry grant for the land would be a huge help, providing a stay of execution for the whole estate. I had planned to offer them something else in exchange.'

Fiona took hold of Stan's hand. 'There's no point in beating yourself up. But you don't think Jim did this to himself, do you?'

He shook his head. 'I can't imagine Jim taking his own life; surely it must have been an accident. What about Lizzie? I bet she's in bits.'

'Stan, don't overthink it. As you said, the three of you have been friends since childhood.'

He nodded, knowing he'd have to face Lizzie as soon as possible.

As Fiona, with her breakfast things balanced on a tray on her lap, wheeled herself over to the sink, she asked, 'By the way, have you seen anything of Matt Hill? I haven't seen him since the morning of the dance.'

'No, with all this dreadful business with Jim, I've not given him a thought.

'I never expected to have a physio session yesterday, knowing Friday would be a late night and he would want a lie in, but I'm increasingly concerned that he's never replied to my texts. Even when we were snowed in, he phoned every day to talk me through my exercises, so not hearing from him since Friday is a worry. I've not seen him going for his usual morning jog round the estate either. I'll go across and check at the gatehouse.'

***

There was no sign of Matt at the gatehouse or the gym and it looked as if his personal things had gone. There was something seriously amiss, but Fiona was reluctant to tell Stan. That night she was woken by a text message. She looked at her alarm clock. It was 1.00 am.

Meet me at the fishing lake. Monday 7.00 am. Will xplain Matt x

She wondered what on earth was going on. It wasn't

even Matt's usual style of text. The fishing lake was where they sometimes met for a picnic. She slept badly and got up at 5.30am. She made some sandwiches, a flask of coffee and filled another flask with some leftover chicken soup. She found half a pack of sausage rolls in the fridge and some ham that needed using up. She left a note for Stan:

I'm just popping out early into the village to do some errands.

See you soon. F xxx

***

The lake was down a secluded country lane about twenty-five minutes' drive from the house. There was a slight breeze and waves lapped gently onto the bank. Matt was sitting in his car, parked in the lay-by next to a wide jetty, leading to a fishing platform for disabled fishermen. Further along there was an accessible bird hide where people could watch the waterfowl, reached via a broad walkway. She wondered why on earth he wanted to meet her here at this unearthly hour.

As she approached his car she waved. He waved back with hardly a movement of his hand, almost as if to indicate stop. She was shocked to see the state of him; he was unshaved, and his right eye was bruised with a nasty cut above it. He gave a tiny flick of his head towards the back of the car. The hairs on the back of her head stood up. Something was very wrong.

She drove straight past the car, then revved up the engine and sped along the narrow winding road as fast as she could. She heard a roar. A black BMW, with heavily tinted windows, closed the gap behind her; with stones flying, it overtook her on the left, almost clipping her wing mirror. It swerved in front of her, coming to a sudden halt. She put her van into reverse, but as she looked behind her, Matt's car roared towards her. It stopped inches away from her bumper. She gasped. She was trapped between the two cars. To her astonishment, a man with a black woollen hat pulled down close to his eyes was sitting in the back seat of Matt's car with a gun to Matt's head.

The doors of the car in front flew open and the driver, dressed in a fishing outfit complete with a canvas hat, got out. A large man dressed in camouflage gear lumbered out from the passenger seat. He strode angrily towards her then halted at the driver's side of the minivan. He waved a gun at her.

'Okay, Lady Scott. Open the doors. Now! Do as you are told, and no one needs to get hurt.'

Reluctantly she unlocked the door of her van and indicated that her wheelchair was in the front passenger seat so he would have to get into the seat behind her.

He was so heavy she felt the van sink with his weight. Holding the gun to the back of her head he shouted down her ear, 'Now phone your husband and put me on the phone. Just do it. Now.'

***

Stan's mobile phone rang at 7.45. It was Fiona's number. He wondered where she was and why on earth she was phoning him so early in the morning.

'Fiona, what's wrong? Where are you?'

A man with a strong Newcastle accent answered. 'Lord Scott. I've got your wife here. You need to pay £50,000 in cash by the end of the day, or you won't see her again. Don't contact the police.'

'What the hell are you talking about? Is this some sort of prank?'

'Here, speak to her yourself.'

'Stan, there are three of them. They've got Matt. He looks injured. They are holding guns to our heads. You need to pay the money.'

The man grabbed the phone back from her. 'Scott. Phone back when you have the cash. We'll tell you where to leave the money. One of our associates is watching your property, so don't try and call the police or another match will drop in the stables.'

Stan heard Fiona gasp at the last remark. So they – whoever they were – had set the fire in the stables. A fleeting thought came into his head that he was glad it wasn't Kirsty Ainsworth who had been responsible. He wondered if it was the same people who had left the blackmail message, except they asked for £30,000. Where the hell was he going to get £50,000? He felt nauseous and despite the early hour poured himself a large single malt. Taking a deep breath, he phoned his agent, Hamish Braverman. It was a long shot but he had to try.

'Hamish. Sorry to phone you at home so early but now Jim Young's dead we'll be able to put the farmhouse up straightaway for sale. I'm looking to raise some immediate cash. How much can you free up by the end of the day?'

'Cash? No chance. What's wrong with you? Are you being blackmailed or something? Level with me, Stan. What's going on?'

'Ehm. No, I'm not being blackmailed, but I do need the

cash pronto.'

'Stan, I don't need to know what's going on, but you sound desperate so leave it with me. I'll see what I can do and phone you back. As you are fully aware, the Stanton Holm current account is massively overdrawn. There are a couple of other avenues I can explore, but it can only be temporary.'

His next phone call was to Todd Richards, Fiona's financial advisor, who didn't seem surprised to hear from him.

'Hi there, Stan. Good to hear from you. Has Fiona spoken to you about her proposal then?'

'No. What proposal?'

'If it's not about the divorce settlement, why did you phone? It's early for a social call.'

'What divorce?' What the hell are you talking about?' Stan yelled down the phone. He felt he had been punched in the stomach. Shocked, he blurted out the real reason he had phoned.

It was Todd Richards' turn to be stunned. 'What? Kidnapped and held for ransom, did you say? Was the physiotherapist Matt Hill with her by any chance?'

'Yes. How the blazes did you know? She said one of the kidnappers had a gun to his head.'

'Look Stan, Fiona is my client, but I advised her to be careful of Mr Hill. I spotted him gambling heavily at one of the casinos in Newcastle not long ago, so I did some investigating and I don't think he's all he makes himself out to be. Fiona is vulnerable since her accident, and I think he has been after her money. From what I can gather he has been pressuring her to leave you.'

Furious, Stan roared down the phone, 'The bloody

scumbag. She never said a damn thing. I was suspicious but thought the better of it. Do you think it is a set-up to extort money from me? But it doesn't make sense. Fiona knows I can't put my hand on that kind of money.'

'Fiona could have asked for money to be freed up from her own investments, but it would take time. It's not possible to raise £50,000 just like that. Do you know where she is?'

'No, but wait. I'd had suspicions there was something going on between the two of them a while back, and set up a tracking app on her phone. Let me check. Just give me a minute... Oh my god, they're at the fishing lake. It's not far from here. I've an idea. But see if you can come up with the money – as much as you can, just in case nothing comes of it.'

'Okay. Leave it with me. But Stan, please be very careful. This Matt guy could be mixed up with some unsavoury people.'

'I'll need to go. I've got Ted Dixon, my keeper, coming any minute.'

'Is that the one who has been in a spot of bother?'

'Yes. He flatly denied any wrongdoing and I believe him. The estate's reputation was at risk so I got him a good lawyer. He got off with a warning, on the basis the bird could have flown in from elsewhere and there was no proof he was responsible for the poisoning. Since then, I have been meeting up with him weekly.'

'Stan, please be careful. Keep me posted. It sounds as if Fiona is in real danger.'

***

It was 8.15 in the morning. Kirsty and Euan worked

together cleaning the cow shed; it gave the two of them a chance to talk without Lizzie overhearing. The police had allocated them a Family Liaison Officer (FLO) and she was due to visit at 9.00. Since Jim's death Lizzie had spent most of the time either asleep or in tears. She was still in bed.

'I'm really worried about Ma. I don't know what to do about her.'

'Hopefully the visit from the Liaison Officer will help to settle her.'

'Do you think?'

'I'm not sure. But at least it's someone else to speak to. Maybe it will give her some answers.'

'I'm surprised Fiona hasn't been to see her. I thought they were close.'

'Speaking of close. What about us? Are you okay after what happened between the two of us on Friday night?'

'Yes, Euan, more than okay.' Kirsty lifted the last bale of silage into the pen and leaned over the fencing to kiss him.

'Kirsty, I have deep feelings for you, you know that. I really appreciate the support you are giving me and my Ma. But she is my priority till things settle down. We need to put "us" on the backburner for a while.'

'Of course I understand.' Trying to hide her disappointment from Euan, she suggested, 'You finish up here and I'll start on breakfast and see if your mum will eat something and get dressed before the liaison officer comes.'

As she ran through the boot room holding back her tears, Kirsty heard the house phone ringing and rushed to answer it. It was Dixie. 'Are you two busy? I wouldn't ask but it is an emergency.'

Kirsty listened intently as Dixie explained what was going on. Her mind was in overdrive as she told him, 'The Family Liaison Officer is due at 9.00 but given what you have just told me perhaps it could be delayed a day or two. To be honest, Lizzie is in no state to be meeting strangers, but someone needs to be in the house with her. Do you think Netta Grieve would be willing to come and keep her company? I'll explain to Euan what's happening, if you could phone Netta.'

'Thanks Kirsty. I'd better get on, there's a lot to organise.'

Chapter 26

Rescue

Fiona tried not to panic. Ever since she was a young girl and taught how to school horses, she had learnt not to show fear. It was a way to keep horses and now her kidnappers calm. She knew she should just sit tight. She heard one of the other men call the man in the camouflage suit 'Dave.' He was clearly the one in charge. He was a large, haggard-looking man, somewhere between late fifties and mid-sixties. She wouldn't like to have met him on a dark night, but even with a gun in his hand, she knew she was safe, at least till they got the ransom. He barked instructions to the other two men.

'Okay. Let's move the cars back to the lay-by and wait it out.'

The man dressed in the fishing outfit set up a spot by the water; he'd come prepared with all the gear, including a folding seat and fishing umbrella. The man with the gun to Matt's head moved from the backseat to sit next to him. His hat was pulled right down, but now he was in the front seat she could see he was a good-looking Black man in his thirties. He produced a newspaper and a flask. To anyone passing by they would look as if they were enjoying a day out fishing.

She asked, 'Is there any chance I can sit outside in my

wheelchair? It's not good for my circulation to be cramped up in the car so long.'

'Okay, but no funny business. And I'll keep your mobile with me in case that husband of yours phones.'

Fiona's fingers shook as she used her control pad to swivel the driver's seat round so she could transfer into her wheelchair. Then she exited the van by the ramp at the back doors, and carefully manoeuvred her chair next to the van.

Her captor paced up and down next to her. She looked up at Dave and smiled. 'I thought Matt and I were going on a picnic so I packed some coffee, chicken soup and a substantial quantity of sandwiches. There's plenty. If you bring the hamper from the back, we can share them round.'

'Under the circumstances that's very civil of you, Lady Scott.' He smirked at her. 'A lady by nature as well as by name.'

While Dave went to get the hamper Fiona looked across at Matt. He mouthed 'Sorry.' He held up his hands, which were fastened together with cable ties.

Fiona balanced the hamper on her lap and sorted through the food, chatting away, trying to pump Dave for information. His mouth watered at the sight of the sausage rolls and ham sandwiches. 'It's days since we've eaten properly. We only had time this morning to stop off at the local shop for a few bags of snacks. The old biddy with a row of heavy beads round her neck who served me snapped at us, saying we were too early for ham rolls.'

In spite of the tense situation, Fiona couldn't help but grin at the thought of Netta Grieve unwittingly being first to make contact with the kidnappers. She handed Dave a sausage roll and a paper napkin.

'Thanks pet.'

'Oops, sorry, butterfingers. You're making me nervous, my hands are shaking.'

The napkin slipped from Fiona's fingers to the ground.

As Dave bent to pick up the napkin she slipped a paring knife from the hamper into a pack of egg sandwiches. 'I'm not hungry, so you can give my cheese and pickle sarnies to the guy fishing, and some for the chap in the car. You can have the sausage rolls and the ham sandwiches if you like. I'd made these egg sarnies for Matt. They stink but he likes them. Be sure to tell him I made them especially for him.'

When Dave returned from distributing the food, Fiona handed him a coffee. He took out a hip flask and poured in a generous glug of whisky. 'Want some? It's cold by the lake.'

'No thanks. Did you guys know Matt previously?'

'I didn't know him personally, but he has owed the boss money for a long time. We're just the collection agency. Apparently he knew Carl, the guy who's in the car with him, from his army days.'

'What!' Fiona roared at him. Unable to contain her fear any longer, she let her calm façade slip. 'This just gets better and better. So why the hell did he have a gun to Matt's head if he's in on the kidnap?'

'We warned him of the consequences if he did not pay up. We thought he'd cough up after the unfortunate fire in the stables. So we had to take charge.'

'But surely he never owed £50,000.'

Dave grinned. 'No, he didn't. But we topped it up as a bonus for the stress and inconvenience he has caused us. As an enforcer I've my reputation to uphold; besides, the person who contracted us to do this job is getting very impatient.'

***

The wind dropped and an eerie silence settled over the pond, broken only by the occasional plop on the water as the fisherman cast flies. A pair of buzzards screeched overhead. Fiona positioned her wheelchair so she could see Matt in the front seat of his car, which was parked on a curve in the lay-by. As the morning wore on the lake got busy. A white minibus with a group of bird watchers pulled up. She watched curiously as a woman with a walking stick, a Black girl with her hair hidden under a dark cap, and a young man wearing a navy baseball cap, alighted from the vehicle. All wore binoculars round their necks and walked purposely along the walkway towards the hide. The driver parked the minibus further along the road several hundred yards down from the lay-by but didn't join them.

Fiona thought she recognised some of the birdwatchers but they never let on to her. Ten minutes later two groups of fishermen turned up, parked their cars in the lay-by and set up further along the bank of the lake either side of the jetty.

'I thought Matt said this would be a quiet place spot to wait things out,' Dave complained. 'It's busier than a hen night in Newcastle town centre.'

'What? Matt suggested here? So, he was in on the plan.' Fiona gasped, shocked at this revelation; a shiver ran down her spine.

'Matt sure did. It's a bit public but it's great to be

outdoors after being stuck in my place for the last few days. You see, we've never had to kidnap someone in a wheelchair before. The places we usually use are down flights of basement stairs or at remote hideaways. Not wheelchair friendly, as Matt put it. He was in over his head in debt and couldn't keep up with the payments, giving us a couple of thousand here and there. Not sure where he begged or stole the money from. We threatened him but after the fire he panicked when the groom nearly died.

'We told him to blackmail your husband but the fool Scott went straight to the police. Like I said before, we're only the collection team. We'll cop it if we don't get the money. We told Matt to kidnap you and demand a ransom but he tried to do a runner after the dance. But we caught him before he left the gatehouse and could get away. The roads were teaming with police because of the shooting up at the farm, so we had to hold up in my pad for a few days.'

'So you were holding him prisoner?'

Dave shrugged his shoulders. 'No comment.'

'What! This is just unbelievable.' She'd shrieked so loudly the fishermen by the lake turned round. She thought one of them looked familiar, but could not see his face clearly at that distance. The guy within the car moved suddenly as if he were going put his gun back against Matt's head.

Dave called out to him, 'It's okay. Cool it. Her Ladyship here is just getting hysterical.'

The guy in the car withdrew his gun from Matt's head, took off his hat, wiped his brow then calmly replaced his hat.

***

Feeling she couldn't cope with all the revelations about Matt, Fiona closed her eyes and wondered how on earth she'd let herself get so involved with him. Following her riding accident Stan had tip-toed around her, unsure of how to treat her. She'd become despondent at any lack of progress in her mobility, and was feeling very depressed, staying in her room most of the time. She'd felt guilty at not being able to be a proper wife to him in the broadest sense.

She had come across Matt's advert for a physio post on the internet by sheer chance. After her badgering away at Stan over several days, he reluctantly agreed for her to employ Matt as a live-in physio. She provided the money for Matt to set up the gym with basic pieces of equipment plus an examination couch and a set of handrails.

She smiled as she remembered their early physio sessions. The daily exercise programme Matt put together for her was intensive but she soon saw an improvement. In spite of his being a hard taskmaster, he was great company and good to look at. Gradually the boundaries of their professional and personal relationship blurred. Slowly her spirit, which had become trapped inside her after her accident, re-awakened and to her surprise a close physical relationship developed between them.

Now she could manage a few steps from her wheelchair to a firm surface. She'd even been able to get back on a horse, with encouragement and physical support from Matt and Summer Dixon, so in many respects life was much better. She'd known it wouldn't be long before Matt would have to move on and he had been putting her under pressure to leave Stan and move away with him. She imagined what it would be like to live with Matt as his partner. She saw them living in London in a ground floor flat in an exclusive apartment block with a gym and swimming pool. She imagined herself swimming up and down the pool; with each length her limbs getting stronger and stronger. Then she saw Matt standing over her asking for a bigger allowance...

'Lady Scott, Lady Scott...' She heard her name called and was brought abruptly back to the present.

It was almost 2 pm when her phone rang. Dave answered it.

'It's Stan. First let me speak to my wife. I want to know she's safe.'

'I'm fine, darling, but cold and stiff sitting here by the fishing lake all day.'

'Look, I'm struggling to get £50,000 in cash. It's been jolly difficult, I can tell you. I've got a proposition to make to your kidnappers. Let me speak to them.'

She nervously handed the phone back to her kidnapper.

'You got the dosh?'

'I can bring you £30,000 in cash, then once I get my wife back safely, I'll make the rest by bank transfer. Just let me know where to meet you.'

Dave grunted. 'If I give you longer can you come up with more cash?'

'Look, I don't know who you are, but my wife will tell you raising that amount of cash wouldn't have been easy. It really is the best I can do, old boy.'

'Okay and less of the "old boy". Come to the fishing lake. I think you know where it is. No funny business or your wifey here will be having another accident. Her wheelchair is facing the lake. Pity if the brakes fail. I don't fancy her chances in the freezing cold water.'

'Okay. Okay. It will be about forty minutes by the time I get there.'

Dave shouted to the others, 'Right lads, that's a result. Forty minutes. Let's get packed up.'

Suddenly a burst of loud music blasted out from the white minibus. Almost immediately the birdwatchers came out of the hide and walked along the walkway and stopped opposite Fiona's vehicle. Fiona recognised Kirsty Ainsworth, who was carrying a walking stick, as well as Sia Laidlaw, who was dressed in jeans and sweatshirt. Euan Young was at the front of the group; he stopped to speak to her. 'Good afternoon, Lady Fiona. Have you been doing a spot of fishing?'

'She's busy, mate,' Dave snapped, getting agitated. 'We're meeting her husband. He'll be here shortly.'

'*Aye*. Right enough,' Euan replied but didn't move on. Sia Laidlaw positioned herself next to Fiona.

The fishermen from either side of the jetty headed towards their cars and one stopped to speak to the other kidnapper who was hastily packing up his gear.

She instantly recognised him... it was Dixie Dixon. The white minibus reversed at speed towards the lay-by, parking right in front of the BMW, blocking it in. The back doors opened, out jumped Stan with half a dozen pheasant shooters, all carrying guns. Dave and the other two men were caught off guard. They were surrounded.

'What the hell is going on?' Dave roared. Then everything happened almost at once. Sia Laidlaw moved in front of Fiona. Matt jumped out of his car, throwing the cable ties away, and dived towards Dave, knocking him to the ground. He held the paring knife Fiona had hidden in the sandwiches, to Dave's throat. Matt looked towards a shocked Fiona.

'I'm so sorry, Fiona. I never meant for you to get caught up in all this.'

Sia moved swiftly forwards, knocking the paring knife from Matt's hand; at the same time Stan charged towards him from the opposite direction, shouting

'You bastard. Leave my wife alone.' He pointed his rifle at Matt, who leapt up, knocked the rifle out of his hands, and dived headfirst into the lake before anyone could stop him.

Sirens could be heard approaching the lake. Several police cars came to a sudden halt and a dozen police officers poured out. The kidnapper wearing the hat, who had been sat next to Matt, ran from the car and evading the police threw himself at Dixie. He punched him in the stomach and tried to kick him. It took three police officers to pull him off and restrain him. Dixie was winded but yelled at him.

'I know you, Carl Noble, what the blazes are you doing mixed up in all this nasty business? Wait a minute... do you know anything about the poisoned bird? I bet it was you who set me up.'

Chapter 27

The investigation

Fiona was overwhelmed with gratitude for the lengths Stan, Dixie and all the others had undertaken to organise her rescue. Dixie happily recounted his part in the tale to anyone who would listen. He boasted it only took him two phone calls to get the ball rolling; one to the pheasant shooters, another to the syndicate of local fishermen who regularly used the fishing beat. Soon the phones in and around the estate and village were alive with messages back and forth as the plan took shape.

It was out of season for pheasant shooting so took a while for people to dig out their gear and get everything together. They were sat cramped in the white minibus with Stan, and had to wait it out so the kidnappers wouldn't be suspicious. She appreciated the help from the fisherman who had sat in the cold by the lake, waiting to pounce as soon as the signal of loud music was heard coming from the minibus.

Dixie confessed, 'It was the most fun I've have ever had fishing,' and even presented her with a couple of brown trout.

She'd laughed at the thought of the part Kirsty and Euan played sitting in the bird hide watching through binoculars then relaying information to Stan, while Sia

Laidlaw kept the constabulary updated. Kirsty told her how as soon as she saw the kidnapper in the car take off his hat to wipe his brow, she'd recognised him as Summer's ex. 'I suspected it was him from the photo Summer had shown me, but with the binoculars I was able to get a close up of the scar above his eyebrow, which confirmed it.'

***

While Sia had been busy with her role as police liaison officer, Kirsty and Euan spent the time in the bird hide quietly discussing their future.

'I'm really worried about Ma. She's taken my *faither's* death badly.'

'But it's only three days since the accident. She is bound to be still in shock. It must have been traumatic for you on the hillside, but at least you know you did everything you could do to help him. But your mum is getting everything second hand, it will be all a blur to her. It is to be expected she still can't get her head round it. It's no wonder she blames herself for not stopping him going after the fox.'

'*Aye*, maybe you're right, but it's not only that I'm worried about. I don't think I can keep the farm going on my own. Then there's the letter from the estate. I'm sure Stan has been scheming for months to put us off the land to plant it up with trees.'

'Don't get ahead of yourself. Let's concentrate on what's needed now. You've got me. And what about Dixie and Billy Moffat? Can't you give them more hours?'

'But how will I pay them? There's no extra money.'

'Oh, I never realised things were so tight financially.

You took me on to help with lambing but I could stay longer if you asked me.' It was dark in the hide but she could see Euan looking at her imploringly. She squeezed his hand and whispered, 'Of course I'll stay.'

They sat close together and Kirsty was comforted by the warmth of Euan's hand in hers. From their vantage point they watched for any sign of activity at the water's edge. In the long periods when there was no activity from the kidnappers there was an awkward silence in the bird hide. Neither Kirsty nor Euan knew what to say to Sia, uncomfortable with her role in Kirsty's arrest. Then Kirsty remembered Netta Grieve had told her Sia was a musician.

'I heard you play the guitar. What kind of music do you play?'

'I do play the guitar, and have been experimenting with music from my mother's homeland in Tanzania; drums and other percussion instruments. We left when I was young so I don't remember much about it, so it's a way of connecting with my roots.'

Euan was impressed when he heard Sia talk so enthusiastically about traditional music and that she even composed her own songs.

'I'm surprised our paths haven't crossed before, eh... socially I mean,' he added remembering how angry he had been with her when he'd thought she was accusing Kirsty of setting fire to the tack room. 'With lambing, the band hasn't been able to get together as much as we would like. When things have settled down, why not come along to one of our practice sessions. Bring your guitar with you. It could be great to get some new ideas. And I think you and Dixie will get on *gie* well... he might even let you use his drums.'

Kirsty couldn't help laugh at his last remark knowing how precious Dixie was of his drum kit and wouldn't let anyone else near it in case they 'bashed the hell out of it.'

***

While Matt Hill was on the run Sergeant Elliot was under pressure. In spite of an intensive search of the lake there was no sign of the fugitive. It wasn't his fault Matt's car had been left unattended at the kidnap site but he had borne the brunt of Inspector Thompson's anger. He'd been nervous when he phoned him at 7.30 am the morning after the kidnap.

'Boss, Sergeant Elliot here. I'm at the fishing lake. We've got a problem. Matt Hill's car has gone. Vamoosed. Vanished.'

'What the blazes?'

'I went to meet up with the car transporter at 6.30 am, to move it, and it had gone. We've searched the entire area and there's no sign of it.'

If Inspector Thompson had been short with him over the phone, by the time he'd returned to the station, even a mug of fancy coffee and tray of doughnuts from the supermarket failed to calm him down; if anything it made him uncharacteristically angry. The inspector called him into his office and gave him a severe dressing down. The air was bluer than the players' dressing room after the local rugby sevens team had lost to their arch rivals.

'Don't be such a cliché, Elliot… as if a bloody donut is going to make up for losing Hill's car.'

'S… sorry boss, it wasn't my fault.' Sergeant Elliot's explanation was abruptly shut down. While the inspector took a drink of the coffee and a large bite of a pink iced donut, he tried again. 'Sorry boss, but the recovery contractors had been overloaded with work and had only sent a vehicle big enough to take the kidnappers' car away. There wasn't another one available till this morning. How was I to know he'd come back for it? Assuming it was him and not some opportunistic thief.'

'Opportunistic thief, my eye. It should never have been left there overnight. It's a catastrophe. The man's a trained soldier and a cunning bastard to be sure; he'll be miles away by now. I've put out an alert.' He paused to finish off the donut, and then carried on. 'I'm waiting for someone from the Major Investigation Team, MIT, to come from Edinburgh, to investigate the kidnapping. I don't want them to think we're an incompetent shower of country bumpkins in letting a key suspect escape.'

They got their hopes up at reports of the car being driven down the M1 at speed. But when the driver was apprehended after a chase through the suburbs of Birmingham, it turned out not to be Matt Hill. The driver claimed he'd found the car abandoned on the motorway service station at Forton. He'd had a row with his mate who'd driven off and left him stranded on the motorway; the keys were still in the ignition so he just got in and drove off without thinking of the consequences. He was charged with theft and a series of motoring offences. Matt Hill was spotted as a passenger in a range of vehicles on various cameras up and down the motorway but they were no nearer to finding their runaway.

'He's a conniving bastard that one,' Derek Thompson complained to anyone who would listen. He knew he was letting the missing Matt Hill get under his skin but the man was making fools of them. It took him some time to piece together the events leading to Fiona Scott's kidnap and eventual release. She was unharmed, but the doctor advised her to take things easy for a few days.

At the team briefing, Sergeant Elliot told them, 'I've got some information about the physiotherapist, Matt Hill. It turns out he was court martialled from the army for attacking an officer. He looks like he's got a serious gambling problem, hence the contact with the loan sharks.'

PC Laidlaw then explained she'd spoken to Lady Fiona Scott. 'When she employed him she understood he was ex-army and had been in the SAS. He had provided references from senior officers, but it appears the references were fakes.'

Inspector Thompson continued, 'We are putting the spate of burglaries in the village down to Matt Hill. He faces charges of housebreaking, attempted blackmail and extortion as well an accessory to kidnap. There was no sign of him after intensive searches of the fishing lake or anywhere in the Scottish Borders. We've traced his previous contacts in the Newcastle area and come up with a blank. His name has been added to the National Crime Agency Most Wanted List. I'm sure it will only be a matter of time before he's found.'

***

Detective Inspector Tulip Sharma, from the Major Incident Team, MIT, in Edinburgh, was drafted in to investigate the death of Jim Young and Fiona Scott's kidnapping. She read through Jim Young's autopsy report then laid out the photographs taken by the Scene of Crime Officers, SOCO. She carefully studied the position of the body lying against the stone wall, and the angle the gun lay on the ground, then read the statement from the son, Euan Young. She would need to write a report to pass on to the Procurator Fiscal Service, before they could weigh up all the evidence to pronounce a verdict declaring the cause of death as suspicious, accidental, or unexplained.

The local policing team had helpfully printed out a list of housebreaking and various other incidents that had happened in the locality that they had put down to Mathew Hill. For a small village a lot of things had happened in the preceding few months, culminating in the kidnap of the landowner's wife. As far as she could see there was nothing to connect any of these incidents to the farmer's death. However, she prided herself in being thorough and didn't want to miss a connection.

The Englishman Matt Hill's name figured in a number of reports. She wondered if there was a link. Perhaps Jim Young had stumbled across the loan sharks and had been shot by them, or perhaps he had found out what Matt Hill had been up to and had been shot by him, although there was no evidence of either of these two scenarios. The bullet clearly belonged to the gun which he'd been carrying and which according to the son was an old one belonging to his great grandfather.

The name of the Australian, Kirsty Ainsworth, kept coming up. She'd been living with the Youngs since January. There was something about this girl that puzzled her. Perhaps there was something in her past that could shed light onto matters. If she made a request for information from Australia to check if she showed up on their records via formal channels, it would take weeks to get a reply. However, one of her former colleagues, who'd left to take up a job in Australia two years ago, owed her a favour. It was time she called it in.

A week later she received an email dossier on Kirsty Ainsworth from the Sydney police. It made interesting reading. She breezed into the meeting room. 'The info from Sydney is enlightening.' She held up the documents. 'It appears Kirsty Ainsworth was something of an animal rights activist. In early 2017 she was part of a group "freeing" test animals from a cosmetic research lab but was let off with a warning. In August of the same year, following the death of 2,400 sheep on route to the Middle East, animal rights activists tried to blockade the port. She was arrested for criminal damage when she, along with several other activists, glued herself to a truck being used to transport live sheep to the port. She was given a suspended sentence. She was very lucky not to go to prison. Given her strong animal rights views I just don't understand what she is doing working on a sheep farm. Is there a local link?'

Sergeant Elliot and Sia Laidlaw exchanged glances. Detective Inspector Sharma looked directly at them. 'You're the ones with your ears to the ground. What about Stanley Scott? Where does he fit in with all this? I believe he and Mr Young were friends.'

'*Aye.* Right enough,' replied Sergeant Elliot. 'Stan, Lord Scott, is a few years older but they grew up together. They both went to Australia on some sort of exchange trip, when was it? Let me think. It was before the son, Euan was born, so about nineteen, twenty years ago. But I've heard they were seen arguing a *wee* bit back. And of course the Youngs received a letter from the Stanton Holm Estate the morning he died, offering them the opportunity to buy the farmhouse, otherwise they would be evicted.'

'Would that be enough to tip Jim Young over the edge? Betrayal by his long-time friend; facing losing his job and his home. Seems a strong motive to me. Wait, did you say they went to Australia together? When was it?'

'Ehm, I'm not sure, but maybe sometime before the Millennium. I vaguely remember Stan saying he wished he'd been there to see the fireworks on Sydney Harbour Bridge. What are you thinking, ma'am?'

'The girl staying at the Youngs', she's eighteen, isn't she? Check her date of birth and see if you can find out when they went.'

Chapter 28

The Revenge List

Since the shock of Jim's death, Lizzie was in a daze. She blamed herself for his death; if only she'd stopped him going out on the hillside that night, he would have still been alive. At least Euan was with him at the end so he didn't die alone.

Waves of sadness were liable to engulf her without warning; one minute she would be working on plans for the next event at the 'big house', and the next minute she would be fighting back tears. The slightest thing reminded her of Jim and their life together. She'd lost everything. She even missed the sound of his whistling round the house; it used to get on her nerves but now she would have given anything to hear it again.

Euan was a great support, as was Kirsty, who was like the daughter she and Jim had never had. Thankfully, the lass had agreed to stay on for a while till things settled down. Today Euan and Kirsty were out preparing some sheep ready to sell. That was the thing about farming; nothing ever stopped it, even death. It was almost two weeks since the accident and they were still waiting for his body to be released, which was dependent on the completion of the autopsy report. The family liaison officer had explained this was separate from the fatal accident enquiry which would take some time to complete.

She wandered aimlessly round the house and found herself on the top floor. She opened the door of Kirsty's room to see if she'd stored any family photos in boxes under the bed, thinking there might be some she could use when they were eventually able to hold a funeral. Something caught her eye. There was a book of poetry sitting on the bedside table. She wondered if Kirsty had borrowed one of Jim's books from the bookshelf. She picked it up but didn't recognise the red cover. It was a first edition of *Border Poems of Will Ogilvie*. She looked at the inscription:

To my dearest Janine, thank you for a wonderful time.
I will always remember you,
all my love,
Stan xxx
December 1998.

Why would Kirsty have a poetry book signed by Stan, to someone called Janine? Puzzled, she sat on the bed and flicked open the pages and an airmail letter fell out. She knew it was wrong to pry into the lass's belongings but felt compelled to find out what was in the letter. She picked it up and gingerly opened it; her heart raced as she read the letter which to her astonishment was written by Lady Isobel. Why on earth had she sent this girl a cheque for a thousand pounds? An abortion, a pay-off, an airline ticket to Scotland? It wasn't clear. As she put the book back on the bedside table, a grubby handwritten piece of paper fell to the floor.

She read the 'revenge list' line by line, hardly able to

process the enormity of the implications.

REVENGE LIST. My plan to get revenge on THE BITCH and DADDY DEAR

send condolence card/s to Stan for THE BITCH √

send funeral flowers for THE BITCH √

put death notification in local paper ... xxx paper refused without ID

send hearse ... xxx too expensive

dig up dirt on THE BITCH & DADDY DEAR ???

start gossip in village – NG – good for this

create tension between DADDY DEAR & wife. Ask for selfie, flirt with him

let rats & mice into house ....

pretend attempted break into the house

set up fake events/house party to attract 100's of people

put negative reviews of events on internet √

set traps/poison raptors on hills without creating actual damage to wildlife

blackmail THE BITCH /DADDY DEAR ... demand money ... threaten to contact local/national press if they don't pay up.

My god! Stan was the girl's father. After they had made her so welcome, the girl had brazenly lied. Lizzie was furious, but Kirsty could wait. The police would deal with her.

Lizzie flew down the stairs, jumped in the car and headed to Stanton Hall, where she found Stan in his study, and without stopping for any niceties burst straight in.

'You lying bastard. You're manipulative and downright evil. What everyone says about you is true. You are an entitled, pompous and arrogant liar. You told me nothing happened in Australia. I believed you. Just as I believed you had no choice but to marry Fiona.'

Stan recoiled in horror at the barrage of abuse Lizzie had hurled at him.

'Wow, steady on, Liz. Tell me what's happened.'

'I found the letter from your mother offering to pay off Kirsty's mother. And Kirsty had made a list of all the ways she was going to get her revenge on you and Isobel. She sent the funeral cards, wrote the bad reviews, everything. That's what happened. Here it is.' She waved the airmail letter and revenge list at him and thrust them into his hand.

'Hey, steady on, Liz. Slow down, one thing at a time. Firstly, I'm 100% sure I am *not* the girl's father, if that's what's bothering you. Now sit down and take some deep breaths.' He poured two glasses of whisky and handed her a glass. 'Now drink this. You've had a shock.'

He took a couple of sips of whisky then continued, 'The police are still carrying out their investigations into Fiona's kidnapping and all of its ramifications. Let them sort it out. Please believe me, Liz; I never had any choice but to marry into money. I was twenty-two years old, my father had recently died and there was a huge inheritance tax bill to pay. I know it makes me sound like some sort of Jane Austen character, whose mother was trying to marry her off for money. It just happens to be true. My mother made it clear, if I didn't marry Fiona, the estate would be ruined and all the workers' jobs would be wiped out, including your own father's job. I thought I was doing the right thing in marrying Fiona, even though I loved you. For what good it did.'

Lizzie looked up at him. 'So you did love me?'

Stan nodded. 'Of course I did, you must have known that.' He took a deep breath then carried on, 'Now the estate is on the verge of bankruptcy again. That's why I've been advised to sell the farmhouse and plant up the fields for forestry. It was the only way to save the estate. I told Jim about it but didn't go into practicalities, but didn't realised the letter would go out so promptly. I feel so ashamed. I'm truly sorry about Jim. He was like a brother to me. I intended to come to see you to explain, but then there was all that business with Fiona being kidnapped.'

Lizzie nodded. Then the tears started to flow.

'Come here. Let me hold you.'

They clung to each other till Lizzie calmed down and then they held each other for a while longer. Stan poured them both another drink.

'Here, drink this. We've both had a shock.' He took Janine Ainsworth's letter from his jacket pocket and gave it to Lizzie to read. He read the reply from his mother with horror.

'Do you know, she never even asked me about it. She must have assumed I was the father and didn't want to risk the match with Fiona.'

'Well, if you aren't her father, who is? Perhaps it is someone else her mother met in Australia.'

Stan shifted uncomfortably in his chair. He frowned and took another swig of his drink before answering.

'This is rather delicate. I know the timing is terrible. But the possibility is something Jim and I talked about.'

'What possibility?' Lizzie interrupted him. 'Hang on. Why Jim? Why would you two discuss it?'

Stan didn't answer. There was an uncomfortable

silence. He watched her face as the truth gradually dawned on her.

'What? You can't really think my Jim is her father?'

He nodded.

They both jumped guiltily when they heard Fiona's wheelchair coming along the corridor. 'What's going on here?'

***

When Kirsty came into the kitchen with Euan from rounding up the sheep, she immediately spotted the red poetry book on the kitchen table, alongside two red and blue edged airmail letters and the revenge list.

Lizzie was angrily pacing the kitchen floor. 'Euan, can you make some tea and fetch over the plate of scones and then make yourself scarce,' she said, giving him one of her 'don't you dare argue with me' looks, so he did as he was told.

He glanced across at Kirsty, who had gone as pale as a sheep on its way to the knacker's yard.

'It's okay, Euan. I'll be fine,' she assured him. In many ways she would be glad for the pretence to be over. She steeled herself for the confrontation she knew was coming. She read the two letters in silence.

Lizzie took a deep breath before speaking. 'I've spoken to Stan and he assured me there is no way whatsoever he is your father. There has obviously been some sort of misunderstanding. Have you asked your mother about it?' Lizzie asked gently.

'So you're telling me Stan isn't my father after I came all this way to find him. Are you trying to fob me off with a load of lies?' Kirsty demanded angrily.

Lizzie put her hands over Kirsty's. 'I'm sorry lass, but Stan is definitely not your father.'

Kirsty hung her head and sat silent for a few moments. She needed time to take in what Lizzie had just told her. Gathering her thoughts she explained, 'My mother would never tell me about my father. So that's why when I found the poetry book and letter, I came here to find him. Are you absolutely sure it's not Stan?'

'Yes. I'm sure.'

'But if Stan isn't my father, then who is?'

'Perhaps it is someone else your mother met in Australia. I've spoken to Stan and Fiona this morning and the only way to confirm this is with a DNA test. Stan has agreed to pay for it. But you must speak to your mother straight away... but before you do, tell me about this list. There are some pretty nasty things on it.'

'I didn't mean any harm. I was angry. I thought Stan didn't want anything to do with me and Lady Isobel was sending the money to pay for my mother to have an abortion.'

'Stan knew nothing about it. Lady Isobel didn't tell him about the letter until recently when she became ill. It came as a complete shock to him.'

'I wrote the list on the plane coming across. I had plenty of time to make it up. When I arranged this placement with Euan, I didn't know it was so near to Stanton Hall. Yes, I did a couple of things on the list, I sent the condolence card and funeral flowers. I shouldn't have sent them. It's unforgivable of me. Apart from taking the silver cross, I promise I never stole anything else. Oh, and about the bad reviews. It was just after I got here. I know now it was mean of me and you were all so kind to me, I felt guilty afterwards.' She paused and took a deep breath. 'But I didn't do anything else. Some of the things I was accused of *are* on the list, but I promise I didn't do it. I even wondered if someone in the house had found the list and was setting me up.'

Lizzie looked horrified at this last remark. 'What, are you trying to turn it back on us? How dare you!'

'No, no, Lizzie. You have all been wonderful to me. I quickly put the thought out of my mind. I'm not trying to deflect the blame but... I was suspicious of Matt Hill. When I was with him he kept ignoring persistent phone calls and I saw him spying on Stan and Jim when they were arguing by the long field.'

Lizzie's stomach tightened. 'Do you know what they were arguing about?'

'No. You'll have to ask Stan. Wait. My cousin, Emma, in Australia recently found out there might have been another young man staying at my uncle's sheep station, at the same time as Stan. Someone called Gillespie. She didn't know his other name.'

Lizzie turned pale.

'What is it? Do you know him?'

'*Aye*. My husband.'

'What?!'

'He hated the name, Gillespie, which was his mother's family name, so he used James, his middle name.'

Kirsty shrieked, 'What? Jim could be my father? I can hardly believe it... I've been living with my father all this time and I never knew.'

Lizzie wiped tears from her eyes; she looked up. Euan was stood by the door.

'How long have you been stood there, son?'

'Long enough, Ma.'

He turned abruptly and walked out of the back door.

Chapter 29

Fair girls

27th May 2018 Sydney

Janine Ainsworth was surprised to get a text message from her cousin Emma, asking her to contact her urgently. She assumed Archie had suffered a relapse so she phoned her back straight away.

'Janine, I had to speak to you. I'm worried about Kirsty. I'm breaking my promise not to tell you where she is but I'm really concerned about her.'

'Why? What's wrong?'

'The farmer where she is staying has been found shot. He's dead. They think it was an accident. She's in bits.'

'I knew she was in Scotland. But do you know where? Do you know the name of the family she's living with?'

'She is staying near a village called Stanton Holm. The family are Jim, Lizzie and Euan Young. She previously sent me a photo of them. I'll send it to you now if you want. And then I will text you the address.'

Janine's mobile pinged. She stared in horror. Even after twenty years, he still looked the same: tall, slim, dark haired. She immediately phoned her cousin back.

'Are you sure the farmer is called Jim Young? Did she

mention anyone else?'

'She mentioned someone called Stan a lot; she's convinced that he's her father. She hates his mother, Lady Isobel. And the way she talks about Euan Young, I think she's fallen for him. She doesn't want to leave him and his mother to come home. Janine. Are you okay? You've gone very quiet.'

'Do you have a photo of this Stan person by any chance?'

'Actually I do. He looks very pompous. I'll send it to you.'

Janine's phone pinged again. She looked at the photo of the squat, middle-aged man with thinning fair hair. He was dressed in shooting gear, posing with a party of pheasant shooters in front of a large house. He hadn't aged well but there was no question about it. He wasn't the boy she'd fallen blindly in love with all those years ago. He was the one who had introduced his friend to her as 'Stan.'

'Emma, I've had a terrible a shock. I can't explain. I must go to find Kirsty. You must promise not to tell her we've had this talk. I've let her down badly. I have to go to Scotland before it's too late. I'm going as soon as I can get a flight. Can you find me a contact number for the Scotts and Lizzie Young? Whatever you do, don't tell Kirsty I'm coming.'

***

Stan woke up abruptly when he heard the landline ring. It was gone midnight. Half asleep he stumbled downstairs to answer it, unsure who could be phoning so late, hoping it wasn't more bad news. He didn't recognise the voice, but picked up on the accent straight away.

'Hi Jim, or should I say Stan? Sorry to phone so late. It's Kirsty's mother, Janine Ainsworth here. You might remember me, Archie Ainsworth's niece. I'm actually phoning from the departure lounge at Sydney airport. I'm having breakfast before I leave for the UK.'

'Janine Ainsworth did you say?' Suddenly wide awake, he asked, 'Are you the stunning Sydneysider in the blue dress, who stole poor Jim's heart? Thank heavens. I'm so glad you contacted me. I didn't know how to reach you. I promise I never knew about your letter until recently. I'm afraid I've some bad news. Do you know what's happened to Jim?'

'I heard from my cousin Emma that he's died in some sort of shooting accident. Do you know when the funeral is?'

'No. I'm afraid not. The family are waiting on the results of the autopsy, which are due any day now, before the body can be released. There's also going to be a fatal accident enquiry, but that will take a while. Have you spoken to your daughter recently? She's been in a bit of bother over here.'

'I haven't spoken to her, only Emma, so you'll have to fill me in. I'm very worried about her. I don't want her to know I'm on my way. Could you arrange for someone to pick me up at Newcastle Airport?'

'Yes, I can do that, no trouble. Do you have somewhere to stay?'

'No, not yet. But I was hoping Lizzie Young might put me up, if it's not too awkward.'

'We have plenty of space here. You can stay with my wife Fiona and me at Stanton Hall.'

'Thanks. That will be brilliant. I must go now, my flight is being called. I'll text you my email address so you can fill me in with what's been going on.'

***

When Janine arrived at Newcastle Airport her stomach turned somersaults at the thought of facing her daughter. She recognised Stan straight away from the recent photograph. Wearing a tweed jacket and deerstalker hat, he looked completely out of place amongst the casually dressed throng waiting in arrivals. She was amused when he threw his arms around her like a long lost friend. Freeing herself from his grasp she blurted out, 'I can't wait to see my daughter. This is my chance to build bridges with her. I just hope I'm in time to stop things going too far with Euan Young.'

'Look, just come back to Stanton Hall and get settled in. It will be late by the time we get there. So why don't you get some sleep and I'll take you to see Kirsty in the morning.'

***

On Friday morning after an early breakfast Kirsty told Lizzie that she'd go and help Euan finish cleaning out the cow barn.

'Okay lass, you do that. I've plenty of jobs to do around the house to keep me busy.'

Lizzie was washing the breakfast pots when she heard the postman at the door. He handed her two large envelopes, both addressed to Jim. She opened one of the envelopes, unsure what to expect, but was shocked by what she'd read. Her hands were still shaking when she phoned Stan.

'I'm in a bit of a state. Two official-looking letters came this morning addressed to Jim. I opened one of them. It was a DNA test. It's as you suspected, it says there is a 98% match, so he is Kirsty's father. I can't stop shaking. I don't know why but there is a second envelope. I've not dared open it.'

'Do you want me to come across while you open it? It might just be another copy of the same letter sent by mistake.'

'Would you?'

'I'll ask Fiona to take care of things at the house and I'll come straight away.'

Stan was apprehensive as he opened the second envelope. He scanned the contents then gasped, 'Oh my god, Liz. I never expected this. Why the hell didn't you say something?' He quickly passed the document to her, as if the pages were burning his fingers.

Lizzie looked at it just as stunned, not wanting to believe the truth. 'Believe me; this has come as much as a shock to me as it is to you. I suppose we should have realised long ago, but we'll deal with it. We have to for the kids' sake.'

***

As Kirsty and Euan mucked out the cowshed, neither spoke until the task was nearly completed, when Kirsty broke the silence. 'Euan, after we slept together the night your dad died, I thought we had something special. Then you said you needed to put your mother first, but I still cared for you and I think you still care for me. Now we know we are half-brother and sister, I don't know how to be around you. My feelings are still the same.' Kirsty brushed tears from her eyes with the back of her hand.

'Don't do that, you'll get muck in your eyes. Come here. You look as if need a hug.'

They heard a cough. Stan was stood at the barn door.

'Erm, these cows must have the cleanest barn in the region, but you two need to leave it now and come into the house. We have something important you need to see.'

***

Euan and Kirsty followed Stan into the kitchen. Eyeing the piles of food, Euan said nervously, 'I'm always suspicious when tea and scones appear. These days it's never anything good.' Then he spotted two large white envelopes and a bulging brown envelope on the table and blurted out, 'I'm sorry, Mum. We didn't mean it to happen, it just did.'

'I wouldn't have said anything,' Stan said looking directly at Kirsty and Euan as he joined them round the table.

'Am I missing something? You didn't mean what to happen, Euan?' Lizzie asked as she poured out the tea.

Kirsty turned to face Lizzie. 'I'm really sorry, Lizzie, but we didn't know we were half-brother and sister when we fell for each other.'

Euan moved the chairs so he could sit next to her and held her hand.

Stan smiled. 'Look, you two don't have anything to worry about. You are not blood relatives. There is no reason why you can't marry – if that's what you both want.'

'What? How?' Euan asked, surprised.

'Okay. I'll explain. Before he died Jim sent off a DNA

test for you, Kirsty. He must have taken a handful of hairs with follicles from your comb. I'd been telling him to do that for a while so he would know if you were his daughter or not. The results show there is a 98% chance of his being your father.' He handed her one of the white envelopes.

'What, so Jim was really my father and not you, Stan? I can't believe it. All this time I was looking for my father, I was actually living with him and never knew it.'

'Oh my god, it's true,' Euan mumbled looking at Kirsty in shock. 'So that's what dad meant on the hillside when he was dying, when he kept saying he was sorry to you and Ma.'

'Why didn't you say something?' Lizzie asked, aghast, wondering how many more shocks she would have to endure.

Kirsty then asked, 'But if Jim is my father, surely Euan and I are half-brother and sister?'

Stan looked up at Lizzie, who nodded to him.

'Go on, Stan. Tell them the rest of it. They need to know the whole truth.'

Kirsty and Euan looked at each other mystified.

'I knew Jim was going to send off a DNA test for Kirsty, what I didn't know was that he also sent off a DNA test for you, Euan.'

'Me? But why did he send off a DNA test for me?'

'Please Stan, just tell them the result. We'll come to why later,' Lizzie implored him.

'The test showed you aren't related. I'm sorry, Euan, Jim was your father in every way that counted but he wasn't your biological father.'

'What?!' I don't believe it,' Euan shrieked. 'That can't be right. Ma, what's going on? Tell me he's wrong.'

Kirsty interrupted him. 'But listen. It means if we're not related we can marry and start a family when we are ready.' She turned to Euan to hug him but he put his arm out to stop her.

'Go back a bit. If Jim, isn't my biological father, then who is?'

Turning red in the face, Stan turned to face Euan. 'Forgive me – but I'm your father.'

'What? It must be a mistake. The test is wrong. We'll have to do it again,' Euan shouted, standing up so abruptly the wooden kitchen chair crashed onto the stone floor; the sound waves reverberated through the house.

By the look of pure anger on his face Kirsty thought he was going to punch Stan. 'Don't. Please don't do anything you'll regret.'

'I'm sorry, son,' Lizzie said reaching towards Euan, intending to stroke the back of his hand, but he snatched it away abruptly. 'We don't need another DNA test to confirm it. But you can have one if you wish. I was already pregnant when your dad and I married, but I didn't realise how far gone I was. I just took it for granted you were Jim's. When you came early we were just so pleased you had arrived safely; you were underweight and I assumed you were premature but I didn't think to check the dates.'

'Dates?'

Stan stood up next to Euan. He spoke hesitantly, 'Jim knew Lizzie and I went out for a while before I got engaged to Fiona. We even used to joke about it.'

'What? You joked about screwing my mother! Was it one of the perks of being the heir to the estate? You bastard!' he shouted.

Kirsty stood up as well and whispered in Euan's ear.

'Please darling, calm down; we need to know the truth.'

Euan picked up the chair and held on to it. There was a brief moment when there was a possibility he would smash it over Stan's head. Then taking a sharp intake of breath he put the chair on the floor and reluctantly sat down again.

'Euan, it wasn't like that,' Lizzie said looking across at Stan. He nodded encouragement so she continued. 'Stan came to say goodbye to me the night before he and Jim went to Australia. One thing led to another. You know how these things happen.' She looked at them pointedly, as tears ran down her cheeks. 'I promise it was the one and only time. I suppose I am guilty of not considering the possibility the baby was Stan's. As far as I was concerned we were a family, Euan was our son – Jim's and mine.'

Kirsty got up and fetched a box of tissues from the dresser. As she passed the box to the older woman she gently squeezed her on the shoulder.

'So, my *faither* was second best to him, then?' Euan asked angrily glaring at Stan.

'No love. I had loved your dad since we were children. That never changed. Never will change. Stan, tell them about the letters Jim left.'

'Not long before Jim died he asked me to keep a letter for you, Kirsty, just in case you turned out to be his daughter. At the time I wondered why it was in such a thick envelope, which was addressed to me. Anyway, when the letters came in the post this morning with the DNA results, I opened it. There were letters for me, Lizzie, Euan and your mother as well as you, Kirsty.' Stan handed Euan and Kirsty their letters. He left the one for Janine Ainsworth on the table.

‘Wait, if he wrote letters before he died does that mean his death wasn’t an accident?’ Kirsty asked putting her envelope down abruptly in front of her.

‘No, lass,’ Lizzie reassured her. ‘I’ve read mine. It certainly does not mean that at all. Don’t be nervous about reading it.’

They heard a car pull up in the yard and stop outside the boot room. A few moments later Fiona knocked at the kitchen door. She opened it, popped her head round the door and asked, ‘Is it okay if we come in? I’ve got a visitor for Kirsty.’

‘G’day,’ a voice called out. Kirsty leapt out of her seat and rushed to the door.

‘Mum? Is that really you? What are you doing here?’

‘What do you think? I came to see you. I heard you were having a tough time. Come here girlie and let me give you a hug.’

***

It took some time before they all caught up with their news and sat round to read their letters. While this was happening Euan hardly said a word, and Lizzie and Kirsty both worried about him. Lizzie looked completely stunned by the revelations but held onto her composure as best as she could. Stan had phoned Fiona as soon as he had read his letter and forewarned her about the DNA tests. She’d long suspected there had been something between him and Lizzie in the past so wasn’t totally surprised at the outcome. She wheeled her chair next to his, to give him moral support, then suggested, ‘Stan darling, you have already read your letter; if it’s not too personal, why don’t you read it out?’

Stan held up his envelope so everyone could see it. It was marked: OPEN FIRST. Taking a deep breath he read the letter out slowly.

Dear Stan,

Could you please hold onto these letters for me until the DNA results come through? I wrote them to get my thoughts straight. I don't want to destroy them but I'm concerned in case they are found if I keep them here.

I have thought long and hard about this and have finally taken your advice and sent off DNA samples for myself and Kirsty. I've also taken the liberty of sending one off for Euan. I am not sure what results I am hoping for, but in event of the DNA tests coming back positive could you please return the envelopes so I can give them out in person? Otherwise return them to me and I'll burn them.

You have always been like a brother to me and my best friend, apart from my dearest Lizzie. I hope whatever the results; they don't change things between us.

Your dear friend,

Jim

Kirsty read her letter silently then smiled. She read it out slowly. Her mother was amused to hear she'd picked up a slight Scottish accent.

My dear Kirsty,

If you are reading this letter then it means I am your father. Please forgive me for sending off the DNA test without your permission. I hope you are not too disappointed Stan isn't your father. You have been like the daughter Lizzie and I never had. Don't worry about Lizzie; she has such a kind heart, she will love you as much as I do.

I've written a letter to your mother apologising for not contacting her when I got back to Scotland and for pretending to be Stan. It was such a childish prank. If you will give me her address I can send it to her.

When you first came you were so nervous around the sheep I wondered what on earth our Euan was doing taking you on, but you have turned out to be a natural with the sheep, a true Borders shepherd at heart.

I have loved having you staying at the house and hope you will stay on and help with the farm for as long as possible. Hoping we can get time to spend together and get to know each other as father and daughter,

Your loving father,

Gillespie James Young.

Janine dabbed at her eyes as she read her letter.

Dear Janine,

I've asked Kirsty for your address to send you this letter. It has come as such a shock to realise you had my child. I never knew anything about it until recently. It must have been hard for you bringing her up on your own. She is a grand lass and I already love her like a daughter.

I'm sorry for not keeping in touch when I got back to Scotland. I never should have pretended to be Stan – it was childish. I suppose I lacked confidence in those days. You were so beautiful – my 'Barefoot

Girl.' I thought you wouldn't look at me if you knew I was just a farm worker.

Perhaps you could come across to Scotland and we can all meet up. I'm sure you will love the Borders countryside and being able to visit the places you will be familiar with from the book of Border Poems by our favourite poet, W.H.O.

Looking forward to meeting you again.

Yours

Jim Young alias Stan

By the time it was her turn to read out her letter, tears were running down Lizzie's face. Fiona wheeled her chair next to hers and took her hand, which was shaking. 'It's okay; you don't have to read it out if you don't want to.'

'No, I'll be all right. It's time I faced the truth.' She read hesitantly with her eyes fixed on the page.

My dearest Lizzie,

I'm writing this letter in the middle of the night while you are fast asleep. You must have sensed I have been distracted recently. I've been troubled and been unable to sleep properly for weeks so decided to write letters to people I care about as a way to clear my thoughts.

I have struggled to find the words to express all the thoughts jumbled up in my head. I have finally accepted the possibility that Kirsty could be my daughter. I will ask Stan to hold onto the letters for me until I can arrange some DNA tests. I met Kirsty's mother when we were in Australia. It seems a lifetime ago. I was young and totally smitten. I have seen how Kirsty and Euan look at each other and worry about them being half brother and sister. I did the maths and decided to send off a DNA test for him while I'm at it.

None of this means I love you or our Euan any less. You know deep down we are soul mates, even if we are only human and got a bit distracted in our youth. If Kirsty is my daughter, please forgive me, just as I will forgive you if Euan isn't my natural son. I won't love him or you any less.

Your loving husband,

Jim XXXXX

All eyes turned towards Euan. He stood up and shook his head. 'I can't do it. I can't read it.' He turned and ran outside slamming the door behind him. Kirsty got up to go after him but he turned and shouted, 'No. Don't come after me, I need to be by myself. I'll be a while. I've got a lot to get my head around.'

With that he headed off across the fields and into the hills.

Chapter 30

Mother, daughter, mother, son

Euan was devastated by the news Stan was his father and became increasingly withdrawn, taking himself off into the hills for hours at a time, leaving Kirsty feeling confused and anxious. Although Stan and Fiona had made Janine feel very welcome at Stanton Hall, she decided to move into the farmhouse to support her daughter. She offered to help Lizzie out by doing the domestic chores to free her up to work alongside Dixie and Kirsty with the sheep. It amused her she was staying in the 'shearers' room, which made her feel a little homesick for the Outback.

She enjoyed going for walks with Kirsty when she'd finished her work on the farm. On the second afternoon of her stay at the farmhouse, Kirsty finished her work early. The two of them walked over the hills above the farm and Kirsty suddenly blurted out, 'Mum, why didn't you ever tell me who my father was? It's something I still don't understand.'

'Come here my love, let me give you a hug then let's find somewhere out of the wind to sit for a while.'

They walked further up the hill and sat in the shelter of the dyke by the badger sett.

'You always asked about your dad, but never about your grandparents. First you need to understand about them, so I will start at the beginning...

***

'One morning when I was twelve years old, I came down to breakfast. The table was all laid out. There was a white envelope addressed to Dan, my dad, propped up by his bowl. There was a postcard propped up by mine. I was excited, thinking it must be a special occasion. It was. My mother had left home. My card said:

> My dearest, darling Janine,
> I am ever so sorry to have to do this but I can't live this life any longer. I am leaving your father. I have met someone else and we are travelling far away. I love you and will always love you. Please be good for your father. Work hard at school. I will come back for you when we are settled.
> Your loving mother xxx
> Christine

'The card had a picture of a horse on the front and a verse called "Galloping Hooves". I loved the card and carried it everywhere. I wondered where the poem came from and found a book in the school library by a Scottish poet called Will H. Ogilvie, which led to me finding out as much as I could about him and to a lifelong love of his work. It was if it was an invisible thread linking me to my mother who I never heard from again.'

'Oh, Mum. I never knew. That's awful.' Kirsty leaned over and hugged her mother. The sun was starting to set behind the hills so they headed back towards the farmhouse. As they walked Janine recounted the rest of her story.

'After Mum left I took on most of the housekeeping tasks: washing, cooking and cleaning. Dad hardly ever spoke to me. He was either at work or with his mates at the pub. I longed for school holidays and the time away at the sheep station. Archie, dad's younger brother by twelve years, and his wife Mabel became my surrogate parents. Even when Emma and then Drew, were born, they treated me like their older daughter. But I was lonely. All I ever wanted was to be loved and be part of a loving family. When I reached my teenage years, with each boy I met I really believed I loved him, and he was "the one", but they soon discarded me once I'd slept with them.

'Joshua, who was in the year above me at school, joked about my being another notch on his didgeridoo. Tom boasted to his mates in the rugby team I had thighs like a full back, and my nickname became "thunder thighs", so I went on every fad diet I could find to lose weight. Then when I met "Stan", he was leaving within a few days and had no choice but to go back to Scotland, so he couldn't reject me. I was delighted he shared my love of poetry and I treasured the book by Will Ogilvie that he gave me.'

'Was that the one I found hidden in your drawer? The one that brought me to Scotland to find him?'

'Yes. It was, but I never hid it, it must have slipped down. Anyway, after he left I looked up his contact details in my uncle's files, so I could write to him to thank him for the book, but never had the courage to write. Then, just before I was due to go back to Sydney I started feeling sick and suspected I was pregnant. I was thrilled. I would have a child of my own to love, someone to love me back. I thought if I wrote to Stan maybe he would send for me. However, most of all I feared my father's reaction. At Aunt

Mabel's insistence I told him over the telephone. There was silence, and then the line went dead.

'A few days later, early in the evening, I spotted his jeep as it roared up the long drive towards the yard. I'd been chatting to the station hands who were sat outside the shearing shed playing cards. The vehicle came to a sudden halt with stones and dirt flying up behind it. The door of the jeep flew open and Dad lurched out of the driving seat. As I ran towards him I could smell drink on his breath. He grabbed hold of my shoulder, and dragged me by my hair back to where the station hands were standing open-mouthed.

'He bellowed, "If it's any of you who got my daughter pregnant I'll castrate you as soon as look at you." Not one of them spoke.

'He bawled at me, "Tell me, girlie, which one of these no marks got you in the family way?"

'I said, "Dad, stop it will you. It wasn't one of the station hands. It was someone else."

'Hearing the commotion, Mabel and Archie came running out of the house followed by Emma, who was only two years old at the time. Mabel, heavily pregnant with Drew, yelled at Emma, "Go back inside now, there's a good girl." Emma toddled back indoors with Joey, her toy kangaroo, tucked under her arm.

'Archie shouted, "Oy, Dan, stop that. My boys wouldn't touch a hair on your girl's head. Leave them be."

'My father turned on me roaring, "Janine, you're a wayward tart just like your mother. If you keep this bastard you're carrying I want nothing to do with you. If I find out who did this I'll kill him, even if I have to cross to the other side of the world. I mean it."

‘Archie shouted, “Dan, stop this nonsense or I’ll have to ask you to leave.” He approached his brother cautiously.

“‘You don’t get rid of me that easily. Wait, you sly dog, unless you have something to hide. Was it you, the ‘someone else’ who touched my princess?”

‘At that, Archie launched himself at Dad’s throat. The pair of them wrestled on the ground screaming obscenities at each other. The dogs started barking, the horses whinnied and Emma stood at the door of the homestead bawling. In the midst of the pandemonium I sat on the ground and cried for my mother. The fight stopped abruptly. The brothers dusted themselves down, checked themselves for any damage, as if they were schoolboys again having a toy fight.

‘Dan spoke first. “Okay, I’ll get going and leave you to it then.” He tried to clamber into the jeep but Archie pulled him back and grabbed the keys from the ignition.

“‘No you don’t, mate. You’re in no fit state to drive. You can sleep it off in the shearing shed, then leave at first light.”

‘I was left sobbing, ashamed and humiliated. Aunt Mabel put her arm round me and said that I could stay for a long as I wanted. Archie went home with me to collect my belongings. We timed it for when Dad was away working. Fortunately, the letter from Lady Isobel arrived while we there. I’d have hated Dad to have got hold of the cheque she sent.’

***

As they continued walking back to the farmhouse Janine explained, ‘I promise I never meant to hurt you, but the emotional memory of that day was so strong it has stayed with me ever since. I really believed my nasty, vindictive father knew about Stan, and would follow him to Scotland. If I'd thought about it rationally, I should have realised he would never be able to afford the fare. My excuse is that then, I was a frightened, pregnant teenager, but I can't say the same now. When you told me you were going to Scotland to find your father, I wondered if "Stan", or even my own father, had contacted you.'

'Wow, but how would they have known where I lived?' Kirsty asked puzzled.

'I wondered if one of them had seen a photo of you in the papers after all that terrible business last year with the demo and your arrest, and traced you from that.'

'Did you still believe my father was at risk?'

Janine nodded and brushed the tears from her eyes. 'Yes, I did. I was deeply hurt when Stan's mother had written such a cold reply to my letter telling Stan that I was pregnant. It was another rejection: first my mother, then my father, and then Stan and his mother. Deep inside I felt an emptiness that could never be filled, except for the baby growing inside me.' She looked across at her daughter and smiled. 'Every night I hugged my expanding belly, sang to you, recited poetry and told you how much I loved you.'

'Oh, Mum.' Kirsty felt tears run down her cheeks and reached out for her mother's hand.

Janine continued, 'If the baby was a boy I was going to call him William, after Will Ogilvie, the poet whose work gave me such comfort and was the link with my own mother and now your father. If you were a girl I intended to call you Christine after my mother, but when I gave birth to my beautiful brown-haired, brown-eyed baby daughter, I was overwhelmed with love. After much thought, I decided to call you Kirsty, the Scottish version of my mother's name.'

Kirsty said very little as they walked but let her mother tell her own story.

Janine then went on to explain how her aunt and uncle looked after her baby while she went away to train to be a teacher. Emma was three years older, so the two girls grew up together like sisters. Drew, Mabel and Archie's second child, followed Kirsty everywhere. She went back every holiday and weekend to the sheep station to spend time with her daughter but somehow she felt superfluous.

'My parents had a loveless marriage; cold towards each other except for the heat of their fights, but they never laid a finger on me in either anger or affection. I never felt safe or loved. I'd been abandoned by my mother, but Aunt Mabel had become a loving surrogate. However, there were tensions between her and Archie over his drinking and I often heard them arguing about it.

'I promised myself I would love my child in a way I was never loved, but somehow we never got on. Perhaps it was because I'd missed so much of your early years while I was studying, that we never bonded. My father's threat to kill the boy who'd got me pregnant was so deeply etched in my mind, I never dared tell you who he was; it felt safer that way. It became a habit; a dirty secret, which built a barrier between us.

'After I qualified as a teacher, I worked at a school in Bathurst for a couple of years, but it was over an hour-long journey morning and evening. Then one night when I got home from work, Archie was lying drunk on the floor outside the shearing shed. You were stood over him prodding him with your tiny fingers, saying "Wake up Uncle, wake up." He staggered to his feet and started yelling at you. That was the push I needed. You were getting older and I didn't want you exposed to that type of situation.'

Kirsty gasped in horror at that revelation. 'Mum, that must have been dreadful.'

Janine nodded and continued her story. 'I got a job at a school in Sydney; by then I'd saved enough money to buy a small flat and when you were six years old, we moved into the tower block in Redfern. It didn't have the best reputation then but I was determined not to use the money Stan's mother had sent, and had opened up a savings account to pay towards your education. As you grew up you pulled against me all the time as if it was your life's work to oppose me. No matter what I said or did, you did the opposite.'

'Sorry, Mum,' Kirsty whispered, wiping tears from her eyes. The two women walked the last distance back to the farmhouse in silence. Janine felt relieved to finally share her past with her daughter.

***

Kirsty found her mother's story hard to hear and felt guilty for giving her such a hard time while she was growing up. She was relieved Stan wasn't her father, but saddened she hadn't known it was Jim until after he died. She knew she would cherish his letter as long as she lived. She was glad her mother had come to find her, although she knew stitching together the wounds of their long-fractured relationship would take time.

As they approached the boot room door they heard raised voices. Since the bombshell DNA letters had arrived, the tension in the house was palpable. When they had gone for their walk they'd left Euan and Lizzie in the house and they hoped mother and son would at least have a civil conversation with each other. Euan had been devastated to discover Stan was his father and not Kirsty's. He was furious with Lizzie. Previously, Kirsty had been jealous of the close relationship that Euan had with his parents, but in a strange twist of fate, now Euan could hardly stand to be in the same room as his mother.

Euan was raging at his mother. 'How the hell could you keep this from me all this time? If Kirsty hadn't turned up thinking Stan was her father, would you ever have even told me?'

'I'm sorry, son; it never occurred to me or Jim that you weren't his child. In those days there weren't DNA tests you could do. You were our son so I never considered it. When I slept with Stan, your dad and I weren't even engaged. I suppose I was a coward in not confessing what had happened between us before they left for Australia.'

'Well, Dad, or should I say Jim, must have considered it, otherwise he wouldn't have sent off the DNA test.'

'Darling. We both loved you and if Jim were here he would say the same. He was your father. From reading the letters it sounds as if he was concerned about you and Kirsty being together as a couple and wanted the best for you both. That's surely something a good and loving father would do.'

'A loving father who just happened to get Kirsty's mother knocked up and never gave her another thought, so I suppose it got you and Stan off the hook.'

Janine and Kirsty walked into the kitchen. 'Hey, less of that, young man,' Janine interrupted. 'There's no point in arguing about this or blaming people. It won't change anything. I certainly don't blame either Jim or Stan.' She looked across at her daughter and smiled. 'Lady Isobel has apologised profusely to both of us for her part in all this.'

'And so she should,' Kirsty agreed. 'Mind you, the money she sent will pay for my course fees if I decide to go back to university in Australia. I'm grateful to you, Mum, for setting up the saving account. I had thought Lady Isobel had sent it to pay for an abortion.'

Janine threw her arms up in horror. 'Good grief, girlie, that's something I would never, ever have considered. Come here, darling, and let me give you a big hug.'

Lizzie turned to her son, who'd barely grieved over Jim's death; now it was if he had lost him all over again. 'I suppose now you are older there is more of a resemblance to Stan, so it might have occurred to me. But it doesn't take away what I hope was a happy childhood.'

'*Aye*, you are right there, Ma, I did have a happy childhood.'

'And I expect a happier childhood than growing up in the "big house",' Kirsty said smiling. She put her arms round Euan. 'Come, let's go for a walk.'

'And I'll put the kettle on and you can try the scones I've made when you get back,' Janine added grinning.

'Is that a treat or a punishment?' Euan asked, smiling for the first time in days.

'Hey, don't disparage my mum's cooking,' laughed Kirsty punching him playfully on the arm.

Chapter 31

The Truest Friend

I had a comrade tried and true,
Shoulder to shoulder we fight life through;
And whoever spoke light of his name to me
Had a foe to face and a sword to flee:
I'd have staked my life on the grip oh his hand-
But swords get broken and troops disband!

The Truest Friend by Will H. Ogilvie

The autopsy report finally came on 11th June; it declared 'death by bleeding caused by a bullet wound to Mr Young's lower limb.' It was the result that had been expected but it would be some time before the Fatal Accident Enquiry would be completed. The phone call to say Jim's body was finally being released came the following day. Lizzie felt she'd been holding her breath since that fateful evening when Jim had gone to check on the sheep and had never returned. She let out a long, deep sigh. At last she'd be able confirm plans for the funeral, which George Dixon confirmed could be held in a week's time. Finally, there was something she had some control over. She hoped laying Jim to rest would help Euan overcome his anger and resentment towards her and Stan. The funeral would be an opportunity to celebrate Jim's life and a chance for his friends and newly extended family to come together.

After the DNA results Lizzie was apprehensive about facing Fiona, but it was something she had to do, so she invited her to the farmhouse for coffee. Fiona arrived carrying a large Selkirk Bannock, the round heavily fruited loaf that was one of Lizzie's favourite teatime treats. She spoke softly as she watched Lizzie cut several slices of bannock and spread them generously with butter.

'Lizzie, there is no need to worry about my being upset about Euan being Stan's son. It was something that happened before we were married. Stan has been faithful to me throughout our marriage, which is more than I can say about myself. I've told Stan all about my entanglement with Matt Hill and how much I deeply regret ever employing him in the first place. I hope that Stan will acknowledge Euan as his son, although I realise you might not want it to be public knowledge just yet; it's far too soon for Euan.'

'Thanks, Fiona, for being so understanding. I agree with you, Euan is still in shock and has a long way to go to accept the situation.' She poured the tea and handed Fiona a couple of slices of the fruit bannock, arranged neatly on a plate. 'The gossips will have a field day. Janine told me that once Netta Grieve had realised she'd stayed over at Stanton Hall, she was pumping her for information about was going on in the "big house".'

'No surprises there then. I'm glad we all agreed to keep the youngsters' parentage between ourselves for now. I wanted to make sure the two of us are okay. Lizzie, I truly value the support you have given me since I married Stan and moved here. The locals weren't exactly welcoming.'

Lizzie laughed, remembering some of the things the

estate workers had called her. 'I don't want to lose your friendship either. Euan has taken the news very badly. He can hardly bear to look at me. I doubt he has even spoken to Stan.'

'What about Kirsty? How is she coping?'

'She admitted she came with some sort of plan to get her revenge on Stan and Lady Isobel for abandoning her. I think she's over that now. She and Jim got on well, so she's pretty cut up about not knowing he was her father till too late. Now, I wanted to ask you about the funeral. I've some ideas I wanted to run by you and see what you thought.'

***

Euan hadn't gotten over the shock of the DNA results, but putting his feelings aside, he got involved in helping make the funeral arrangements. It helped that Dixie came along with his father, George Dixon, who in addition to running the garage and the local bus service, was also the local funeral director.

The funeral took place on a bright sunny afternoon in the middle of June. Before the service George Dixon lifted the lid of the coffin. The family mourners hardly recognised the man lying in his best black suit, the one he kept for funerals. Lizzie secretly wondered if Jim would have preferred to have been buried in his work shirt, worn dungarees and muddy Wellingtons. She bent down and kissed him tenderly on his lips then brushed a lock of hair onto his brow. She whispered, 'That's better, my love. More like you.'

Euan stood stiffly by the side of the coffin, unsure of how to behave towards the man who was no longer his father. Kirsty nodded to him and smiled encouragingly.

'Darling, he is still your father. A bit of paper doesn't change the years of love he gave you.'

Euan bent down over the body and discreetly tucked an envelope into the jacket's inside pocket.

Kirsty and her mother stood side by side. Kirsty handed her mother the red poetry book that brought her to Scotland. Janine wiped a tear from her eyes and placed the well-thumbed copy of Will H. Ogilvie's *Border Poems* into the coffin. It felt fitting to give him back his treasured book. She smiled thinking of the shy young man she'd met in the Outback and reached out to hold her daughter's hand. Kirsty sobbed as she bent forward and placed a gentle kiss on her father's cold brow.

Lizzie silently watched the two Australian women without any sense of jealousy; they were as much a part of her husband's life as she was.

Stan and Fiona went directly to the church. The entire village and estate workers turned out to say farewell. The minister, the Reverend Jessie Wilson, welcomed everyone, and then gave a brief eulogy followed by the hymn, The Lord is my Shepherd.

'I haven't been your minister for very long so didn't know Mr Young that well. So I now pass you onto someone who grew up with him to share thoughts of their childhood.'

Stan, who was sat at the end of the front pew, stood up. Fiona, whose wheelchair was in the aisle next to him, moved back to let him pass. Stan looked towards Lizzie who smiled and nodded encouragingly to him. He walked purposefully towards the lectern.

'Jim Young wasn't just a tenant of the Stanton Holm Estate; he was my oldest and truest friend and a friend to us all. Jim, Liz and I all grew up together and had many happy childhood years playing round the estate. Over the years our lives have been entwined. Jim will be a great loss, not just to his wife Elizabeth and son Euan, but to everyone on the estate, in the village and the wider farming community...'

Euan moved restlessly in his seat, letting the words of Stan's tribute wash over him. He fingered the photo of the man smiling up at him from the Order of Service; then looked up at the man standing at the lectern. Gradually their two faces morphed into one. Since the shock of the DNA tests, he'd vehemently rejected the idea of Stan as his father. He'd never had much to do with him and had always thought of him as arrogant and privileged. He wondered if the letter offering them the opportunity to buy the farm had in some way precipitated his father's death. Stan would have known they wouldn't have been able to afford to buy it. Anger built up inside him.

Kirsty nudged him gently in the ribs and he heard Stan mention something about Jim's love of poetry and about how proud he was of winning rosettes for his sheep at the Highland Show.

Stan stood down and Kirsty walked towards the lectern. She smiled.

'When I came to stay at Holm Farm, the Young family made me welcome and treated me like one of their own. At the time I never realised that along with my mother, we shared the love of the poetry of Will H. Ogilvie, who is known in Australia as a bush poet. I am honoured to have been asked to read his poem, The Road to Roberton.' She'd checked the pronunciation of some of the place names the night before with Euan and recited the poem from memory.

Netta Grieve whispered to her sister, 'Wow, I'm so impressed she can recite the entire poem by heart word perfectly. I'm surprised at the central role she and her mother are taking in the proceedings. I wonder what that is all about?'

The service ended with a recording of Bellwether playing 'Galloping Hooves.'

As they left the church to walk round to the graveyard for the internment, Euan ran after Stan, who turned round when he heard footsteps behind him. Without warning Euan punched him squarely in the face. Stan reeled backwards and tried to steady himself by reaching for the edge of the nearest headstone. Euan followed up the first blow with a punch to the older man's chest. Stan slid down the side of the gravestone landing heavily on the floor.

He gasped in pain and muttered, 'What the hell was that for?'

'You. You are a hypocrite and a liar.' The words shot from Euan's lips like a volley of arrows, hurting more than the punches. 'How can you say those things about my father? Your truest friend, my eye. You're an arrogant bastard. Wait. No, that's me. I'm the bastard. And my father isn't dead, is he? That's you. Was it one of the perks of being the Laird's son? First dibs on all the village virgins?'

'Euan, please, this isn't the time or the place,' Stan rasped, holding his chest as the pain intensified.

As they came out of the church Netta Grieve and her sister stepped aside to let Fiona pass; the three women had a ringside view of the altercation. Netta's mouth dropped when she heard Euan's angry words. Fiona turned towards her and shook her head. Netta closed her lips, placing a finger over her mouth as if to say she would keep the secret. The juiciest gossip she'd ever witnessed and she would have to keep it to herself.

Fiona wheeled as fast as she could towards Stan. Kirsty, Janine and Lizzie were leaving the church, accompanied by the minister, when they heard the commotion. Lizzie was on the point of collapse, so Janine and Reverend Wilson linked their arms through hers and helped her make her way to the graveside. Kirsty darted after Euan who had run across the graveyard. She found him on his knees by the graveside sobbing uncontrollably. The other mourners stood by unsure of what to do.

'Euan. It's okay. Stan's just winded. He will be okay.'

'No, not that.' He sobbed even louder. 'I never read the letter my *faither* wrote me.'

'Where is it?'

'In the coffin. I put it in his jacket pocket.'

***

Kirsty woke up in the night to hear Euan sobbing. His side of the bed was cold. Turning on the bedside light she saw him in the corner of the room curled up in the foetal position.

'Euan, darling, it will be okay.' She knelt on the floor next to him and stroked his back gently. She felt an overpowering sense of love for him and wanted to take his pain away. He pushed her away sharply as if her touch burned his flesh.

'Leave me be, I don't want your pity, woman. Go back to your own room,' he hissed nudging her roughly with his elbows.

Hurt by his rejection she fled upstairs to her own bedroom. She could still smell the scent of him lingering on her nightie; she buried her head under her pillow and sobbed.

***

Hearing the hurried footsteps, followed by the muffled sounds, Lizzie looked at her alarm clock. It was 3.30am and she was still wide awake. Pulling on her woolly dressing gown she tip-toed to Euan's room, knocked gently on the door and walked in. He was curled up in the corner of the room sobbing quietly.

'This won't do, son. It won't change things. I can hear that girl of yours crying her heart out. Carry on like this and she will pack up and go home.'

'Ma, help me, please help me.'

'Get up and lie back on the bed. I'll stay with you till you fall asleep. I'll read to you like I did when you were little.' She picked up Jim's replacement copy of Border Poems from the bedside table; there was a marker on the page for the 'Road to Roberton.' She read it slowly, letting the words paint a picture of the Border hills. Eventually Euan relaxed and fell asleep. She tenderly stroked his thick blond hair; in his sleep he looked just like Stan at that age. Her child was so broken and confused; she wondered what she could do to help mend him. She lay on the bed beside him and fell asleep...

Lizzie dreamt of an early November evening. The sky was clear and full of stars. She floated above the scene, looking down below. She watched a girl waiting in the moonlight outside a barn. A young man hurried towards the girl smiling. 'See, I've kept my promise to say goodbye before I leave.'

The girl ran towards the boy and threw her arms round him. She shivered. The young man spoke. 'It's cold, let's go inside.' The girl followed him.

Lizzie floated through the barn door. She saw a tartan rug folded on top of one of the square bales of hay. She watched as the girl undid her thick winter coat. The boy spoke again, 'You are wearing your best dress; it is too thin for the winter. You'll freeze to death. Come closer. Let me warm you.' The dream faded away...

***

When Euan woke up he was shocked to realise it was his mother lying on top of the covers next to him and not Kirsty. The poetry book was in her hand. She'd aged so much; no longer the 'village beauty' he'd heard people call her. He thought to himself, everything must be as difficult for her too; perhaps she felt as lost as he did. She was still the same loving mother who had brought him up, 'his Ma,' and he felt a deep sense of compassion for her. Her dressing gown had come open. As he leaned forward to take the book from her hand and cover her up, he heard her muttering. The words tore through his flesh with the speed of a bush fire. He prodded her shoulder roughly.

'Get up. Get up now.'

Lizzie woke to find Euan standing over her; flushed, she pulled her dressing gown tightly round her. She looked at the poetry book on the bed and remembered reading to her son to help him fall asleep. He had been so distressed during the night; now he looked angry.

'Euan, what's wrong?'

'I heard you mumbling his name in your sleep. "Stan, my darling, Stan." Tell me, how could you have gone with him? Did he force you? Are you still seeing him?'

She blushed. 'I'm not going to answer your questions, other than to say it happened only once. I'll not discuss it again. End of story.'

'But it's not the end of the story for me, is it? Every time I look in the mirror I see him staring back at me. I hate him, I hate myself and I hate you even more for doing this to me. Get out of my room.'

As Lizzie ran from her son's room in tears, she met Janine coming down the stairs from the shearers' bedroom.

'Whatever has happened? Come upstairs and talk to me. Kirsty told me she'd had an upset with Euan during the night. She's gone to check on the animals so we can talk between ourselves. This situation cannot continue. The lad needs help. We must do something before there's another tragedy.'

Chapter 32

Moving Forward

Lizzie insisted Euan faced up to what had happened at the cemetery so four days after the funeral they went to visit Stan at Stanton Hall. Stan had suffered two cracked ribs, which the doctor who'd checked him over at the local hospital assured him would heal on their own. He had a badly bruised face and a graze down his side where he had fallen against the headstone. He refused to make any charges against Euan; instead, he tried to find ways to connect with his son, realising it would take far longer for Euan's emotions to heal than his injured ribs.

Euan reluctantly followed his mother through the side entrance into Stanton Hall, and down a narrow corridor. As they crossed the spacious entrance hall, their footsteps echoed on the flagstone floor. The space was sparsely furnished; there was a pair of ornate wooden chairs placed in opposite corners with a suit of armour in another corner. He grinned. A pomander that his mother had made Fiona as a Christmas gift was hung incongruently from its wrist, any scent long since evaporated.

Paintings of long dead members of the Scott family hung on the walls. He stopped and stared at them, wondering who they were and how he was related to them: army officers resplendent in their uniforms, horses and riders ready to follow the hunt, elegantly attired women with dutiful children at their feet. Others were painted in front of huge hayricks with fields of cows and bullocks in the background. He shivered, unsure if it was the weight of history on his shoulders, but more likely it was just the cold. Dust motes floated in the shafts of light which illuminated the room through the two large rectangular windows.

Lizzie called to him, 'Hurry up, Euan; we're not here to sightsee. Hurry now. Stan's still in a lot of pain so we don't want to keep him waiting.'

She took him past several rooms; some with their doors left open were devoid of any furnishings. He heard a sound behind him, turned round and saw Lady Isobel peeping round the door of her room, watching him. She never acknowledged his presence.

'Come this way,' his mother called again. 'We're meeting Stan in the snug, it's just along here.' He reluctantly followed her.

The room was indeed snug. Two tall bookcases full of old books stood either side of the door. From the look of the faded floral wallpaper and worn velvet curtains, it was apparent the room hadn't been decorated for decades. There were a number of faded family photos in silver frames displayed on the marble mantelpiece. He wondered if the photos were Stan's parents and grandparents... his grandparents and great grandparents.

Stan was casually dressed in dark green jogging bottoms with a grey sweatshirt. He sat bolt upright in a worn Chesterfield armchair, with a cushion on his lap.

He motioned them to sit opposite him, on a pair of worn brocade armchairs of indiscriminate colour. There was a long coffee table in front of the armchairs, with a tea trolley stationed next to it.

'I'll be mother, shall I?' Lizzie offered. 'Do you want tea, Euan?'

He nodded.

Stan, what would you like?'

'Coffee please, Liz. But in a mug for me.'

She poured the drinks, placing a slice of Victoria sponge cake onto two china plates on the coffee table. The two men sat staring silently at each other. Euan was completely shocked when he saw the damage he had inflicted on the older man; Stan's face was swollen and bruised, his left eye completely closed up. Euan took a sip of the tepid tea and, with shaking hands, carefully placed the cup and saucer on the table. He looked down at his clasped fingers; gathering his courage like a fragile butterfly fluttering in his palms, he tried his best to express his feelings.

'I'm... I'm so sorry, Stan. I don't know what came over me. I'd hardly had any time to grieve for my father... eh, I mean Jim. His death was so traumatic, I'll never forget finding him slumped over the dyke bleeding to death.' His voice kept breaking but he continued. 'I've been angry and confused ever since I found out you were my actual father. Everything I knew about who I was, who I am, who I'm meant to be, was whipped away from me in one sudden blow. It was as if the floor beneath me disappeared leaving me freefalling into an abyss, tumbling, tumbling over and over.'

He took a deep breath then continued. 'Ma and Kirsty tried to reason with me but I wouldn't listen and literally pushed them both away. There were so many conflicting thoughts whirling round my brain. I couldn't reconcile going from being the son of a sixth-generation tenant farmer with being the illegitimate son of the landowner. Then, during the funeral service I listened to you at the lectern telling everyone that Jim was your "truest friend" and all my anger bubbled up, exploding like a volcano. I was consumed with such a humongous rage that I couldn't control myself. I am truly ashamed of how I behaved.'

'It's all right, son, Stan understands.' Lizzie moved towards him to try to comfort him but he put his hand out to stop her.

'It's okay.' He took another sip of tea to give himself time to pull his thoughts together. 'Tell me, Stan, how can you possibly understand how I feel? You've been brought up in a life of privilege.'

They were interrupted when Fiona came in to give Stan some painkillers, a glass of water, and bring a fresh pot of tea. After she'd left and Lizzie had finished refreshing their cups and offered them the slices of cake which had been untouched, Stan turned directly towards his son. He spoke hesitantly, afraid of further alienating him. He started to cough.

'Are you okay, Stan, is the pain bad?' Lizzie asked.

'I'll be okay, once the painkillers kick in,' he answered.

He turned back to Euan. 'I loved Jim like a brother and am devastated by his death. It hit me hard, blaming myself for sending out that letter, even though I had warned Jim about it. Erm... I thought maybe it had contributed to what happened.' He took a swig of water, then looked directly at Euan and Lizzie. 'I realise all the business with the DNA tests would have come as a shock to both of you. I'd been telling Jim to send one off for Kirsty for weeks. I never considered he would send one off for you,

Euan. Your mother never knew anything about it. It was a double shock for her. With hindsight I realise I could have handled it better. But... with the way things were between you and Kirsty, when the results came I thought it was important to clear things up straight away. I should have taken time to consider the enormity of the revelations.'

Lizzie nodded and smiled at Stan encouragingly, and he continued.

'As far as privilege goes, I never felt privileged. In fact I was jealous of the upbringing that both Jim and Liz had. I hated being sent away to school in Edinburgh at such a young age. I thought it was because I'd done something wrong or... because my parents didn't love me. My mother was never what you'd call "motherly".'

Euan and Lizzie nodded agreement at this comment.

Stan paused, took a deep breath and continued, 'Euan, it might come as a surprise to you but I fully understand what you mean regarding the hierarchy on country estates. It all seems rather feudal. I'd grown up with Jim and Liz and always thought of them as equals, but your father must have felt the disparity... but I never realised.' He shrugged his shoulders, wincing in pain. 'When we were in Oz, Jim borrowed my jacket, giving an impressive impersonation of my public school accent. I thought it was hilarious and introduced him to Janine as "Stan". With hindsight, I realise he was telling me what he thought about our respective roles in society but I was too wrapped up in myself to see it.'

He hesitated then said, 'When you're both ready I'll be proud to tell the world you are my son.'

Then, Euan blurted out something that had been bothering him since the morning of the Spring Fling. 'But what about the farmhouse? Do we have to move out so you can sell it? And what about the animals? I'm a livestock farmer. I don't know what else I'd do.'

Stan looked across towards Lizzie. 'Selling the farmhouse and planting up the fields with trees is the only way to save the estate. I told Jim I would find somewhere else for you to live with enough acreage for some sheep or cattle. It was never my intention for you to be thrown out with nowhere to go. There are a number of possibilities to consider when you are ready.'

Euan thought for a moment. 'Wait a minute. These "other possibilities". Does that involve putting someone else out of their homes so we can farm their land?'

'Well. It depends how much acreage you wanted. I never discussed the details with your father.'

Sensing the increasing tension in the room, Lizzie leaned forward and started to clear the coffee table. 'I think we have talked enough for today. How about we come back when both of you are stronger.'

***

Amidst all the turmoil, Kirsty found solace working with the animals, with an unexpected satisfaction at watching the lambs growing bigger and stronger, ready to be sold or kept to be put to the tup in autumn. Although, with the likelihood of the farm being sold she'd never see the ewes produce lambs of their own.

Slowly an idea germinated in her head. Picking up her sketch pad she pencilled in some suggestions; soon she had several pages full of ideas. She was so engrossed she never heard her mother come into the kitchen.

'You look busy. It reminded me of when you were little.

You loved doing your colouring-in books.'

Kirsty looked up. 'Jim got a letter just before he died to say the farmhouse was being sold. I expect that might still happen.'

Kirsty's voice became tense, and she started to scribble tiny doodles in the corner of the page of the sketchbook, just like she'd done as a child when she was upset.

'That must have been shock for the family. So where will they go?'

'No idea. Stan has never said anything about it since. It's an extra pressure for both Euan and Lizzie who still don't know if they will actually have to sell up all the stock and move out of the farm.'

'I suppose Stan's still in shock, like everyone else. Are you going to let me look at your drawings then or is that a secret too?'

Kirsty laughed. 'No of course not, but don't mock my drawing ability, some of them are a bit iffy. I'm thinking of ways the estate could be viable without sheep or cattle and at the same time better for the environment, although I think Euan might still like some cattle. Mind you, if we still had enough land for animals, I'd prefer goats; they are much more environmentally friendly. This is a sketch of the estate and village with all the different ideas.'

'Eh, what's this?' Janine asked, turning the page from side to side.

'That's meant to be a llama and these are yurts.'

'I'm not sure what Stan will make of that.'

They both laughed.

'What's this? Is that the stables?'

'The ramp wasn't damaged in the fire, but we would need a couple of ponies for the younger riders; it would be perfect as a small riding stable with facilities for the disabled. Summer could be employed to look after the horses.'

'Wow, you have been giving it a lot of thought. What's that? It looks like the Eiffel Tower with wings on it.'

'Thanks very much. It's meant to be a wind turbine, but I hadn't finished it yet. I can't stop thinking of different ideas. Another idea is to convert the barns at the farmhouse into craft workshops or even a micro-brewery.'

'Wow. The micro-brewery sounds great but would be a big investment. A riding school would need money put into it as well, but would have a lot to offer the community, but would these projects raise enough money to keep the estate going?'

'Netta Grieve, you've met her, told me a friend of hers lives in a village that is making an application for a community buy-out of a large area of hillside from the landowner. Perhaps that is something to consider. Do you think Stan would be open to that idea?'

'Wouldn't that involve a large amount of money?'

'I suppose so but there would be grants. Either that or some sort of joint estate and village enterprise.'

'Sounds like a possibility. Have you spoken to Stan about it?'

'I've not seen him since the funeral and in spite of Lizzie's best efforts, Euan's hardly on speaking terms with him. She's trying to help them patch things up today, which is why I'm trying to distract myself.'

'I've an idea. Stan and Fiona were so welcoming to me when I stayed with them that I should go across to the see how he is. If you like, I'll take your sketch pad and see what he says.'

‘Thanks Mum, that would be brilliant.’ She leaned over and gave her a hug.

***

The next day, Janine came back from her visit to Stanton Hall, carrying the sketchbook in her hand. Kirsty rushed to meet her.

‘How did it go? Did Stan like my ideas?’

Janine shook her head. ‘Sorry, darling but he never even looked at it.’

‘What? Why ever not?’

‘Sit down. I have some bad news. The situation with the estate is worse than we thought. Stan expected the farmhouse to be put up for sale at around the million-pound mark, and to apply for a grant to plant up the fields for forestry, but he’s been told the farmhouse is only worth half that without the land. To make matters worse he and Fiona are thinking of splitting up. If she withdrew her financial support, the estate would face certain bankruptcy. He might have to sell up completely and anyone who bought the estate would be unlikely to keep the farm going.’

‘That’s terrible. Do Euan and Lizzie know?’

Janine shrugged her shoulders. ‘From what I can gather things are as bad as ever between Euan and Stan. Poor Lizzie is stuck in the middle.’

Just then Lizzie came into the kitchen. ‘Did I hear my name? What’s going on? By the expression on your faces it looks serious.’ She sat down at the kitchen table and picked up Kirsty’s sketchbook and turned the pages. ‘I love these ideas. Did you do these drawings, Kirsty? I never knew you could draw.’

'Mum just took them to show Stan but he was too preoccupied to even look at them. I expect you know about what's going on up at the Hall?'

'I'm afraid I do. It isn't good.'

***

The three women sat in the farmhouse kitchen and, over copious cups of coffee came up with a plan of sorts. Lizzie took charge.

'Jim would have hated to see all his hard work lost. We must do something. We just need to get Stan, Fiona and of course Euan on board with it. First things first, I'll phone Fiona and see if she can join us tomorrow morning. She's key to any rescue plan. Janine, you're a neutral party in all of this, so we'll need you to act as sounding board cum referee.'

Janine laughed. 'That sounds like a typical day at work.'

Feeling more optimistic, Kirsty offered to contact her old school friends Tahnee and Ash. 'I've been in touch with them since I've been here; they're both involved in some interesting sustainable projects, which could give us ideas of how to make the farm viable. Because of the time difference, we're unlikely to hear from them before we meet with Fiona, but I've some photos and links to projects I can show her. I just hope we can get her on board.'

Lizzie and Kirsty turned the farmhouse kitchen into the base for a 'Save Holm Farm' rescue plan. Fiona was impressed with Kirsty's ideas and added some of her own, confessing there was so much more she'd wanted to do with the wedding and event business. Netta Grieve was invited to join them and shared her idea of setting up an

Estate and Village Trust and applying for grants. It was harder to sell their ideas to Stan and Euan, who were both reluctant to get involved.

Stan was nearly lynched when he said, 'If Hamish Braverman couldn't do anything, no disrespect, but how can a bunch of housewives save the estate?'

'Exactly!' Fiona replied coldly. 'Hamish was looking at it through a pair of financial advisor binoculars and not at the bigger picture. If we put all our heads together we can surely come up with something workable.'

'Hear, hear,' Netta Grieve shouted.

'Hear, hear,' the other women chimed, determined to prove Stan wrong.

***

After his public breakdown, Euan's doctor had recommended complete rest and plenty of relaxation, but he insisted on carrying on as normal. His visit to Stanton Hall had left him angrier than before and he had showed no inclination to get involved in the farm rescue plan. He sat round the kitchen table with Kirsty, Lizzie and Janine for their evening meal in a sullen mood, when Janine casually suggested, 'It sounds like a good holiday is what you need; get away from it all for a bit. I've nearly used up all my holiday allowance and must get back to work. Why don't both of you come to Australia with me? You can do the tourist thing in Sydney, visit some of the sustainable projects Kirsty's friends are involved with, and then spend some time at the sheep station. When school term finishes I can join you. We can travel further into the Outback and I can show you round Bourke, where I understand there's a wonderful exhibition of Will Ogilvie's work. I had wanted to take your father there but there wasn't time. It would be a fitting way to honour his memory.'

'Sounds like you've got it all mapped out,' Euan mumbled unenthusiastically.

'Why not? I think it is a brilliant idea.' Kirsty could hardly contain her excitement at the thought of going home and looked at Euan hopefully, worried he was going to walk out of the room before they had a chance to discuss it.

Lizzie agreed. 'It's a fantastic idea. It will give us all time to catch our breath and decide what will happen with the farm. Dixie and Billy Moffat are available to help me with the animals and organise the sale of any stock if that's what you want to do, Euan.'

'I'm not sure,' Euan replied, aghast at the suggestion.

'Look Euan, it's perfect timing, I get to go on a trip home and we get a chance to check out some projects that might just save the farm, and you get a change of scenery, then some time to relax, so that will benefit everybody.'

Euan was hesitant about making the journey but the three women convinced him it was the right thing to do, deciding a six week holiday would be long enough to fit everything in. Euan reluctantly accepted Stan's offer to pay for his fare, with the promise he would pay him back after the sale of any of the farm stock or equipment.

***

Before they left, Kirsty arranged to meet with Sergeant Elliot, who updated her on the progress of the investigation into the items stolen from Stanton Hall and elsewhere.

'Thank you for coming in, Ms Ainsworth. I'm pleased to say the forensic lab was able to lift Matt Hill's fingerprints from the paring knife that was recovered from the scene, and link it to some of the stolen items. As far as we can tell he was responsible for the thefts at Stanton Hall and round the village. We also have an admission of guilt from someone else regarding the fire raising incident at the stables. Therefore all charges against you will be dropped.'

'Does that mean I can leave the country with a clear slate?'

'Yes, we can complete the formalities now.'

'That'll be great. It's a huge weight off my mind.' Kirsty sighed with relief.

Chapter 33

The Back of Bourke (Back of Beyond)

She has hidden each footprint of mine
With a swirl of her drifting sand;
My camp-fires leave no sign
And nowhere my tent-pegs stand;
On her tracks I have left no trace,
Yet my heart to her heart shall cling;
I shall remember her face
To the end of remembering.

Australia by Will H Ogilvie

End of June to mid-August 2018: Australia

Kirsty and Euan spent the first two weeks of their six-week stay in Australia with Janine at her flat in Sydney, in the inner city suburb of Redfern. It took several days for Euan to recover from jet-lag and Kirsty was impatient to show him where she'd grown up.

'Wow, this is just fascinating. I really love the colourful street art. It couldn't be more different from life on the farm.'

'You're right; I'm glad you like it.' Kirsty squeezed his hand as they explored the streets. 'The paintings reflect the area's strong Aboriginal culture. The district's become increasingly gentrified in the last few years; we certainly wouldn't be able to buy anything here now.'

It took Euan some time to get used to the bright sunlight and perpetually wore sunglasses. Kirsty teased him, 'It's winter, so the mild temperatures are perfect for sightseeing, but you look like a typical English tourist on your summer holidays.'

'Less of the English tourist, if you don't mind.'

'Oops, sorry... you look like a typical Scotsman abroad.' They both laughed.

They explored Sydney's many art galleries and museums. Late one afternoon they met up with Tahnee and Ash, Kirsty's friends from school, who Euan had heard so much about. The four of them sat outside, and chatted over a pizza and cold drinks at a café overlooking Sydney Harbour.

'How are you liking being in Sydney?' Ash asked, not sure of what to make of the quiet Scotsman.

'The views are absolutely wonderful.' Euan waved his hand in the direction of the Opera House, across the harbour. 'There can't be many cities with this combination of sea, wonderful buildings, art and shops... so many shops. I'm glad Kirsty knows her way around. I certainly wouldn't like to drive in the city; there are too many one-way streets, underpasses and the like. As I expect you can tell, I'm not a city person.'

Kirsty looked across and smiled. '*Aye*, he's more used to being on the farm with only the sheep and cattle to talk to. Aren't you, Euan?'

Afterwards they went to a popular local bar which had live entertainment and Kirsty's friends saw a different side to Euan. He got into conversation with Mick, one of the regular performers, and showed him videos of some of Bellwether's gigs on his mobile. Mick handed Euan a guitar and invited him to join his folk group on stage. After encouraging him to accompany the group on a few cover tracks he thrust Euan to the centre of the stage.

'This is Euan Young, visiting us from bonnie Scotland. A shepherd by day but a musician by night, who plays with a fabulous group called "Bellwether". Give him a right Aussie welcome.'

The customers momentarily put their drinks down and gave a lukewarm hand clap. By the time Euan had sung several verses of 'Galloping Hooves', the audience were tapping their feet in time with the beat and several sang along with the chorus. Mick nodded and signalled he could continue playing.

'For my second song, I'll sing one that reminds me of home.' Turning down the tempo, he sang 'The Road to Roberton'. Glancing up he noticed Kirsty dabbing her eyes then quickly shove her handkerchief into her jacket pocket.

The crowd cheered and clapped. Mick stepped forward. 'Thanks, Euan. That was great. I think there'll be more than a few pints of amber liquid lined up for you.'

As Euan made his way back to his seat, several people patted him on the back or punched him playfully on his arm. Ash moved up closer to Tahnee to make a space for Euan to sit down.

'Well done, mate, that was great. You had the crowd eating from your hand. They're not known for being the easiest audience. How would you two like to join me and Tahnee on a bushwalking and camping trip at the weekend?'

Having seen Euan pacing the floor at the flat like a caged animal, Kirsty knew he would appreciate spending time outdoors. 'If you do all the planning we'd love to go, wouldn't we, Euan?'

'*Aye*, that sounds a *gie braw* idea. It'll be great to get out of the city for a few days.' He lifted one of the several bottles of beer left for him in the centre of the table and drained the bottle in two long gulps. 'Singing is thirsty work. Help yourselves, I'll never get through all these and make it back to the flat in one piece.'

Tahnee helped herself to a beer and raised the bottle. 'Cheers, Euan.

Kirsty had told us you were good but I was supper impressed with your performance. You're part of our mob now.'

***

The four of them went on a three-night camping trip to Ku-ring-gai Chase National Park, just north of Sydney, where they explored a bushwalking trail and visited sites of Aboriginal art. Ash had worked as a guide in the park during school holidays; he planned the trip so they arrived to view the best of the traditional rock engravings in the late afternoon or early morning, when the light was better to see the large outlines of animals and human figures etched into the rock formations. Resisting the temptation to touch the actual outlines, Kirsty slowly traced her fingers in the air above the shapes.

'Wow, I'd forgotten just how amazing these are. I can't believe they are over 5,000 years old.'

***

Euan sat quietly letting his thoughts race round his mind. He watched Kirsty laughing and joking with her friends as they shared exploits of their teenage years. He'd never heard her laugh so much and wondered if he'd be able to make her happy. Looking at the ancient Aboriginal art around him, his life felt insignificant. Would he leave his mark on the world? Here, his anger at Stan and his mother felt unimportant. What mattered was that he'd had a happy childhood. If he and Kirsty ever had a family he would do his best to make them happy.

Before they'd left for Australia, Stan pointed out to him that legally he was heir to the estate, so unless he met someone else and had another child, he would eventually inherit the title. He'd angrily thrown the words back at him. 'Heir to nothing, you mean. Money and titles mean nothing to me... as if I care about all that mumbo jumbo.' But he did care – he cared about the lives of the people who worked on the estate and those who lived in the village. What would happen to them if the estate was sold? He had to play his part in the rescue plan and vowed to make the most of the opportunities Kirsty's friends had arranged. He turned to Ash and asked him how he became a guide.

'After we got into trouble with the law for all the animal rights stuff, my folks encouraged me to work at the park. Respect for nature is part of our tradition, so it wasn't so much as a punishment, but more a way for me to reconnect with the land and my heritage.'

'Kirsty has mentioned she was involved in animal rights but she has been a bit coy about the details... haven't you?' Turning to her he gave her a playful nudge on the shoulder.

'Coy is never a word I've used to describe Kirsty before,'

Tahnee said laughing.

After the three friends got bored re-living their teenage exploits, Ash and Tahnee talked enthusiastically about the organic and sustainable farming projects they were now involved with. Euan was curious.

'The estate at home is on the verge of collapse so Kirsty has been exploring ideas of how we can rescue it and at the same time make it more sustainable. We're looking forward to visiting some of the projects you're involved with, although I'm not sure how applicable they would be to Scotland.'

Ash and Tahnee had put together a short itinerary of projects for them to visit. Euan was particularly impressed with a small farming project not far out of the city. The owner, Jed Thomas, showed them round the fields. 'We grow organic vegetables, as well as flowers for cutting. We have recently introduced Farm Stay holidays and have just set up a small herd of goats to produce our own cheese and yogurts.'

Kirsty was keen to explore non-agricultural options. 'I'd like to look round your Farm Stay properties, that is something I'm sure we could do. Providing accommodation for tourists potentially could be a real money spinner.'

'Certainly. I'll arrange for our project manager to show you round, while Euan and I go round the dairy.'

Euan was enthralled with the entire cheese production from grass to finished product. He asked lots of detailed questions about the breed of goats, as well as the milk yields, and was fascinated by the actual cheese-making process.

Jed explained, 'We have to keep the goats shaded from the heat and we have to make sure we have a good supply of water.'

'That shouldn't be too much of a problem for us.'

Euan was intrigued when Jed told him, 'Our next step is to develop our own range of ice creams. We've got a few samples if you'd like to try.'

'Sure, but can we wait till Kirsty gets back? I'd like to get her impression.'

Several hours later they were sat in the farm office. Jed had only been too happy to share his knowledge.

'We feel having a range of different projects is the best way to increase biodiversity. Of course, the seasons and the soil in Scotland will be different from here, so you'd need to adapt to the environment where you live. But please keep in touch and let us know how you get on.'

'Thanks, Jed. Your enthusiasm is catching. We really enjoyed our visit and you have given us some *gie braw* ideas.'

Kirsty added, 'Let us know if you are ever coming to Scotland and we can show you round. Maybe even stay in one of our own Farm Stay properties.'

Next day, Tahnee arranged for them to visit a city farm and a community gardening project which used local volunteers. She was also involved in a project which made use of unused residential gardens to grow vegetables for a share of the produce.

'It's awesome,' Kirsty replied, inspired by their visits. 'I never knew there was so much going on. Thanks for showing all this stuff. You've given us plenty of ideas.'

'I'm glad you enjoyed it. It's certainly more rewarding than gluing ourselves to the back of lorries,' chuckled Ash.

'I wish Stan could see the farm projects. I'm sure he would find it enlightening.'

‘Let him know if he ever visits we can set up some introductions for him.’

***

Before they left Sydney they even managed to watch a game in the local rugby league tournament. The stadium was packed; the roars and cheers of the crowd felt so familiar to Euan that he experienced a sense of homesickness for the first time since he had been in Australia.

‘Wow, that was fun. It certainly rounded off an action-packed two weeks.’

‘Now for the best bit. I’m impatient to show you round Uncle Archie’s sheep station. Emma and Aunt Mabel can’t wait to meet you.’

***

They caught the train from Central Station in Sydney, which ran on the country line through the Blue Mountains, travelling to Bathurst, the nearest sizable town to where Kirsty’s family lived. Euan spent most of the three-and-a-half-hour journey with his nose pressed against the window. Bored at the lack of conversation, Kirsty glowered at him as she rooted in her bag for another book to read.

‘You’ve hardly said a word since we left Sydney. Are you ignoring me?’

‘No, of course not, but I can’t remember when I was last on a train, so this is a real novelty for me. The views are breathtaking. I can’t believe that you, and Janine, had to travel this journey every school holiday.’

‘I can’t speak for my mother, but for me it was a relief to get out of the city. Emma and I get on well. We are more like sisters than second cousins, but the downside was her father was often drunk and short tempered. Her mum, who I call Aunt Mabel, had her hands full looking after Emma and her younger brother Drew, as well as the homestead.'

When they got off at Bathurst, Emma was waiting for them outside the ornate orange and cream station. She ran towards them arms outstretched and hugged Kirsty. She turned to Euan and looked him up and down.

'Ah, so this is the famous Euan Young.' She grasped hold of his hand and shook it firmly. 'I've heard so much about you, Kirsty never stopped texting me about you from the minute she clapped eyes on you.'

Euan blushed.

They had a short walk round the town and ate lunch at a small café.

Euan marvelled at the black and white photos of old Bathurst. 'Gosh, this is fascinating. I never knew Bathurst was the centre of the Australian gold rush. Can we come back and have a proper look round?' His eyes sparked as he looked at Kirsty. 'I bet this would be a great place to buy gold jewellery.'

Emma giggled. 'I'm sure we can arrange it.' Turning to Kirsty she mouthed, 'I can see an engagement or even a wedding on the cards.'

***

Emma drove the final leg of the journey; leaving the main highway, habitation became sparser with '*beware of kangaroo*' signs at the sides of the road. When they arrived at Migaloo Sheep Station, Mabel ran out to meet them. 'G'day, Euan. I'm delighted to meet you. Come out the back, Archie has got the barbie going in your honour.'

Archie was waiting for a kidney transplant, and was having dialysis at home. His condition varied from day to day. On a good day, he and Mabel enjoyed sharing amusing stories about what Stan and Jim had been like as teenagers and the mischief they had got up to.

'They were good lads. Worked hard enough, except when one of them kept sneaking off to be with young Janine.'

'They don't need to hear all that,' Mabel hushed her husband. 'I doubt you knew anything about it, otherwise you'd have taken your shotgun to him.'

After the bustle of the city Euan appreciated the wide open space of the Outback and learning about life on the sheep station. He was keen to help out Emma's brother Drew, who had taken over the running of the sheep station.

***

Janine was due to come to stay overnight before the six-hour drive to Bourke. That afternoon Euan and Kirsty were relaxing by the creek. They lay under the shade of the three old gum trees, which reminded Euan of the photo in the calendar that Kirsty had brought with her when she first came to stay. There had been heavy rains further up the valley and the water in the creek ran swiftly. Euan sprawled out on his back on a large rug; he let the sounds of the Outback wash over him and casually batted the flies from his face with a crumpled envelope.

Kirsty lay next to him. She turned to him. 'It's time. You can't put off opening the letter from your father any longer. Dixie got there just in time to ask his dad to retrieve the letter from his jacket pocket before he was buried. Don't think about it – just do it.'

Euan sat up and looked hesitantly at the envelope. He took a long deep breath, opened it, read it slowly then let his tears flow.

My dearest Euan,

This is the hardest of all the letters to write. It is nearly dawn and the paper basket is overflowing with my failed attempts to explain how much you mean to me. No matter what the DNA test results says – you are MY son. I loved you even before the first moment I felt you kicking in your mother's belly. Lizzie and I were always meant to be together. Please forgive both of us if we got a little lost on our way.

I can see how you and Kirsty look at each other, so I hope that you are not half-brother and sister. I want you both to be happy. If Stan turns out to be your biological father – it doesn't change a thing. You are still MY precious son, no matter what a bit of paper says.

I'm looking forward to planning our future together with Lizzie – and Kirsty, if that's what you all want.

You are always in my heart,

Your loving father,

Jim xxx

Euan sobbed. Kirsty leaned forward to hold and comfort him...

***

When Janine arrived at the sheep station she went to look for Kirsty and Euan. If they were going to make the most of their trip they would need to leave early next morning. She smiled as she spotted them lying by the swollen creek and quietly turned back, not wanting to disturb them.

Memories of the young man she still thought of as 'Stan' came flooding back to her. Perhaps it was time she let go of the love she carried for him and let someone else into her life.

Next day they left early to drive north west along the Mitchell Highway towards Bourke. Kirsty passed Euan a bottle of drinking water, and he took several long glugs.

'Thanks. I'm excited to travel deeper into the Outback and see more of the country, it's so different from home.' He clutched a fistful of leaflets about the area as well as a folder he'd put together about Will Ogilvie and the other bush poets.

They stopped off a couple of times to eat the picnic Mabel had prepared, reaching Bourke in the early evening. Euan, exhausted by their long journey exclaimed, 'Wow, Bourke really does feel like the back of beyond.'

They were booked in for three nights at the Back O'Bourke motel. Bourke was an old mining town, with a large exhibition centre with sections devoted to the bush poets. They spent the day there, absorbing the sights and sounds. Enthralled, Kirsty and Euan held hands as they walked round the exhibits. They enjoyed looking at photos of Will Ogilvie, who'd left his home near Kelso, aged twenty, to work as a drover at a sheep station in Belalie. He was known as a wandering station hand and bush poet.

The following day Janine took them on a cruise along the Darling River on the PV Jandra, a replica of an old paddle vessel. They sat on the deck taking in the scenery. It was cool on the water; watching the light play on the ripples of water and listening to the squawk of the birds, Kirsty felt more at peace than she had done for a long time. She took a deep breath.

'Mum, why did we never come here before? It's great.'

'I've never been here either. It is always somewhere I wanted to go. My parents never took me anywhere, except to Uncle Archie's. When you were little I was always working.'

'What about the school holidays? You could have come and taken me on holiday.'

'Oh, my darling, I wish I had, but I was working at least two jobs during the holidays just to be able to afford to run a car.'

'I never knew. I always imagined you were lazing about... or seeing men.'

'Good grief, girlie, whatever gave you that idea?'

'I don't know. I thought maybe you were lonely.'

'I was lonely. But it didn't mean I was off chasing men. What on earth did you think of me?'

'Sorry Mum. I didn't mean to offend you. I was only a kid.'

Euan smiled as he watched the two women embrace each other. 'I can't believe how wonderful this is, my *faither* would have loved it.'

Janine drove them back to the sheep station for the rest of their holiday. Euan enjoyed helping Drew, while Kirsty spent time helping Mabel and running ideas past Emma of how to make the estate more sustainable. Sad as she was to be leaving Australia, Kirsty was excited about returning to Scotland with Euan and sharing their ideas.

Chapter 34

Change is in the air

Stan and Fiona dined together in her sitting room, talking late into the night.

'Stan, it's for the best. There is no point in dragging this out any further. We've talked about it long enough. Let's face it, our marriage is over; it was over before I got involved with Matt Hill, it was over even before I had my accident. This is about the longest time we have even been in the same room, just the two of us, for ages. We are only just in our forties. There's time for both of us to start again.'

Stan nodded his head. 'Jim's tragic death has brought it home to me as well. Life can be gone in a millisecond; there's no point in living a half life. You're right, we should make the most of it while we can.'

Fiona reached over and squeezed his hand. He asked, 'What will you do?'

'I'll go to stay with my old school friend, Suzie Maitland, for a while. You remember her, she came to our wedding. She lives in a lovely country house in Kent. It has a ground floor flat she'd adapted for her mother, who sadly died last year. It will be ideal for me. She says I can stay as long as I want. What about you? '

'Well, I can't just up sticks and leave the estate,

especially now… there is so much work to do if the rescue plan has any chance of succeeding. There's my mother to consider; her treatment is going well, and she should soon be back near enough to her old self, but she'll not manage to run the estate on her own. Then there's Euan. I desperately want to get to know him. It's hard for me, realising how much he hates the idea of my being his father.'

'I'm sure he'll come round. It's been a lot for him to take in. What about Lizzie? Do you think there's any chance of the two of you getting together?'

'Now that is a question and a half. I've absolutely no idea.'

'But do you want to? Think truthfully. Take your time.'

Stan took a slow swig of his whisky. 'I'm really not sure, but if we did, we'd face opposition from my mother and my son. A double whammy.'

They agreed to divorce. It would take some time sorting their financial affairs, but Fiona agreed to keep her partnership in the estate business, to be reviewed every five years. 'I don't want to see Stanton Hall and the entire estate sold off. I think the youngsters have some great ideas; we need to give them a chance. You never know, it might pay off.'

***

Fiona forgave Summer her involvement with Matt, realising they had both been duped by him. Her horses were still being stabled elsewhere and she planned to send for them once she'd found somewhere permanent to live with suitable stabling.

Dixie had been devastated to discover Summer had

been involved with Matt Hill. She assured him that nothing physical had happened between them; she'd simply been lonely and had enjoyed his attention. She'd been humiliated when Dixie was charged with wildlife offences. She'd got it into her head that Kirsty was the one who had reported him. Although she'd told the police she didn't know the coat belonged to Kirsty, she'd recognised the bright red and orange beanie hat. Agreeing to help Matt Hill pawn the items, which he had assured her belonged to his grandmother, was somehow her way of getting her revenge, not realising the seriousness of her actions. She had been thankful the police had let her off with a caution. They agreed to give their marriage another go.

Fiona also met up with Lizzie, who wanted to explore the viability of keeping the events and wedding business going. She confided, 'I always felt under pressure from Hamish to raise a minimum of £30,000 a year from the various events.'

'Was that separate from the shooting and fishing?'

'Definitely. The bulk of the income from the shooting paid for Dixie's wage, then there was the cost of the birds, the food, fencing etc. When that was all paid for Stan was left with hardly more than bird food.'

They spent several hours going through the records for the last couple of years and updating the list of contacts. Lizzie was shocked to realise how expensive the events were to set up and how little income was achieved given to amount of work it took to ensure they ran smoothly. She wondered if they were they worth the effort and it made her realise why Stan had to take drastic action to save the estate.

Stan had expected the farmhouse, with a small amount

of land, to be put up for sale at around the million-pound mark. The Home Report, from the surveyor, highlighted that a lot of money would need to be spent on the property to bring it up to modern standards. He was bitterly disappointed to be told that without a substantial amount of land it would raise less than half the amount he had expected.

A few weeks later Fiona travelled by train to London to stay with her friend, Suzie Maitland. She was at the station when she was shocked to spot a familiar figure. Her first instinct was to rush towards him and throw her arms round him; her second was report him to the police. Instead, pushed for time, she grabbed her mobile phone and contacted Lizzie.

She spoke at the speed of an express train: 'Hi, I'm at Euston Station. I've just seen Matt Hill... it was definitely him. I'd know him anywhere by the way he holds his head and moves with long lolloping strides.' She took a gulp of air then continued, 'He looks like a tramp with long hair and beard. I lost him in the crowd. Lizzie, I'm sorry... but I really need to get my connection or I'll have hours to wait... could you contact Sergeant Elliot, and let him know?'

'Yes, sure thing. But be careful. Don't think about approaching him. He's a very dangerous man, so don't take any chances.'

***

Matt Hill was all for taking chances; after Stan caught the kidnappers off guard at the fishing lake, he'd taken a deep breath, dived into the freezing lake, and grabbing hold of one of the pillars of the birdwatching hide, he hid underneath it. He swam just below the surface of the water, holding his breath for as long as possible, then, periodically surfacing for air, swam to the far side of the lake. He hid in the woods till he thought it was safe then went back to where he'd left his car, which to his relief, was still parked exactly where he'd left it.

His old army rucksack, lightweight camping tent, change of clothes, and basic food supplies were still in the boot. He had planned to go on the run after the Spring Fling to avoid the loan sharks, so had everything he needed to hide out for a while to give the search time to die down. He changed into camouflage trousers, sweatshirt and reversible quilted jacket and strong walking boots. Luckily, he'd filled the fuel tank for his getaway, so was good for around four hundred miles, but he didn't intend to drive that far.

He drove through the night; packing basic camping gear in his rucksack, he abandoned the car at Forton service station on the M6, leaving the keys in the ignition. From there he hitched a series of lifts across the motorway network, doubling back, laying false trails for anyone looking for him.

He was aware of the irony of his situation; he had the army to thank for training him in methods of escape and evasion. One of the key parts of the SAS selection process involved living off grid and being hunted down by an opposing army, so he was able to put into practice what he had learnt. Except this time there was no room for failure; his life and freedom depended on it. He was afraid whoever had employed the loan sharks might have 'put a hit' on him.

The police would have the advantages of technological

resources, with access to vehicle registration numbers and CCTV footage at their disposal. Maybe he'd been watching too many gangster movies, but he couldn't rule out a 'dirty cop', working with or being blackmailed by the loan sharks.

He cut across to the A66 and arrived in the south of England near Dover. If he was being tracked it would look as if he were heading to the Port of Dover, planning to cross the English Channel to France. At a truck stop he was amused to see that The Daily Star had a photo of him with a list of wanted men under the caption: *UK's Most Wanted.* He hardy recognised his photo, taken when he was arrested by the army. He looked a real villain. He didn't think of himself as a villain but someone who had made a series of bad choices.

He headed for the North Downs Way walking trail. On clear nights, before crawling into his tent, he lay on his back and watched the constellations slowly revolve above him; all the tension that had built up over the preceding months dissolved into the night sky. More and more his thoughts turned to Fiona; she was one of the few women he had ever truly cared for. Maybe, just maybe, he even loved her.

After several months camping out in the North Downs Way, he made his way to London. Hoping people had got fed up looking for him, he risked going to Euston Station, where he had stowed a change of clothes, some cash and personal belongings in the left luggage lockers. As he left with his holdall he thought he saw Fiona in the distance – it was a total shock, but he knew it was wishful thinking. What would she be doing in London? He wished it had been her so he could have apologised for all the trouble he had caused her.

After a quick freshen up and a change of clothes, he ventured back to Walthamstow. He went into the local corner shop to buy food; he overheard a woman telling the shopkeeper the people who lived in the house where he'd stayed previously were abroad again. He went to the house and rang the doorbell to check there was no one in; after some searching he found the backdoor key tucked under a watering can. He wasn't sure but thought he saw the curtains in the upstairs window of the neighbouring house twitch, but hoped he was mistaken and let himself in.

It was like coming home. He showered, shaved off his beard and changed into clean clothes he found in the wardrobe. After putting his musty clothes into the washing machine, he made a sandwich of thick white bread, with half a pack of ham and a generous dollop of French mustard. He settled down in front of the television to catch up on the news.

He jumped when he heard the doorbell. Wiping mustard from his chin with the back of his hand, he looked through the translucent glass panel in the front door and saw the outline of two policemen. Turning towards the back door he hesitated – should he try to escape?

The months he'd spent on the run flashed through his mind. The doorbell rang again. He opened the door.

'Excuse me, sir, are you the owner? We believe the owners are away and the next door neighbour alerted us there was someone in the property. Can we see some identification?'

'Yes, of course, officer.' Matt calmly took out a driving licence from his jacket and handed it to them.

'"Edward Smith." Is that you?'

He swallowed hard and looked the officer directly in the eye as he handed over the stolen driving licence, replying with as much confidence as he could muster, 'Yes. I've lost some weight and grown my hair since the photo was taken.' He hoped the officers would go away without asking any more questions.

Just then one of the officers moved aside to answer his radio. He nodded to his companion.

'That was the station. Something has cropped up. We need to ask you to come with us to the police station to answer a few questions.'

***

Sergeant Elliot phoned Lizzie with the news that Matt Hill had been arrested in London and was being transferred back to Scotland.

'Thanks. So Fiona was right when she'd spotted him. I'll phone her and let her know. She will be relieved.'

That evening Lizzie and Stan met over a drink at the Ogilvie Inn. Lizzie knew people would talk, but since the news of Stan and Fiona's pending divorce they weren't sure of how to act towards each other. They were more comfortable to meet away from Stanton Hall, especially as Stan's mother was hostile towards Lizzie. She was furious when she found out Stan was Euan's father and had ranted at him for being as she put it, 'careless'. She didn't care she'd got a grandson or even asked how he was.

'Your mother's always been a law unto herself.'

'You know Euan was correct. It's so damn feudal. My mother apparently thought it was fine to sleep with the farm workers' daughters so long as you didn't get them into trouble.'

'Stan. You know you never took advantage of me. If I remember rightly, I was more than willing.'

Stan grinned. 'Yes, you certainly were. There was chemistry between us in those days.' He leaned over and touched the back of her hand. Looking up at her, he asked, 'Do you think we can find it again?'

'Hi, you two.' Netta Grieve appeared next to their table, looking round as if Fiona was suddenly going to appear and catch them out. She would almost have certainly heard their conversation. 'I've heard that Matt Hill has been arrested. I hope he gets his comeuppance.'

Stan looked towards Lizzie, 'Are you okay if Netta joins us?'

Lizzie nodded. 'What a good idea.'

When Netta was settled with a double gin and tonic, Stan told her, 'Now we have finalised plans for our divorce, Fiona has gone to stay with a friend in Kent for a while. She spotted Matt Hill at the station, which helped to lead to his arrest, so we're celebrating.'

'Well, I hope it works out for you and Lady Fiona. Good luck to the pair of you. Divorce doesn't have the stigma it used to have, but it will be bound to have big implications for plans to save the estate.'

Draining her glass, Netta turned to Lizzie. 'How's your Euan getting on with Kirsty in Australia? He was so distressed at his father's funeral. I worry about him, poor lad. I miss the girl. We were friends, you know. She always stopped for a chat. I bet she's loving being back home.'

'We keep in touch, mainly by email. I've just let them know Matt Hill has been apprehended. They're all relieved.'

'Lizzie, are you going to be able to stay on in the

farmhouse?'

'We've plenty of ideas, Netta, but we'll need to wait till Euan and Kirsty get back from their trip to be able to work on them.'

Chapter 35

A fresh start

On their return from Australia, Euan and Kirsty stayed at the farmhouse for a couple of months while things were being sorted out. Euan was on reasonably good terms with Stan, having been in regular contact while he and Kirsty were in Australia. Stan supported Euan through the sale of the farm machinery and remaining livestock.

He assured Euan and Kirsty, 'You're more than welcome to move into Stanton Hall, till you decide what you want to do. There's plenty of room. Mother and I tend to keep to our own rooms so you would more or less have the run of the place.'

'Thanks for the offer but we'd like our own place,' Euan and Kirsty replied in unison and then burst out laughing.

'Now that Dixie is working part-time at his father's garage and he and Summer have moved into the village, we'd like to move into their cottage. It will do us perfectly till we see what happens with the plans for the estate,' said Euan.

'Sounds like an admirable idea.' Stan grinned at seeing them so happy.

He added, 'Because the farmhouse is worth less than we anticipated, it's not worth selling it, so there's no hurry to move out.'

There was a good turnout for the farm equipment sale with interest from out of the area as well as locally. Many people knew Jim and they came to pay their respects. Even though none of agricultural equipment was new, Jim had ensured it had been well maintained. The large equipment went for good prices. The highest amount was for their Massey Ferguson tractor and trailer which went for £25,000. Other pieces of machinery went for reasonable prices. They were pleased with the outcome, which raised more than expected. They decided to keep the quad bike, which would be handy to get round the estate.

Euan insisted he paid back Stan the money for his fare to Australia.

'Are you sure? You really don't have to, you know.'

'No, it's something I need to do. Then we can make a fresh start.'

The two men shook hands. Then Stan put his arm round his son's shoulder and gave him a brief hug.

While Euan and Kirsty had been in Australia, Dixie had sold off most of the sheep for them, with the breeding rams fetching good prices at the livestock market in Longtown. Euan decided he would take his precious herd of cattle to the annual blue grey sale held in Lockerbie in October.

Stan had said he could have some grazing land, so he planned to invest in a small herd of goats. Then there was the rest of the remaining livestock to sell as well as the farmhouse to empty.

'You know, Euan, I'm so impressed by the reports you sent me from Australia about the projects you visited. I can't wait to book my own trip. Kirsty, do you think your friends would arrange to show me around too?'

'Of course. And Janine says you are welcome anytime.'

'Yes, she's made that clear when I spoke to her.'

'Oh, yes, I'm sure she did,' replied Euan grinning.

***

Once they were settled in the cottage Kirsty and Euan were able to concentrate on developing their ideas. They met regularly to firm up ideas with the newly formed Stanton Holm Estate and Village Trust, which comprised themselves, Stan, Lizzie, Summer, Dixie plus his father George, Netta Grieve and Sia Laidlaw.

While Stan was in Australia, it was Euan's responsibility to chair the meeting. He called the meeting to order and asked everyone to report where they were with their various projects.

Kirsty was the first to answer. 'The trip back home gave me lots of ideas but initially I wasn't sure how they could be applied in the Scottish Borders.'

'What do you mean?' Netta asked. She'd volunteered to take the minutes and held her pen poised expectantly above her notepad.

'Well, the weather's totally different and there are no cave paintings, for a start.'

Euan, laughed. 'Darling, I *ken* you were *gie* taken up with Aboriginal art but the Borders has plenty of its own history. Besides, since we got back we've got lots of ideas from the agricultural projects Dixie and I visited in Dumfries and Galloway. The environmental conditions are similar to the Borders. Try these.' He handed round a plate with samples of cheese. 'Tell me what you think.'

'Wow, this is delicious. It has a lovely creamy and tangy flavour. What type of cheese is it?' Netta asked helping herself to another piece. The others all nodded agreement.

'Glad you all like it. It's made with goats' milk. Having a small herd of goats is a more viable option than dairy cattle and is a definite model we can follow.'

Lizzie spoke next. 'Kirsty and I have been looking at the possibility of a camping or glamping set-up. However, the main issue is the cost to set it all up.' She patted the large pile of catalogues for yurts, shepherd huts and cabins in front of her.

George Dixon talked through some ideas he and Netta had been looking at. 'Farm tours, guided cycle or walking tours. Even Will Ogilvie tours across the Borders, which of course would link in neatly with my bus company.'

Netta smiled, knowing George was always ready to pursue a business opportunity. As far as she was concerned the project needed someone with a good business head to get it off the ground.

Sia reported back on the educational ideas she and Kirsty had been looking into. 'Art and writing sessions, and history trails, music sessions are all possible. Again the issue is finance.'

Summer added, 'We could develop the horse riding for the general public and not just disabled people. Could we breed horses? Maybe set up horse trails through the woods?'

Euan gave an update about the work he had been doing with Hamish Braverman, who was in discussion about obtaining a forestry grant. Then Dixie reported on the wildlife management aspect of the project and the feasibility of keeping the pheasant shooting going.

Kirsty then gave a presentation of ideas for an 'Eco-hub.' 'We could hold courses to teach people how to live in a more sustainable way. Sessions would be housed partly in the farmhouse and it would not be too costly to convert one of the barns into a demonstration area.'

'Wow,' Euan exclaimed impressed at all the suggestions. 'I think we need to cost some of the most practical ideas then discuss the finance side with Hamish Braverman, when Stan he gets back from Oz.'

***

Lizzie moved into the gatehouse, which was furnished, but chose some items of sentimental value from the farmhouse to take with her. She told Netta they no longer wanted Euan's parentage to be kept secret and gave her the go ahead to tell people. To her surprise it took a while for the news to get round the village.

She'd taken over the running of the events side of the estate business from Fiona. She kept herself busy during the day but the nights were long and lonely. She missed Jim terribly and wondered what he would have made of the changes taking place on the estate. She couldn't help dwelling on about what might have happened on the hillside that fateful night.

Eventually the fatal accident inquiry was held at Jedburgh Sheriff Court in December, seven months after Jim's death. It was a tense affair; with what in the tragic circumstances was the best outcome they could have hoped for. Kirsty emailed an extract from the local paper to her mother in Sydney.

A FATAL ACCIDENT INQUIRY AT JEDBURGH SHERIFF COURT

into the death of Mr Gillespie James Young.

On the evening of Friday 25th May 2018, Mr Young's son found his father wounded on the hillside above their property. In spite of first aid at the scene the injury was fatal. Mr Young had gone to check on their sheep after a number of incidents in which the sheep had been attacked by foxes.

The Sheriff's verdict was accidental death. In his written findings, Sheriff Pearson said, 'Mr Young had gone onto the hillside to check on his sheep. He was carrying a hammer gun that had belonged to his grandfather. When the gun was examined, it was found that the right-hand barrel had a trigger pull of only 12oz instead of the normal 3½ to 4 lbs. This resulted in the trigger being too light. Mr Young was suffering with pain due to arthritis in his knees. It was thought that in the dark he tripped over his dog, dropping the gun which accidentally discharged. In spite of first aid by his son, Euan, he died at the scene.'

The Sheriff ruled that using such an old type of gun was in itself a hazardous action and should be avoided.

Chapter 36

A Wee Scotch Night

If you chance to strike a gathering of half-a-dozen friends
When the drink is Highland whusky or some chosen Border blends,
And the room is full of speirin' and the gruppin' of brown han's
And the talk is all of tartans and plaidies and of clans,
You can take things douce and easy, you can judge you're going right,
For you've had the luck to stumble on a wee Scotch night!

A Wee Scotch Night by Will H. Ogilvie

24th January 2019: Newcastle Airport

When Janine Ainsworth arrived back at Newcastle airport she looked around for her daughter and her future son-in-law. She grinned when she spotted them in the crowd at the arrivals gate; they were wearing matching tartan hats and waving at her frantically.

'Very funny,' she laughed as she threw her arm round her daughter. 'My darling, I didn't recognise you at first, I thought you were a rather rotund Scots woman. Being pregnant suits you.'

'Thanks a lot, Mum. I've still got four months to go.'

She hugged Euan. 'Now tell me, what's with the funny hats?'

'It's a bit of a joke. I was wearing one when Kirsty arrived. And well, you would come in time for Burns Night. Kirsty missed it last January, so we promised her the real deal this year. Where's Stan got to?'

'He's gone to get our luggage. Six weeks in Oz was more than enough for him. He couldn't wait to get back and see what you've been up to without him.' Then her expression became serious. 'We were so relieved to hear the result of the fatal accident enquiry. It must have been a relief.'

'*Aye* it was. But didn't bring my *faither* back though.'

'True,' Janine agreed, giving him another hug.

Kirsty spotted Stan heading towards them and couldn't help but giggle. He was wearing a bush hat complete with corks, plonked so far down on his head he could hardly see where he was going. He dragged a heavily laden luggage trolley behind him.

'G'day mates. Do I look like a proper bush ranger in this get-up?'

They laughed so much that other passengers turned round to see what the commotion was about.

On the journey to Stanton Hall, Stan told them about his research into sustainable farming projects.

'I wasn't sure about meeting some of your environmental activist friends, but Tahnee and Ash are a fascinating couple and were very helpful. We visited the various places you suggested. They were a real eye-opener. Although I'm not sure how they will translate to Stanton Holm. But as you said, Kirsty, the secret is to be open-minded and flexible.'

Kirsty grinned, glad the excursions had gone down well.

Stan continued. 'The trip to the Outback to visit Migaloo sheep station and meet Archie and Mabel again after all these years was enlightening, as was the visit to the Back O'Bourke and the Will Ogilvie Exhibition. Of course, the highlight for me was the New Year's fireworks at Sydney Harbour Bridge. I just wish Jim would have been there with us. He'd have loved it.'

'*Aye*, he would that.' Euan agreed, blinking back tears. 'He'd have loved all of it. Though I'm not sure what he'd make of all the changes happening on the estate. I'll drop the ladies off at Stanton Hall, then I'll show you round. I can't wait to show you the stable conversion and the plans for the Eco-hub look really good as well.'

***

Lizzie was waiting at the hall to greet them. 'It's lovely to have you both back. It's been so quiet while Stan's been away. Janine, I've made up a room for you in case you want it. Although I expect you might prefer to bunk in with Stan.'

'Thanks Lizzie, you have become such a good friend. I thought the two of you would get together and I had no chance with Stan. I think you knew there was something between even us before we did,' she laughed.

'When you came to find Kirsty, I saw the way Stan couldn't take his eyes off you. I'd like to think of us as family. After all, your daughter is going to marry mine and Stan's son. So, we are going to be in-laws and share a grandchild soon.'

'Yes, my daughter is absolutely blooming. I hope the cottage is going to be big enough for the three of you,' she said turning to Kirsty.

'Don't worry, Mum. We'll show you round later. It is perfect for the two of us and a wee one.'

'I heard Lady Fiona is coming for the Burn's Supper and staying for the weekend. I hope it won't be awkward with Stan and me together.'

'She'll be fine about it. I'm sure she wants the chance to wish you both well. I'm pleased to say everything is on track for the Burn's Supper. We're looking forward to it, aren't we, Kirsty?'

'It's been hard work. I never knew so much organisation went into organising a wee Scotch night.'

***

The dining room at Stanton Hall was transformed. It looked resplendent in an array of tartan and heather. It was the first time the annual Burn's Supper had been held there instead of the village hall and it was important everything went off perfectly. Lizzie and Kirsty had sent out invitations to the estate workers, villagers and to the invited guests who usually gave the toast and speeches. Summer and Netta Grieve organised a team of helpers to prepare the food: Scotch broth, neeps and tatties and the all-important haggis. At Kirsty's insistence there was an option of vegetarian haggis. The dessert was whisky trifle followed by oat cakes with a sample of goats' milk cheeses from the new Stanton Holm dairy. The plans to develop a range of ice creams were progressing, but there wouldn't be enough samples to serve on the night.

There was a panic when they found out the usual bagpipe player would be away on his honeymoon. 'Very remiss of him,' Netta complained. 'Fancy letting us down. You can't have a Burn's Supper without someone to pipe in the haggis. We'll have to call the whole thing off.'

'I'm sure he never planned it on purpose,' Euan said trying to placate her. 'I'll go through my phone contacts and see if I can find someone else.'

Bagpipe players were in great demand to celebrate the Bard's birthday and he had to make several phone calls before he found the daughter of one of his musician friends who agreed to pipe in the haggis.

Dixie volunteered to set up the bar. Lizzie produced the programme for the evening which followed the standard Burn's Night order with a mix of toasts, food, poetry and traditional music, but putting in their own twist with poems by Will Ogilvie.

Stan was in his element; he beamed broadly as he welcomed the guests.

'Ladies, gentlemen, laddies and lassies, welcome to Stanton Hall's very own Burn's Supper, hopefully the first of many. It's a far cry from the simple corrugated tin hut where Will Ogilvie and his compatriots held their Scotch nights. I doubt it will be such a boozy night, but hopefully, it'll still be a *gie braw* do, with food, poetry, music and drink.'

There was laughter from the assembled crowd.

Getting into his stride, Stan continued, 'This evening is also a way to celebrate the success of the Stanton Holm Estate and Village Trust. The options and plans for the various projects, including the Eco Hub and the Education Centre in the farmhouse. Plans for the glamping pods, with examples of various designs, as well as outlines of the mountain bike trails through the forest, are on display in the entrance hall. Without further ado, let's get on with our evening.'

George Dixon recited the *Selkirk Grace* and the *Ode to the Haggis*, which was admirably piped in by the young bagpipe player.

When it came to the *toast to the lassies*, Stan excelled himself.

'I want to make a toast to all the wonderful lassies here this evening and any that can't be here. Firstly "good health" to my mother Lady Isobel, who is recovering well from her illness, but not well enough for such festivities. I'd like to welcome Janine Ainsworth, our newest Stanton Holm resident, and to give a big thank you to my future daughter-in-law, Kirsty Ainsworth, who convinced me there needed to be change. Without her, none of this would be happening. The estate hasn't been viable for a long time, in truth, not since my father's day.'

Stan paused and took a sip of his whisky then continued, 'I can't let this opportunity go by without thanking Netta Grieve, recently elected Chair of the Stanton Holm Estate and Village development project, for all her hard work in getting the project off the ground. There's plenty of time ahead of us to develop our plans. I'm delighted to say that Summer Dixon has achieved the certification for the riding stables and it will be open for business shortly. I can't finish without a vote of thanks to all the lassies, Lizzie, Sia Laidlaw and Netta, for this wonderful meal they have prepared this evening. Please raise your glasses to the lassies.'

Fiona then gave a *toast to the laddies*. 'Welcome to all the laddies and gentlemen here this evening. Thanks to all the hard work of Euan and the team at the Stanton Holm Dairy. I'm sure we will all enjoy the sample of their cheeses and wish the project every success. There is so much more to enjoy this evening; as well as verses by the Bard, Bellwether will be giving us some of the poetry of Will Ogilvie, set to music, so raise your glasses to the laddies. And I should add that the wonderful Sia Laidlaw, the newest member of the group, will join them on her guitar.'

The evening flew by with a surfeit of food and drink accompanied by a whirl of bagpipes and traditional music. Kirsty looked around the room. Here were the people she'd got to know and grown to love over the last year. She patted her stomach protectively. Her child would have a happier childhood than she and her mother had. They would be loved unconditionally. Her 'walkabout' had not only transported her across the world but to another life, bringing her past and her future together. She loved the simpler life; experiencing nature first hand, and watching the cycle of life unfold, was changing her even more than knowing her true parentage. She'd come to Scotland determined to extract revenge on her father and grandmother, when all she really need to do was make peace with her mother.

She turned to Janine and Lizzie.

'I can't believe it is only a year since I came to Scotland. It's been a real rollercoaster ride. I came to find my father. I was so angry and wanted to punish him for abandoning me. Instead I found my wonderful dad – and lost him again.' She hesitated, brushing tears from her eyes with the back of her hand.

'Don't fret, lass, Jim knew you cared about him,' Lizzie reassured her.

'It took time but I eventually realised I had rushed to judgement of a man I never even knew. Stan's not so bad a father after all.'

Euan smiled. '*Aye,* I'll drink to that. *Slainte,* good health,' he said raising his glass.

'To the future!' Kirsty beamed happily at the thought of all that lay in front of them.

Glossary of farming terms

'in-bye' sheep: kept in the fields nearest the farmhouse on low lying ground

Mules: a cross between two pure bred breeds of hill sheep

tups: young rams

first crop ewes: first time mothers

geld sheep: barren sheep not carrying any lambs

gimmers: young female sheep

crutching: shaving the ewes under the tail and between the legs to remove any clumps of dirty wool known as 'dags'

mulesing: a controversial method used in Australia with Marino sheep which involves removing the skin round the buttocks and the base of the ewe's tail, to reduce soiling and the chance of attack by flies, whose larvae could infect the sheep.

Scottish words

aye= yes
braw = fine or good
bothy = a small shelter
driech = dull or gloomy weather
dyke= a dry stone wall
faither = father
gie = big or good
hame = home
ken = know
lass/lassie = a young girl
laddie = a boy
messages= shopping
peely walley = off colour/under the weather
pele tower = fortified dwelling.
skelp = slap
slainte = good health
wee = small
yersel = yourself

Australian Slang

amber liquid = beer
arvo = afternoon
barbie = barbeque
bludger =lazy person
cobber =friend
sangers = sandwiches
Sheila = woman
tucker = food

About the author

This novel was inspired by my love of the Scottish Borders, where I have lived in a number of places over the past forty years, always surrounded by wonderful scenery, hill farms and of course lots of sheep. My career was in adult social care. I have always wanted to write and in 1999 I attended workshops offered as part of the Scottish Borders' Writer in Residence programme. Since then, I have had poetry and short stories published in the Eildon Tree magazine as well as in other anthologies.

You can follow me on Instagram:
https://www.instagram.com/bgoldbooks/

Acknowledgements

Thanks to the many people who have given generously of their time to help with the research for this novel, especially the Mercer family of Stirches Mains Farm, who answered my many questions about sheep and farming and even let me feed their pet lambs!

I am grateful to members of Kelso Writers for help with various aspects of research, in particular Alister Ferguson for his advice about guns. Thanks to members of Gala U3A, Borders Writers' Forum and Hawick Library Writers for their support and encouragement. Many thanks to my first reader, my sister Sharon Goldman, beta readers Cathy, Marjorie Bromfield and Susan Carew plus everyone who has offered their advice and support. A big thank you to Susan Allen for the use of her photograph on the front cover.

Many thanks to my editor, Lin White, for her infinite patience and support.

Author's note

The title of the novel, Comfort of the Hills, is from my favourite Will H. Ogilvie poem which means a great deal to me. I am indebted to Will Ogilvie's great granddaughter, Catherine Reid, for permission to use his poems. I also appreciate the advice and support of members of the Will Ogilvie Trust.

Will H Ogilvie, 1869 – 1963, wrote over a thousand poems, many set in the Scottish Borders, but with numerous poems set in Australia where he is known as a wandering station hand and bush poet. He was born at Holefield Farmhouse near Kelso on 21st August 1869. Aged twenty, he was sent by his family to Australia to work as a drover at a remote sheep station in Belalie. Bourke was the nearest town.

If you would like to know more about the poet and his work, see the Will H Ogilvie Memorial trust webpage: whogilvie.co.uk

Feedback

If you have enjoyed this book, please leave a spoiler-free review on Amazon or Goodreads.

Proceeds from the sale of this book will go to cancer charities.

Printed in Great Britain
by Amazon

61845968R00188